By Way of Reunion

First Love, Second Time Around

Suzanne Morell Velarde

To My Beautiful Grandmother,
Olga Fernandez,
Who taught me about love
and family

Acknowledgements

What a truly, wonderful experience writing this novel has been. I want to lovingly thank Anna Maria Basile, Laura Bielma, Ami Shill and Jimmy Velarde for helping me through the editing process. Your help and advice has greatly enhanced this amazing story of love and renewal! Thank you all for your support in my journey.

A huge thank you to everyone at *Create Space* who has helped me bring this novel to life.

But one always returns
to one's first loves.

~Etienne

One

$\mathcal{S}$able woke early and thought of all the things she would have to accomplish that morning. As sole owner of the restaurant *Amor Mio,* her daily responsibilities and tasks were countless. The tasks were all consuming, but they gave her a sense of accomplishment and pride that nothing else had ever had. She loved this restaurant with all her being and she loved the purpose that it had given her. Her parents and all who knew her saw in her an inspired sense of being and inner happiness. Although extremely busy, to the point of sheer exhaustion some nights, Sable couldn't imagine her life any other way.

She had purchased the restaurant a mere eleven months ago and was succeeding well past what she had dared to dream. She was a conservative person and she assumed that the first year would be quite a struggle in the ways of building a clientele, fine tuning the menu, finding a chef and staff that would support her ever-changing decisions, advertisements…But, counting her blessings, everything at *Amor Mio* was a grand success. She didn't take anything for granted and knew that the restaurant business was hard, especially for new ventures, and especially for female proprietors.

Sable was now 28 years old and lived in Manhattan Beach, California. She was a graduate of UC Santa Barbara and had majored in Business. She never dreamed that she would go into the restaurant business when she was younger. But after graduating at 23, she worked for 4 years at a company who did advertising for restaurants, *Cuisine Ads*. It was during that time that she attained her extensive knowledge in marketing and promoting all facets of restaurant life. It was because of her great rapport with the restaurant owners and managers who were her clients, that she started internalizing their love of cuisine. Little did she know that very soon she would own a restaurant instead of marketing for others.

After 2 years of working for *Cuisine Ads,* when Sable was just 25, she had bought a small 2 bedroom cottage in Manhattan Beach. She used all her earnings to buy the small house and furnish it. It was her great artistic outlet to make her little house a home. She pored over magazines and gained inspiration on how it would look, but more importantly, how she would *feel* in her home. Sable was always drawn into her deep white couches against the pale blue walls in the living room. She chose that color palette to mimic the blues of the ocean's water outside. She loved to sit on her couches and gaze outside her large windows at the crashing waves.

Her bedroom was done in soft golds and creams with small red accents. Her second bedroom was used as an office and she was most comfortable there with her oversized desk and floor to ceiling bookshelves. It had the aura of an old fashioned bookstore and she loved that. Her parents visited her often and she enjoyed serving them breakfast on her front porch to enjoy the breathtaking views of tourists walking, waves crashing and sunbathers enjoying their day. Sable couldn't imagine a home more peaceful for herself.

She lived modestly and after furnishing her home in this relaxed, airy beach style, she had been able to save $25,000 over the last couple of years. She did not know what drove her to save so consistently when she knew that most girls her age were busy traveling and buying expensive purses, designer clothes, overrated cars and such. But she never was a frivolous person. Her motivation to make her house inviting pleased her. After she had met that goal, her next goal had been saving for the future. It empowered her to feel that her financial independence would cocoon her in its security.

The year after she bought her home and decorated it, her parents wondered what kind of gift they could give her for her upcoming 26th birthday. They worried that Sable wasn't dating much or having the social life they assumed all young women her age to have. They also knew that in the last decade, Sable had been so dedicated in her path: college, great job, home…that they decided to get her something frivolous and fun. So they gave her a 10 week cooking class as a present. She absolutely loved the experience. Although she knew she would never be a great cook herself, the class opened up yet another facet of appreciation for the restaurant world, besides the world in which she dealt with from 9-5. It intrigued her how creative the world of food was and she felt surprised that her vision of restaurants had only been business based thus far. She soaked in the demonstrations, the projects, and the fun of it. After class, she would spend hours talking to the instructors about the minutest details of cooking and presentation. She was especially interested in cooking for very large groups of people in terms of organization, and balancing the delicate harmony of elegance with delicious flavors.

It was in that period of Sable's life that an idea was born. She would buy a restaurant.

Back when she was 17 years old, her grandmother Olivia had died and bequeathed her $25,000 of which her parents had subsequently invested for her for the past eleven years. Sable knew that her grandmother had left her money, but since her parents had paid for her college education, there had been no need to spend it back then. She hadn't even needed a car because her college campus was famous for its bike use; plus she had lived across the street in off campus housing. Later, because she had been earning such a great salary with *Cuisine,* she had been able to buy her home, again, not needing to touch her inheritance.

Now was the time. A gift from her grandmother used in the most loving way. A restaurant to honor her and the close relationship she had had with her as a child.

Olivia was an adoring grandmother and always filled her ears and her heart with amazing stories of Spain, namely the Canary Islands off the coast of Spain. Sable even looked a great deal like Olivia. Both had auburn hair and hazel eyes. Sable was a few inches taller than

Olivia at 5'5, but anyone who had seen them together had known they were close family. Their closeness had been a true gift to Sable as she was an only child and her grandmother had always looked after her when her two parents, both teachers, were at school.

Now, with her own savings and her grandmother's gift, she had enough to attain a great, small-business bank loan and bought her beloved restaurant. Although *Cuisine* was sad to see her go, they knew they saw success in her eyes.

The name *Amor Mio,* was a name that came instantly to her mind the moment she had decided on this business venture of the heart. Not only was the name reminiscent of her parents' and grandparents' Spanish roots, the name meant *my love.* If she wasn't going to live a life of love in the traditional sense, she'd have "love" in her romantic restaurant for her guests and their families.

But she knew that deeply *Amor Mio* also made her feel nostalgic of a time in her young life when she'd been the happiest she'd ever been. She often dismissed that time as a silly school girl's first love, but deep in her heart, she knew that that love had been so genuine and so pure that she'd never chance trying for that perfection again for fear of always coming up short in comparison.

As she peered out her living room window and looked across at the beach, she breathed in deeply and smiled. Today, she felt, would be a very busy day at the restaurant and she welcomed the challenge it would bring. She grabbed her keys and quickly hurried out to *Amor Mio.*

mor Mio was a handsome restaurant in Los Angeles, not far from Sable's home. It had a red brick walled exterior and many trees lined the sidewalk in front of it. It had one huge window in the front with twinkle lights all around its perimeter reminiscent of soft Christmas lights. Inside, the windows were draped with heavy, red velvet curtains and 7 crystal chandeliers provided the ambient lighting. In all, there were 30 tables for her guests and Sable could accommodate 140 in her restaurant. It wasn't the largest of settings, but its soft elegance had already won over the hearts of many.

Sable walked straight to the back upon arriving and spoke to her chef Miles.

"Good morning Miles, how are you today?"

"Great Boss, ready for another big day." Miles responded.

"What are our two specials today?" Sable inquired.

"I have prepared for today, a classic Spanish Seafood Paella—simply delicious. I think it will be a big hit tonight. Also, we have a T-bone steak with baked sweet potato and asparagus for our second special. I've already checked the reservations for tonight and we have 14."

"That's great for a Wednesday. Keep cooking like that with those kinds of dishes and there's no telling how much we'll grow." She smiled. "I'll be in my office calling some purveyors, if you should need me."

Sable worked a full 5 hours before she realized it was 2 pm and she hadn't even stopped to think about lunch. She went into the kitchen and made herself a quick salad, grabbed some delicious garlic bread that she couldn't resist and headed back to her office for more paperwork. But she wouldn't work for long before her best friend, Toni called.

"Sable, have you seen your invitation?" she abruptly asked.

"No, what invitation are you talking about? I have to admit, I didn't even walk to the mailbox last night."

Toni sighed, "Sable, you know our reunion is this year! We all promised each other as kids 10 years ago that we wouldn't miss it. I don't know if you've talked to Rick about it, but if you haven't, I was thinking we could go with Diane as Clark's leg is broken and he obviously can't go."

Sable had been casually dating Rick for about 5 months and frankly, didn't even know if he'd be willing to go. Their other close friend, Diane, had been to Colorado recently on a skiing trip and her husband had gotten a hairline fracture in his left leg after attempting a diamond trail he had no business on.

And as for Toni, she'd been single for so long, it was assumed she would go solo.

"So what are you thinking Sable? Want to make it a girls' night out at the reunion and not worry about the male component? I know Diane would think that's fun and it would spare me the trouble of finding a date."

"I don't know Toni. You know how busy I am. My whole life is wrapped up in the restaurant. And with Rick traveling as much as he does, who knows if he'll want to go, which actually....suits me just fine....when did you say it was anyway?"

"It's in about 9 weeks. The invitations are out early to ensure the most guests I imagine. Say you'll go! I really would love to see Ryan Walker again, who knows if he'll even attend—but you know how I felt about him!"

Sable had to laugh at her best friend's school girl squeal. "Yeah I remember the love affair you had in your mind about him. That was ages ago Toni! Well, let me think about it. I'll see what Rick says about the date and I'll talk to Diane to see if she thinks Clark will be better in time."

"You can laugh at me all you want Sable Franco, but I'm telling you right now: You're Going!"

ꙮ ꙮ ꙮ

Walking back to the front door of her home with the thick envelope in her hands, Sable couldn't get Toni's words off her mind for the rest of the day. Try as she might, her thoughts kept returning to high school and all that it had meant to her. She had fallen deeply in love at 15 with Phillip McNeil and even now, so many years later, his name could still generate many goose bumps on her skin. The reunion however, was safe from providing her a chance encounter with him since he was 3 years her senior. But still, all of Toni's enthusiasm had reignited a sense of loss that she always felt when thinking of him. Through the years, Sable had become very good at concentrating on different aspects of her life other than her love life. After losing him she concentrated on finishing high school with honors, and later that same focus grew into studying hard at UC Santa Barbara. After that, she dominated her thoughts on finding a job and working at *Cuisine*. Then it was buying the house and decorating in its picturesque beach fashion. Finally, *Amor Mio* had replaced all other thoughts in her true dedication to getting the restaurant up and successful. She had always been a *very* focused young woman, and although, she focused on normal goals that anyone would deem appropriate for each phase in her life, she knew deep within her, that part of her focus was to bury the idea of love. There had been a few boyfriends sure, but they were always kept at bay. Even now, given her age or her parents' motivation towards a committed relationship, she only casually dated Rick. More specifically, she knew they were still very far from falling in love.

Sighing again, she grabbed a pillow off her sofa and snuggled against it with the invitation in her hand, and gave herself a rare gift: letting her mind drift back to a time of pure magic.

Three

Phillip got up early to enjoy his daily 3 mile jog around his neighborhood in El Toro, California. He simply loved the morning air and the time he spent with his dog Joey beside him. He'd been a runner for as long as he could remember, even before High School when he was on the Track and Field Team. At an even 6'0 feet tall, the olive skinned and dark haired Phillip, looked very handsome running down and in and out of the cul de sacs around his home. He liked the way running made him feel strong and energized for the day. Phillip owned a photography studio in his same town of El Toro and it was his pride and joy.

In the early days of his business, he had been a photographer himself at high-end weddings and parties, but now that he had saved for so many years, he had been able to expand his dream business.

Although he was very busy with new contacts, clients and upcoming proposals, he still managed to enjoy photographing projects a few times a month. He couldn't bear to stay away from the camera for too long.

The new project that had just landed in his lap was a contract with a Reunion company who organized High School Reunions in Southern California. It entailed photographing the couples at the actual reunion and binding all the photos taken that evening in a pamphlet style book to give to the guests. He had to admit, it wasn't as fancy as some of his weddings, but it was very lucrative and he couldn't turn it away. At 31, he knew how to make a good profit.

As he wrapped up his run, he and Joey walked the remaining 3 blocks to their home to cool down. It was a glorious sunny day and he knew that this was the only time he'd spend outside as he usually worked 11-12 hours in his office at the studio. Glancing at his watch he noticed it was already 8 am and he wanted to shower, grab a bite and hopefully be at the studio by 9. He peered down at his Golden Retriever and quickened his step.

Upon reaching his 4 bedroom ranch-style home, he dashed into the kitchen to make himself a sandwich. His kitchen was very sleek with stainless steel cabinets and appliances and navy blue granite counters. He loved his kitchen, it almost seemed sterile to him which made him smile associating that detail with his surgeon father whom he was so close to. He imagined that his dad's OR, operating room, might have a thing or two in common with his kitchen.

He had purchased the home just 2 years ago and he was proud of its minimalist style. The only rooms he had splurged on were the kitchen and the bathrooms. The living room had 2 basic sofas facing his black upright piano, which sadly he didn't play as often as he'd like. In the family room, he had a big sectional, cream colored leather couch that faced both the fireplace and the plasma TV above it. The family room connected to the kitchen which was ideal for when he entertained. His master bedroom had a contemporary 4 poster bed and a tall armoire that hid yet another TV. His favorite part of his master bedroom was actually the adjacent master bath that had travertine tile that reached the ceiling and bounced light from the skylight above the oversized tub. Another room was used as an office and yet another room was a guest room for his parents when they came to town. Phillip had a 4th bedroom but it really didn't have a purpose and it was virtually empty. He had a couple of bookcases in there and he had decided to put Joey's dog bed in there to give it some life.

Phillip had grown up in Los Angeles and had graduated with high honors. He had won a partial scholarship to Princeton and leaped at the chance to go to his parents' alma mater. His parents had met there 25 years before and once he was awarded their acceptance and scholarship, he knew Princeton was his destiny. While Phillip had been in Princeton, his parents had sold their Los Angeles home and moved to Texas where his father had been given a top position at a Dallas hospital as a surgeon. That was the same year that his younger brother, Sinclair, had decided to join the navy and live his life abroad. His mother worked in an Art Gallery.

After college, Phillip had seen no need to return to Los Angeles since his parents had moved to Dallas during his absence. So at 23 he had moved in with his parents and had felt lost for a while. At that age he, like so many other college grads, felt the anxiety of finding their "career" after spending so much time and effort earning their degree. The stress that most felt after college and the big hype about starting one's life was anticlimactic after graduation and Phillip was no different. His parents were well off so he didn't have the financial stress of finding a great job in a hurry as many of his friends did. So the year he returned home, he felt somewhat lost in his identity. He was no longer a kid. He no longer lived in LA or even in Princeton and here he was living under his parents' roof again with no job or prospects to speak of.

With a degree in art history, inspired by his mother's love of art that he had shared with her his whole life, he now felt at odds with any career decision in that realm. He loved art, had even studied it with a passion, but knew that it wasn't for him long term. Luckily, what the scholarship hadn't covered, his parents had gladly paid so he didn't have financial responsibilities such as loan repayments. Looking back, he wished he *did* have debts, maybe, that would have spurred him to really anchor in on what he wanted in life.

But self doubt about his career path and no real motivation led him to pick up a new hobby to keep himself busy while everyone else was gone in the house. So a new passion emerged when he bought himself his first camera. He started photographing all of Dallas, and loved the freedom and creativity that photography offered him. He spent the next two years photographing everything in a photojournalistic style that he particularly grew to love. He visited Sinclair who was stationed in Sicily and traveled all over Europe photographing everything that inspired him. Later, Sinclair was stationed in Puerto Rico and Phillip followed him there as well. He loved the Caribbean just as much as he had loved Europe. During that time, he sold a few pictures to periodicals and newspapers but he felt that wasn't his true niche either. So after 2 and half years of meandering photography, he decided to head back home. Phillip valued the time he spent with his brother Sinclair and he would always be grateful of their fun together, but Phillip was approaching 26 by this point and he felt he needed to start making long term decisions about his life.

As soon as he walked into his parents' home in Dallas upon his return, he knew that that wasn't quite right either. His heart longed for California, where he had been born and raised. So after the holidays that year, he decided to move back to Southern California and start his life anew. His parents were sad to see him leave Dallas, but understood that he had been roving for quite a time after his Princeton graduation. They knew that a young man needed to settle down at some point and that familiarity to his birthplace would make that transition easier.

When he reached California, he decided to go south of Los Angeles to try something different while still being close enough to his familiar roots and settled in Irvine, about an hour south of Los Angeles. Photography was becoming more and more lucrative for Phillip and he was quickly making a name for himself in quite a few arenas such as weddings, magazine work, and even marketing campaigns. He worked for long hours many weekends for those first few years. He didn't have much of a social life, but he didn't miss it. After two years of saving almost everything he earned, namely because he was too busy to spend and enjoy it, he was ready to deepen his roots and commitments to stay in California by purchasing his first home.

After making so many business contacts in Southern California, he felt that his location of being midway between Los Angeles and San Diego was ideal. He told his real estate agent that he wanted to stay in Orange County, not far from his apartment in Irvine. When he was shown the El Toro ranch house, he knew he had found his "home." It embodied everything he wanted, and even what he hadn't known he was looking for. Since leaving high school and moving to New Jersey for Princeton and then later through all his travels with his brother Sinclair, and finally to trying out his parents' home in Dallas, *this* is what he knew was to be *home*. Those all had felt like transition years. Now he was ready for permanence. He could always travel to see his parents and brother, but he just knew that the El Toro house was what he needed and instantly loved.

Shortly after moving into the house, he felt that it was inevitable that he also start his own business. He loved photography and being behind the lens, but he wanted to do more. He loved all facets of art and loved the business world as well, so he knew this was the perfect time to venture into purchasing his photography studio.

He started researching businesses in the world of photography and stumbled upon an actual photography firm that was for sale. That was the event that changed Phillip's course for ever. It was a studio that dealt mainly with high-end weddings and at once Phillip was inspired and felt his calling. The studio's name was *Enchanting* and the owners, a husband and wife team, wanted to retire. Phillip quickly got a business loan and his career was solidified. *Enchanting* experienced a rebirth of new energy and excitement. Because of his experience with weddings, marketing promos, and magazine shoots, the photography studio was thriving, both with the clients that followed him and the accounts that were left to him. He was able to hire 3 photographers and 3 assistants to head each of those departments: weddings, marketing and magazine work. All departments did well, but weddings were his most lucrative sector, and sometimes he still photographed himself on busy multi-booked weekends. Phillip was the heart of *Enchanting* and prided himself in overseeing all of the departments' busy workloads. Although, already extremely busy, he looked forward to new opportunities to strengthen *Enchanting*. He would become ablaze with excitement when he landed new, special projects such as the new business venture with the High School Reunion Company.

For the past three years Phillip had loved everything about his thriving business. Phillip knew that the studio had given him purpose. He had loved his carefree days after college with his travels, but he really felt that the life he led in southern California was what was meant to be. Being the owner of a studio that mostly did "love story" kind of photography, he had become a romantic himself. As he kiddingly told his brother on the phone not too long ago, he was becoming a softie in his dealings with so many brides. And it was that romantic inkling for which he had leapt at the business venture the Reunion Company had offered.

Four

Today Phillip felt particularly melancholy about his youth. The reunion company he was working with had made him nostalgic of his own high school years. As profitable as this new business venture was, Phillip couldn't help feel a longing for the past. He had felt this through the years some, but now he had an overpowering lure to his past. It was uncontrollable lately, his free thoughts always rambled back to his high school. It wasn't just that he was dealing with a reunion company and that the topic was related to their business. It was that across his desk, 3 weeks ago he had seen the name of his own high school represented on the scheduling. It was a 10 year reunion that was coming up in the next 9 weeks time.

Since Phillip was 31, this was not *his* reunion per se, as he had graduated thirteen years before....But why this 10 year reunion had enthralled him so, was that it was *Sable's* reunion….Sable: the love of his life.

He had felt this longing now and again because he had never really felt love, but once in his life. It had felt so powerful, so intense that it had overwhelmed him. He had only been a teenager, but he dared any grown man's love to compare with his own young love.

His thoughts were interrupted when his lead photographer, Shane, entered his office.

"Phillip, when is the next High School Reunion?"

"It's in about two months actually. I just received their contract, and surprisingly, as I read this, I notice that the High School is actually the High School I graduated from, *Madison.* Pretty small world, after all."

"Any chance you might know any of the people there?"

"I very much doubt it since I graduated from High School thirteen years ago and after heading off to Princeton, I never kept in touch with anyone. The people who would be attending would have been freshmen at the time I was there, and you know how little seniors talk to freshmen."

Shane smiled, "Yes, I can agree there. Seniors often feel like the big fish and could care less about the incoming class. I'll make sure to clear my schedule for that Saturday so that I can make it."

"Don't bother," Phillip said slowly, "this is one photo shoot I'll take for sure. It'll be nice to re-connect with my school and maybe chat with a few people about friends we might have in common."

What Phillip didn't say was that as soon as he saw that the contract was for Madison, his blood had run cold. What were the chances that he would land a business opportunity with a client who would put him possibly face to face with Sable again? He had loved her so deeply and had broken her heart when he left for college. He thought he was doing the right thing by not allowing any correspondence and phone calls. He was so busy with the extreme competition for good grades at school, and also for playing tennis on the school's team, that he thought he'd be short changing her by offering her so little. She had begged for him to reconsider, but he thought he was being kind. He also thought that their love was a young love and that he would find love again in school, and if not, definitely through his travels, or even as soon as he started his work connections. But that was not the case. The love he liked to minimize as "young love" was actually so strong that he had never found anything nearly as close or as endearing. Every other relationship he had ever had, had been temporary and mellow at best. His "young love" as he called it still left a hole inside of him. He had thought and fantasized about her so often, that the mere chance that he might see her in a few months left him breathless.

๏๏ ๏๏ ๏๏

Sable snuggled deeper into her sofa and kept letting her fingers caress the lettered embossing of the invitation. High School for Sable had been so bittersweet. Her first year of high school had been a dream, an absolute dream. She had dated Phillip McNeil and had been so enraptured by him that it was a year in her life, that still, hadn't been matched in intensity or feeling.

She had met him the first month of high school in the library and he had asked her out almost immediately.

"Hi, mind if I sit here?" a voice had asked.

Sable had looked up and had looked into the most incredible face. He had warm brown eyes and brown hair. He had wide shoulders and was tall. She thought he was beautiful, although she knew that most boys wouldn't respond well to that word. Still, she knew he was.

"Yes, of course. Let me move some of my books."

"Thank you. My name is Phillip." He outstretched his hand and she put her hand in his for a moment. Sable thought it was a bit formal for a high school library, but his hand touching hers seemed so sensual. She had never felt such a feeling before and smiled at him kindly.

"My name is Sable."

"It's good to meet you Sable. Are you new here at Madison?"

"Yes, I'm a freshman. And it's good to meet you too Phillip."

He smiled at her and she could feel herself blush. She decided to look down at her notes, while he busied himself in taking a notebook out of his backpack. She tried to focus on her papers, but she wanted to gaze at him again. When he asked her a question, she was happy to be able to look into his eyes again.

"Sable, would it be okay if I make a confession to you?"

"A confession?"

"Well, I noticed you a few weeks ago and I was trying to muster up the courage to introduce myself. When I saw you studying here, I just had to come and say hello."

"Really? Phillip, I'm completely flattered. I'm so happy you did."

"I have another confession, I'm afraid."

Sable laughed wholeheartedly, "I can't wait to hear this one."

Phillip smiled his boyish smile and said, "there's no way I'm going to be able to concentrate here sitting next to you. Would you mind skipping the library and going out for a snack?"

Sable felt her skin prickle all over and she could feel her own heart beat faster. "That's a wonderful idea. I'd really like that."

They started gathering their things and stood up to leave and brushed each other's arms accidentally. Sable couldn't believe how happy she felt.

They went out for some soda and onion rings at the local diner and they had talked nonstop. Luckily, she had told her grandmother that morning that she would be working late at school on a project and not to expect her home until six. Her parents were going out that evening to celebrate their anniversary and she knew they wouldn't be home until she turned in for bed. Sable was fifteen, but knew, without a shadow of a doubt, looking across from him at the diner, that this was magical. She wasn't nervous or shy; she was completely the best of herself when she was with him. She knew instantly that he was bringing something out of her that was beyond confidence and affection. It was affirming. Not only was her budding love substantiated that day, but she had the knowledge that he was the loving catalyst to lead her to grow into the exact person she was meant to be. She could feel herself that day sit up straighter, feel inner pride, feel desired—emotions that she had never felt or even thought about before. She loved her new self, she was ready for love.

After they had talked for almost two hours, Phillip asked her, "Sable, may I drive you home? It's getting dark. I don't want this afternoon to end, but I need to be heading home as well."

"Yes, absolutely. I'd love that."

On the drive home, he took her hand and brought it up to his cheek. Just that simple gesture, made her stomach flutter with intensity. Then he held her hand for the rest of the short trip and walked her up to the door. There, he gave her a very sweet, lingering hug, then smiled at her and walked away. When she walked inside, her grandmother noticed how changed she looked. So poised, so tender.

The next morning, Sable thought she would feel insecure. That maybe she shouldn't hold too much credence to talking to him, a senior after all, at school that day. Perhaps, she had only imagined his words to be authentic. However, she believed in him. Deep down, she knew her life had already changed. Phillip would not only speak to her, but he would have a lot to say.

It was about an hour later that he walked up to her at her locker and for the first time, kissed her cheek.

"Hi there," he said.

"Hi Phillip. I loved hanging out yesterday."

"Me too. I was thinking that since tomorrow is Friday, we could go to the movies. I could pick you up at your house."

Sable felt nervous, yet excited. Her father had once teased that she couldn't date until twenty-five, but she knew that her father wouldn't be as strict as that. Or, at least, she hoped he had been joking.

"Well, to be honest, I really don't know. I've never been on a date before and I have no idea what my parents would even say."

Phillip smiled as she said that, as if he liked that she'd never dated.

"Sable, would it help if I came over and talked to them? I'm a clean cut kid with good grades. I think that would be a plus in their eyes."

"You would do that for me? Talk to them, I mean."

"I have a feeling, I would do anything for you." With that he squeezed her hand, smiled, and walked off to class.

Needless to say, her parents weren't thrilled with the prospect of their only daughter going out on her first date with a senior. It wasn't that they were so opposed to her dating for the first time, but they felt that a three year age difference was too much.

"Sable, your father and I think he's too old for you. Your father is not particularly happy with the suggestion of you going out."

"Mom, he's so great. He's very respectful. His dad's a surgeon and his mom is an artist I think. He has one younger brother and Mom, he's so nice. You'd really like him. He says he'd come over and talk to you and Dad."

Well, that surprised her, "You mean he offered to come meet and talk to us?"

"Yes Mom. He's the one who suggested it."

"Well, in that case, I suspect he's a gentleman. I'll talk to your Dad and soften him up. In the meantime, tell Phillip he can pick you up here at seven, but you must be home at eleven."

"Mom, eleven is too early! What if we wanted to go for a snack afterwards?"

"Movies are usually two hours Sable. You have a four hour date, take it or leave it."

Sable sighed, yet tingled with excitement. "Thanks Mom. I know you'll love him." Sable paused and knew it was a start. She looked up at her mother with gratitude.

That Friday night was a big ordeal at the Franco home. Her parents were still a bit apprehensive and Sable was nervous that they would ultimately embarrass her. Phillip decided to arrive twenty minutes early in case they really wanted to interrogate him. His strategy was to be honest and hopefully win them over with his obvious affection for Sable.

"It's good to meet you Mr. and Mrs. Franco, I'm Phillip McNeil. Thank you for letting Sable and I go to the movies tonight."

After they shook hands, Daniel Franco asked Phillip to sit down.

"Well, tell me about yourself Phillip."

"Mr. Franco, I'm a senior this year and I'm in Honors classes. I like to study hard. I am on the track and field team. I play tennis as well. I drive a safe car. And I'm a huge Beatles fan."

Sable smiled to herself from the hallway where she was hiding herself. She had told Phillip earlier that day, that he would score major points with her father if he suddenly developed a love for the Beatles.

"Beatles, huh? Aren't you a little young for that genre of music?"

"I must admit I am sir. My parents usually play older music around the house and my younger brother Sinclair and I decided long ago to not fight it. We ended up becoming fans of all the great musicians our parents loved. In fact, my father only plays oldies in his OR at the hospital."

Sable's dad chuckled at that, "Really, what kind of surgeon is your father?"

"My father is a heart surgeon sir."

"No need to call me sir, Phillip. Well, I think I'm a good judge of character and I like you son. But here's something you need to understand. Sable is our only child and she is the most

*precious thing in our lives. You need to be careful with every-
thing: the way you drive, the way you treat her, the way you
speak to her, everything. You need to respect our home and you
especially need to adhere to her curfews."*

*"I understand completely sir and I would never do any-
thing to hurt your daughter in any way. I'd like to think that
in time, you'll see how much you can trust me."*

*"Well, let's hope for the best. My wife has told Sable that
tonight she needs to be home at eleven. We'll see you then and
have fun tonight." They stood up and shook hands again.*

*In the hallway, both Sable and her mom were smiling and
they hugged. Then Sable walked into the living room and hugged
her father goodbye. As they watched the youngsters drive away a
moment later, they looked at each other and Leslie Franco said,
"Well, our little girl is growing up."*

*"That she is. And that boy is beyond smitten. God help
us."*

*In the car, Sable reached for Phillip's hand and squeezed
it and then interlocked her fingers with his. He winked at her
and she blushed.*

*"You did really great with my dad. He's a real pussycat once
you get to know him. But the whole "only child" thing really
puts a lot of pressure on me to be the perfect daughter. They're so
wonderful to me and I know tonight's a big deal for them."*

"Tonight's a big deal for me too Sable."

"It is? Why so?"

*Phillip quickly looked over his shoulder and veered the car
to the curb and parked the car and faced her.*

*"Tonight's a big deal for me, because it's our first date and
we'll never forget it." He leaned into her and kissed her both
sweetly and deeply. He then kissed her twice more and hugged
her as well. She melted into him. Later, all throughout the
movie, neither one of them could stop smiling.*

Five

*P*hillip called Shane over to his office the next morning and was thinking of having him go to the reunion as one of the photographers after all. That way, in case Sable did go that evening, he would be able to leave the photography area and talk to her. Just the mere thought of that, surprisingly, filled him with more nervous energy than he knew what do with. He hadn't felt this giddy in years. How could it be that she still had so much power over him? She had been a fifteen year old girl, surely, he must realize that time changes everyone. And here he was fantasizing as if they'd just start talking like they saw each other last weekend. Thirteen years is an eternity. What was he thinking? She might have moved out of state, she might be married with four kids. Or worse still, she could hate him. It was no secret to anyone who knew them back then, that Phillip had broken her heart. He had tried to be so stoic when he moved away to Princeton, telling her that she had to forget him. He could not let her wait for him for three years. Besides, he told her, they would grow as people and would soon want other things. It was their time to grow up. He knew long distance relationships never worked and he didn't want them to put themselves through that.

With a lump in his throat and the regret that had eaten at him like acid through the years, he sadly remembered their last exchange.

"Phillip baby, we can make it work. If anyone can, we can. My whole heart belongs to you. I can wait three years, I can wait a lifetime. You're all I want and need. Don't throw us away. Please."

"Sable, we can't wait for each other for three years. And what about after that? Then it would be your turn to go to college and that's four years too. We can't torture ourselves waiting by the phone or writing letters. In the end, we'd be miserable anyway. I'll be three thousand miles away, babe. It would be too stressful, too forced. We would never be happy."

Sable was fully crying by then. "Do you think I'll be happy with this alternative? I won't! I love you! You're not making me wait, I want to! I want to!"

Sable was sobbing so hard that he pulled her into a fierce embrace and while he drew her into his lap, his tears came too. They cried together, holding each other, wiping each others' tears, staring at each other until they were consumed with the love and attraction that was so uniquely theirs. They kissed with an agony that was breaking their hearts.

"I love you Sable. I do, I do love you. I'll never forget this. Knowing you has made me a better man. But some loves I don't

think are destined for forever, some loves are just for right now. And our love has been perfect this whole year, it's a gift, this year was a gift."

Sable cried softly in his arms for awhile longer and finally, broke free from his arms, and said, "I love you Phillip. You've been my greatest gift." With that, she kissed his wet eyes and walked home.

☻☻ ☻☻ ☻☻

Shane walked into Phillip's office and said, "hey, let's grab some lunch."

Phillip rubbed his temples and said, "Yeah, I need to get out of here for awhile. I'm on overload lately. Hey, I've been meaning to ask you to pencil in on your calendar the Madison High School Reunion after all. I'll be there with you, but I thought it would be better if it were a two man job. The Reunion committee said that they're expecting about 100 couples to attend. They're having it at The Oceanfront Hotel. The sunset pictures will be really great with the waves crashing in the background. What do you say?"

"Sounds fine with me, I kinda figured I'd end up giving a hand anyway."

"Great, thanks. Let's try that new Mexican restaurant on Rockfield."

"On you?"

Phillip chuckled, "Sure, why not?"

At the restaurant, Shane was telling Phillip that he and his wife Marli were expecting their second child. They were particularly excited because they had many problems getting pregnant with their first child, Audrey. It had taken them, with the help of doctors, a few years to conceive. Now Audrey was approaching her third birthday, and Marli, miraculously they thought, had conceived naturally.

"I didn't know you guys were trying again. I remember how hard that was on the two of you years back."

"Oh no," Shane answered, "We weren't trying at all. I mean, we knew we would have eventually because we didn't want Audrey to be alone. But, just good old-fashion luck this time, I guess."

"I'm thrilled for you guys, I really am. What a blessing. I don't remember my life at all without my brother Sinclair. Since we're only 18 months apart, of course I wouldn't remember... but I just think it's so nice that my whole life, *he's* in it too. It'll be the same with Audrey and the new baby, you'll see."

"Yeah, that's one great perspective. My sister and I are seven years apart, so that's just too long I think. Audrey, like you, will always remember the baby in her life. Marli and I are just thrilled. Before you know it, the next seven months will fly by and I won't have a moment's rest!"

Philip and Shane ordered just then. Tacos for Shane and Halibut fajitas for Phillip.

"How about you Phillip, you ever think of settling down? Becoming a dad?"

"Yes, I do think about it, but I've never really gotten that far in relationships. My last three barely lasted six months, maybe less. None of them really felt like forever material."

"Well, would you know forever material if you saw it?"

Phillip thought for a moment, "Oh yes, I would recognize it in an instant. For sure, I'd like to marry and become a father one day."

"Well, hey, I got a great prospect for you. Marli's sister is here from Florida and—"

"Stop right there Shane, I don't do set ups and I certainly like to pick my own girl."

"Oh yeah? Well, you got a type or are you just waiting for some love thunderbolt to hit you some day?"

"Haha, you're hilarious my dear friend. Well, actually, I do have a type. I'm partial to medium height girls with auburn hair and hazel eyes."

Sable was just wrapping up her day at *Amor Mio* when she looked at her watch. Diane and Toni would be arriving at the restaurant in about twenty minutes. They loved meeting at *Amor Mio* because the ambience was just so special with the red, velvet drapes and the sparkling chandeliers from above. It looked modern, yet with a romantic, trendy twist. Sable had already picked their favorite wine and was just checking up on a few emails and returning two calls, when her friends walked in.

They usually tried to catch up like this once a month. They were all busy with their lives, but they just had to re-connect with each other. They had been doing it since they were teenagers. It had been a lot of years since milkshakes and cookies, but the result was still the same: a little bit of nonsense, a lot of unwanted advice, some gossip and a whole lot of laughter. Although they had all made great friendships in college, they always were drawn to each other, like childhood sisters.

"So tell us how Clark's doing? Is he still on crutches?" Toni asked Diane.

"Oh yes, he'll be on crutches for at least another month or two. It seems like the ski accident really did a number on him. His hairline fracture just isn't healing like the orthopedist would like. So he'll definitely be home for awhile."

"How's he coping?" Sable asked.

"Well, at first he thought it was fun to miss out on work at the Accounting firm and catch up on a lot of movies he's wanted to watch for years. After the novelty of that was over in about a week and a half, he turned towards books. He read about three novels and even listened to two audio books. Well, that took care of about another two and a half weeks. But now, he's completely going stir crazy. He's irritable, sore, has cabin fever, just the works. We're about to kill each other any moment. Oh, and he's grumpy that he's gained a few pounds!"

Sable and Toni laughed. It sounded like Clark had maximized his own patience with his broken leg.

Diane continued, "At first, I brought him some projects from my classroom. I thought that would distract him. You know, grading, cutting, gluing…but he's tired of helping me too! I'm open to any suggestions from you two."

Sable refilled their glasses while they were all served salads and pasta.

Toni asked, "Well, how about the romance department? Is that still good? That should probably help out with his irritability."

That got a good laugh out of all of them. "Well, you would think, huh? But the reality is, he's so freaked out about the idea that I'm going to hurt him and add time to his disability length, that, it's just not worth it! It starts out okay, but then ends up being a list of requests on 'be careful here, move to the left, watch it, you're hurting me leg, can you move over' that we just irritate each other and stop." Even this made Diane laugh because she heard herself mimicking Clark's voice and they all laughed again. Then they raised their glasses and toasted, "to Clark's speedy recovery" and to which Diane laughed an "Amen!"

"Well, *at least* you can have romance!" Toni squealed. And Toni and Sable clicked their wine glasses high over their table and sang out another, "Amen!"

Their mood was light and festive as it always was and they valued their time together to relax and be like their old selves.

Finally, the dreaded question was asked, that Sable had been anticipating at the end of dinner.

"So what do you guys think about going to the Reunion just us three, stag, with no men?" Toni asked.

"Well, I'll ask Rick about his availability that weekend. And if he's not able to go Ton, I wouldn't mind skipping the whole affair. I don't have a burning desire to remember those tough years. Everyone was great of course, but I'm just so busy here..."

"Come on Sable, don't be such a workaholic. It will be fun! I don't mind that Clark can't attend. It would be fun to simply dress up, have some cocktails and see old friendly faces. It will do your heart good. Plus a little dancing will be great for us! Even if it's only with each other!"

"Well, let me call Rick and I'll see what he says."

"Hey Sable. You've been busy! We haven't talked in two days."

"I'm sorry Rick, it's been really hectic at the restaurant lately. Plus, last night I had dinner with Toni and Diane and I got home late. How've you been?"

"Well, as you know I just got in from San Francisco. I'll be around for a couple of days and then I'm off to Denver to do some fundraising over there for two days. The next couple of months will be sort of hectic for sure."

"Next couple of months huh? Well, I need you to check your calendar for April. The seventeenth to be exact. It's my 10 year reunion and the girls are insisting that we all go and re-live the 'good ol' days'….what do you think?"

"Hmmm, the seventeenth? It looks like I might be in New York that weekend. Of course I can have Jake cover for me if it's real important to you sweetie. I'd like to make it a memorable and fun evening for you. I went to mine five years ago, and it really is a lot of fun to see old faces."

"Well, go ahead and ask Jake, that would be nice. Now that everyone is talking about it, I suppose it really would be a nice occasion. Thanks Rick. Now tell me, when are you going to take me out for a real date? Between both our busy schedules, I haven't seen you in almost three weeks."

"Ahhh, I will see what I can do, I promise."

Sable felt that she couldn't complain. Rick was nice, very nice. He was well mannered and opened doors for her. He called every few days. He was a very "nice" guy. No other adjectives really entered her mind when she thought of him. Their time together was always pleasant. After dating Rick for almost six months, they'd only been intimate a few times. She felt safe with him, knew he wouldn't betray her on his many travels, but by the same token, did not feel any real passion in their relationship. At best, what she felt was lukewarm.

As was becoming the habit lately, she let her mind linger back to the one time she did feel passion. At twenty-eight years old, it was hard to believe that the last time she felt passion, she had been a teenager. What was the matter with her? Now that she was analyzing it, the few boyfriends she had, had always been in the "lukewarm" category. She had tried her best to be open to the possibility of sparks flying or heated romances, but truly, none had ever materialized. Most men told her how pretty she was with her piercing hazel eyes and soft auburn hair that hung midway down her back, but those compliments hadn't ever stirred her emotionally. She knew she had a nice smile, three years of braces had resolved that issue. But she felt she must have some intimacy problems, it just wasn't normal for a young woman to be so neutral about men.

With Phillip, however, she remembered, it had been hard to keep their hands off of each other. It had only taken two months before they had become lovers. She had been shocked at her own behavior, given how young they were. But it just felt so special. None of her adult relationships had ever even been remotely close to the amount of love or passion she and Phillip shared that year. She was grateful that at least love had blessed her life once in a complete and utterly breathtaking way. Yes, yes, yes she had loved him.

◡◠ ◡◠ ◡◠

It had been an ordinary day in October. There had been no indicators to her that morning when she woke, that she would revisit this day in her mind more than a thousand times. The temperature was nice, her classes had been lackluster, her clothes casual. Yet, as soon as Phillip met her at his car after school, her heart was ablaze with feeling. She couldn't quite figure it out, but she was about to have her emotional love for Phillip transcend into the most intense lovemaking she could have ever imagined.

She knew it was just a matter of time, not a question of whether she would decide to or not. She already knew that she would become physical with Phillip. At fifteen, she knew she was young, but her love for him was natural and pure and would eventually be sealed. However, after only a couple of months, it felt a bit too soon.

"I don't think we should do this," she later said to him in his bedroom between the countless kisses that they were sharing.

"You tell me when to stop. I respect you. I'll wait as long as you want. I just want to be close to you."

However, at that precise moment in time, she didn't want to wait or even hesitate. She wanted to experience love in its sweetest nature. She felt treasured beyond belief. Sable knew that he saw her as delicate and would never hurt her. She took a breath and reached for her buttons slowly.

When Sable opened up her own blouse for him to discover her, Phillip didn't think he could contain himself. But he concentrated on pacing their passion so that she wouldn't feel pressured or uncomfortable. He soothingly touched her bra and unhooked it. As he started kissing her breasts, it was Sable who urged him on. She started unclothing Phillip, while her lips never left his. In a moment's haste, they were nude and delicately balancing the possibility of the next moment.

"Baby, we can stop right here I promise. We don't have to go any further. I'll just touch you and kiss you and by God, look at you and taste you. Please don't think we have to. I love you Sable, I swear this is enough if you want it to be enough." He kissed her temple and her cheeks and interlaced their hands.

"I want you," she said, "don't stop please."

In a moment's time, their love was joined. A coupling of minds, bodies, spirit, hope, desire and trust. Sable knew she was safe with him. She wasn't afraid of losing her virginity to him, although very young, it was present in her heart that their love was special and profound. She didn't feel pain, just passion as Phillip continued to make her his. They couldn't stop kissing and devouring each other, it seemed to her, magical. Afterwards, they smiled and laughed and even dozed off for a few minutes.

"Phillip, I can't believe we just did that. I really can't. If my parents find out, first, they'll kill me. Then,…it would be such a disappointment."

"Sable, I know you don't want to hurt them. I love you. You are so perfect. Please don't let nerves ruin this. We'll be careful, I promise. I love you." He had cupped her face in his hands and kissed her lips, her ears, and her forehead over and over again. He held her for a long time until they finally fell asleep again. About an hour later, he awoke and looked at the clock.

"Babe, my parents are going to be home in about an hour. I need to drive you back to the library. Do you feel ok?"

"Yeah, I'm fine. I'm just worried that my mother will be able to tell. It's not going to be easy to act casual around her today. Do I look okay?"

"You're glowing. You're beautiful. You are so mine, all mine. I have a feeling I'll never stop smiling."

With that, she couldn't stop smiling herself. "How much time did you say we had before your parents come home? I don't think I want to leave." She put her hands on his chest and kissed him with a fervor she didn't even know she could muster. For Phillip, it was pure rapture.

Sable sighed very deeply. Enough with the memories, she told herself! Yes, lovemaking was wonderful with Phillip, but that had been over a decade ago. He didn't care enough about her to hold on to her when he left for school. That had been, to date, the worst emotional pain she had ever endured.

Even losing her grandmother Olivia hadn't been so painful because she had died sweetly in her sleep at eighty-four and had always said that her life was complete. She was missed, but so present, in Sable's life.

But losing Phillip had brought on such emotional devastation that when the weeks of tears had subsided, stomach pains and headaches had taken over. She had lost nine pounds almost instantly and the pain in her chest that had manifested was so intense, she had thought in her naivety that maybe she was going to die. Of course she hadn't. After quite a few months of indulging in her misery, she decided to take the higher road. She knew her family was extremely disturbed by her appearance and depression, and for them, she decided to make the best effort to appear calm and resolute. She would no longer act pitifully in front of her

parents. She only indulged in her misery with her closest friends and by herself, late at night, as she re-read
old notes he had written her or traced his image in photographs while cuddling up in a few of his sweatshirts
she had taken from him on cold evenings. There were
countless nights of loneliness and dread, but she had to
move on.

The next few years of high school were hollow. She
had many nice friends and she went to dances and social events, but she was *hollow*. Phillip had taken with
him the best of her youthful self.

Her thoughts were interrupted by a phone call from
her cousin Desiree. "Thank God," Sable said to herself.
"What's gotten into me? I have to stop reminiscing!"

"Hey cous, how are you? Wait. What....what.....
you're what?"

Phillip was out for his morning jog with Joey and his mind was racing about all the things he had to do today. He had two weddings this weekend, one on Friday night and another on Saturday afternoon. One of his photographers was on vacation and his other wedding photographer, Vince, had just had emergency surgery on his appendix. Phillip was glad that Vince was okay, but it really put him in a tight squeeze for the weekend. He quickened his step and told himself, this was what being a business owner was all about, taking care of all the needs—no matter how ill timed.

Next week, his parents would be in town over the weekend. His father had a medical conference in Los Angeles, so his mother would be with him all day. No doubt, she would grill him on his latest dating adventures, or actually, lack thereof and ask about his timeline for the possibility of providing her with grandchildren one day.

So those would be two busy weekends to, at least, divert his thoughts. Lately, he had been spending too much time thinking about old memories, when he needed to focus on his busy schedule and flourishing business.

The Madison reunion was only a month away now and Phillip was almost on the verge of obsession over thinking about Sable's presence there. He imagined their encounter in a multitude of different ways. But none of them satisfied him or assuaged his guilt for breaking her heart. He was never soothed by the logic that he broke up with her to prevent further pain. He had really thought that they were too young to have a long distance, successful relationship. The fact that he hurt her immensely had bothered him for years. How was he to know that their love would haunt him? That no other relationship would ever come close? That he would literally envy his eighteen year old self for the sweetness that his youth had experienced? Her overflowing love for him had left him yearning for more.

"Sable, I can't nap with you here! Your grandmother will be back any minute!"

"My grandmother won't be back for two to three hours! Come on! I was up all night both studying for my algebra test and writing my paper on Macbeth. I'm so tired. Just hold me while I sleep awhile. I love your arms around me and I promise to fall asleep in seconds. I don't want you to leave."

"Okay, I'll hold you for a few minutes, but then I'm going to leave within half an hour, I promise."

"Sure you will, hon. Come on." She walked backwards towards her room, pulling lightly on his hands, smiling softly at his nervous behavior.

"Phillip, don't look so scared. She's not coming back for awhile, she's out shopping with Desiree. You're practically a foot taller than my grandmother ... I'll put my money on you if there's a scuffle!"

He didn't even respond to her teasing. They both kicked off their shoes and climbed into her bed. She closed her eyes and leaned into him, while his arms encircled her waist. Her back was to him, so when he started to kiss her ear slowly, she shivered. Although extremely sleepy, she couldn't help but feel all her senses heighten. It wasn't long before they were kissing passionately and throwing clothes on the floor.

"I love you Sable. I'm sorry, I know you wanted to rest. But you are so irresistible to me." He started kissing her neck and moved above her.

"It's okay. I couldn't sleep after you started holding me. It's like you wake every thing inside of me."

Their lovemaking had been so slow and tender that afternoon. Always stopping to gaze into each others' eyes, kiss hands, entwine fingers, caress everywhere. They were insatiable. They climaxed together and kissed a few more times, professed their love again and again until they softly giggled, encircled their arms around each other and drifted off.

"Dammit Joey, let's get home!" They quickened their pace and were home within minutes. Phillip had been having these strong flashbacks so often now, that he would get angry with himself. "What's the point? She probably hates me and will throw a drink in my face if she sees me. I need to stop thinking about her. Get a grip," he told himself. Thirteen years is a long time, too long. He needed to stay focused on his job. He was very busy this weekend and his parents would be here the next.

"It's in fate's hands," he finally told himself. "I just can't think about this anymore. It's agonizing. I loved her, but that was an eternity ago."

☺☺ ☺☺ ☺☺

"Desiree, how can this happen? You're only twenty years old! You guys aren't even that serious. Dating only three months, how in the world, did you let this happen?"

"Sable, I thought we were being careful. Always using protection until we felt monogamous enough… and closer to one another. Then, all of a sudden, it was understood that we weren't going to be seeing other people, so we started being a little less careful with the condoms. You know how irregular I've been my whole life…I'm just so upset with this."

"What does Dane say about this?"

"He's a total jerk. He's freaking out, says he's not ready to be a father at twenty-three! Well, neither am I! I'm barely a sophomore in college, I don't even have a job! I live off of student loans and the money my parents send me! Give me a break!" Desiree started to cry softly. "I'm so ashamed! I was raised better than this, I just can't believe it!"

"Don't cry sweetie. I'm in shock too, but you have my full support. No matter what you decide, I love you and will help you. You know you're like a little sister."

"Thanks Sable. I need to think about it all. I'll talk to you soon."

After hanging up, Sable sat down on her bed, against all her enormous pillows with a large cup of coffee. She felt so torn up about Desiree's indiscretion. Pregnant at twenty didn't leave her with a lot of options. Two years ago, her aunt and uncle, Desiree's parents, had moved to Spain to live out their retirement. They had had Desiree late in life and now that she had started college, they decided to move back to their homeland of the Canary Islands and visit California twice a year during the Easter and summer breaks. In turn, Desiree was expected to visit them during the Christmas holidays. Sable and her parents were her only family around since their grandmother, Olivia, had passed away years before. Sable felt overwhelmed with this problem. What would Desiree decide? Would she become a single mother here in California as a college dropout or would she move to Spain with her parents for the help, both financial and emotional, that they could provide? Would she terminate the baby or give it up for adoption? Would she try to heavy-hand Dane into a forced marriage? Sable felt so very sad over the situation. A baby should bring the utmost joy into a couple's life… not sheer panic to a young girl's life. No matter what Desiree chose, Sable had already decided, to help her younger cousin in any way she could. Even if that meant helping her financially or with a place to live.

She slipped back into her bed and decided to go over some of the account reports on her vendors. She had been feeling sick and fatigued all day and decided to call Dr. Morgan in the morning. *Amor Mio* was still too new for her to miss work if she got sick. It would be better for her to be preventive in case she was coming down with something, than for an illness to escalate into missing precious days. She felt uneasy, but knew that Dr. Morgan would prescribe something simple. For years, she'd had abdominal discomfort with her menstrual cycles, but lately, the symptoms had escalated into pelvic pain, lower back pain and bladder problems. Surely, so many long hours at *Amor Mio* was the cause of these other ailments.

She smiled to herself thinking of Toni and Diane.... she couldn't get sick now, her friends would kill her if she missed the reunion!

ೞ ೞ ೞ ೞ ೞ ೞ

Later, at Dr. Morgan's office, Sable was waiting in the reception area and was thinking of her cousin Desiree. What would she do in her place? As a young girl, she knew she wanted to go to college....but what would she have decided if she and Phillip had gotten pregnant? They were always careful and wore condoms even in the most spontaneous of moments, but she knew that sometimes mistakes happened with the best of intentions.

Her cousin Desiree had her whole life ahead of her and it pained her that she was struggling with such an emotional decision. She loved her little cousin and didn't want her to suffer now or live with regrets later. It was a delicate balance of misery in both scenarios, that was for sure.

In her place, she wondered what she would have done. In contrast to Desiree who was a young adult of twenty, Sable had been an adolescent when she became sexually active. Her parents and grandmother Olivia would have had a lot to say and would have ultimately influenced her decision greatly. Since she was so young at the time, she knew that her parents would have also involved Phillip's parents in the decision making. On the one hand, it would have been easy to terminate the pregnancy and not stand in the way of her own future and the promising future of Phillip at Princeton. On the other hand, it would have completely killed her to destroy a blessing made between them. Finally, giving away a baby for adoption would have been so unfeasible to her that she would have had to beg her parents to help her raise the baby. In retrospect, Sable was relieved that her young heart didn't have to endure that kind of pain. It was enough in losing Phillip without further complications.

Desiree was such a fine young woman. She was special and striking in appearance. She was about Sable's height, although she had a smaller frame. In contrast to Sable's auburn hair and hazel eyes, Desiree was very Spanish in appearance. She had bright white skin with jet-black straight hair and the biggest black eyes framed with the heaviest of thick eyelashes. Desiree only wore her signature burgundy lipstick and no other make up. When she was a young girl, people often called her *Snow White.*

Because Desiree was born to older parents, she was cherished beyond belief by them. However, she never acted spoiled like many only children of older parents. She was a delight to her own parents, Sable and her parents and, of course, their mutual grandmother Olivia. Since Sable and Desiree were both only children and first cousins, they were raised almost as if they were sisters, regardless of their eight year difference.

Sable longed to take away Desiree's anguish, but knew that life didn't work that way. What she did know was that she would offer her younger cousin her full support, both emotionally and financially. She would also support her decision if she decided to return to Spain and reside with her parents. It would be heartbreaking if Desiree left school, but Sable knew that it might be a result of becoming a young mother.

A nurse called, "Sable Franco" from the doorway and Sable walked in to the hallway to be weighed.

A few moments later, she was speaking to Dr. Morgan about her symptoms. She explained to Dr. Morgan that she was feeling fatigued and that she had lower back pain, in addition to pelvic pain.

Dr. Morgan carefully made notes on her chart and listened attentively to Sable's concerns.

"Sable, I think there might be a few issues going on. First, I think that your extreme fatigue and lower back pain is just an indicator that you are overworked and that you are on your feet too many hours a day. You've been anemic on and off for years and I'd like to give you a supplement of vitamins and iron today and see if that doesn't help with much of your discomfort. But the pain you're experiencing in your pelvis concerns me. Let's set up an appointment after you're next menstruation and we'll do an ultrasound to see if you have any cysts or polyps that should be checked further."

"Thanks, Dr. Morgan. I'll try to reduce my hours a bit and take more breaks throughout the day. And I'll set my ultrasound appointment at your front desk for about three week's time like you suggested."

$\mathcal{P}$hillip was finalizing the paperwork for the reunion of Madison High. His parents had just left his home the week before and he was exhausted. He took them to San Diego, Catalina Island and Hollywood. He had taken more photographs at his parents' request then he did at some of his wedding photo shoots. That made him chuckle, his parents were acting like it was their first time in California, when they had lived in Los Angeles for twenty years!

On their last night in town, Phillip's parents really harassed Phillip on his personal life.

"Honey, when are you going to meet a nice girl? You haven't been in a relationship in years. Your father and I are dying to have grandchildren," Rose McNeil said.

"Yes, we are son. It's a parent's dream to eventually become a grandparent. You're 31. Why, I became a father at 26!"

"Well, Mom and Dad, as soon as I meet a young girl, you'll be the first to know. The reality is, I wouldn't mind settling down in the near future and starting a family. But I haven't met anyone special for years and frankly, I think I might be becoming a cynic about meeting a soul mate."

"Ah dear, please don't feel that way. Look at your father and I and how happy we are. 33 years now. Of course, you'll find that too."

"I hope so Mom. I really do."

"Well, son, have you run into any of your old friends from high school now that you're back in Southern California?"

"Actually I haven't. I've been so busy with the launching of the studio, occasional magazine work, buying and furnishing the house….that I haven't really looked up any of my old buddies."

"That's a shame Phillip. You should really carve out some time for friendships. We're very proud of you and everything you've accomplished, but you need time for fun as well."

"Well, then maybe I should tell you about some news that I really do have. Speaking of old school buddies, I've landed the contract of shooting the 10th year reunion for Madison High next week."

Phillip's parents looked at each other and smiled.

"Phillip, this is great. Reconnecting with some of your old friends would be just what you need. It would be fun for you to distract your mind," his mother said.

But then his father, Blake said, "Well, you really wouldn't know anyone at that reunion. Those kids were much younger than you were. Oh, except maybe young Sable." Once again, Phillip's parents smiled at each other knowingly.

"I caught that little look amongst you too. You're pretty transparent."

His parents laughed at his comment, "Well, dear, we love you and just want you to be happy. To be honest, we've never seen you so gaga over a girl," his mother said.

"Mom, I haven't seen her in thirteen years. Who knows if she'll even attend? This is a professional commitment."

"We're your parents Phillip. We know very well, that no one has ever meant as much to you as that young girl. We thought of it as puppy love at the time, but there was no denying how very happy you were your senior year. We've never really seen you that way since."

Phillip measured his mother's words and so desperately wanted to speak to someone about his feelings for Sable. For weeks, he had been thinking and fantasizing about her, but hadn't uttered a single word to another person. It would be so wonderful to confess his thoughts to someone else, even if it *was* his parents.

"To be honest, Mom and Dad, she's all I think about. Ever since I came back to California, she's been on my mind casually. But it's really gotten bad since I signed the contract with the Reunion committee. It's been a little overwhelming how often I rehash old memories in my mind. I feel so much guilt about breaking up with her and hurting her. I thought it was so adult of me to break up with her to avoid a torturous long distance romance that would end up badly. Or so I thought. The irony is that the kid I was at eighteen felt more love and excitement than I ever have since."

Blake said, "Love sometimes comes to us many times in life son, in different sizes and intensities. But, sometimes love comes but once. What you had was true, pure love, regardless of your young age. Love doesn't have age restrictions. We often assume that young love is less real or perhaps less important. And that might be the case for many young infatuations, but I believe that the love you had with Sable was genuine."

"Genuine it was," Phillip murmured.

"So do you have a plan for the reunion?" Rose asked.

"A plan? Why, no, not really. Part of me fears that she's already married. Although women seem to be getting married later in life, nowadays, so that might be in my favor. All I'm going to do Mom is approach her, say hello, hopefully hug her and if I'm lucky, engage her in a conversation. My worst fear is that she'll throw a drink in my face and leave the party."

"My goodness dear, she's not going to do that. At the very, very worst she'll be aloof. She's not going to be ill mannered or rude to you. You two had too much of a past for that. If anything, I would think she'd honor that memory with good behavior."

"Even if she's still upset with me?"

"Yes, even if she's still upset with you."

Surprisingly, Phillip felt better after talking about his feelings with his parents. He had been tormenting himself with reliving such poignant memories, that it felt good to relieve himself of some of his concerns over meeting her in a week's time.

Since she had no idea that he would be at her reunion, because they were from different graduating
classes, she would never avoid going. Therefore, he was
pretty confident that he would indeed see her. Whether
she was married or not was his next, biggest fear.

ᐸᗧ ᐸᗧ ᐸᗧ

Desiree and Sable had gone out shopping Sunday
at the mall for a cocktail dress for Sable. They were
leisurely walking through the mall and having fun trying on expensive dresses, most of which they'd never
buy. They had already narrowed down their search to
ones that were dark in color and knee length. Sable
thought that the full length gowns were too fancy for
the occasion and she always gravitated towards brown,
navy and black. She felt those colors really highlighted
her auburn hair and gave her a pretty contrast. Pastel
colors looked pretty on her skin and played up her
hazel eyes, but seemed to be too youthful for the
reunion.

Desiree teased, "Youthful? You're only twenty-eight!
Do you view yourself as old prima?" Prima was what
they had called each other their whole lives; it was the
Spanish word for *cousin.*

"Of course, I know I'm not old. But pastels make me
think of dressing up for Easter with a bonnet! That's
one look I'd rather skip out on!" With that, they really
started laughing because they were both thinking of the
big, over-sized bonnets that their grandmother Olivia
had made them wear as young girls. Both Sable and
Desiree started giggling as the sales lady of the boutique
stared at them.

"So is Rick going to accompany you to the reunion?"

"No, he'll be in New York next week. He wasn't able to switch his days around. It's ok. Diane and Toni think it will be fun to have a girls' night out. Rick wouldn't have known anyone and I would've felt guilty if I left him to catch up with others."

They decided to enter Sable's favorite department store and almost instantly, she knew she had found her dress. It was a strapless, knee-length dress in navy. It had white piping around the top bodice and on the hem. At the waist, the dress flared out a bit and had a white organza sash. It was perfect for Sable. She tried it on in a size four and her cousin thought it looked amazing. The dress was $200 but Sable thought it was worth it. It was a style that was timeless and she would get lots of use out of it. Desiree said it had a feeling of an elegant sailor dress, but Sable thought it was completely adorable.

After Sable paid for the dress, they took the escalator down to the bottom floor and were led right into the baby department. Sable quickly looked at her cousin to see if she was upset, but she was wide-eyed and looked peaceful. She walked forward, quietly, and approached some of the newborn dresses. She fingered them lightly and walked to the sweet area of pajamas. She picked up a tiny pajama set with toy trucks on it and brought it up to her cheek. Sable watched her, but didn't say a word. Finally, she picked up a soft chenille blanket in sage, and raised her tear-filled eyes to look at her cousin.

"I can't do it prima. I can't say goodbye to my baby in any way. I think I've decided to be a mom." With that, her eyes finally spilled over and Sable walked forward and took her in her arms. Desiree cried softly for a few moments, but felt empowered in her new decision. She purchased the soft sage blanket and clutching her cousin's hand, happily left the mall.

Phillip dressed that evening with special care. He was a good looking man and loved to dress casually. But tonight, he wanted to impress Sable and hopefully win her heart again. He prayed that she was single and open to give him a second chance. He knew it was highly unlikely given the way he had ended their relationship, but he had been thinking about it for days.

He wore a navy suit and a white shirt. Given his tall stature and with the contrast of the white shirt on his olive skin, Phillip had an attractive lure to his appearance. His brown eyes shined with anticipation and he spent extra time styling his brown hair. He knew he was looking quite traditional and conservative in his navy suit, but he wanted to look respectable. He had gone shopping just two days ago and had spent more money on a tie than he ever had before. The tie was navy and white and had a hint of a nautical whimsy to it. He knew it was perfect the moment he saw it.

He arrived at the reunion an hour before it started to unload all the photography gear and get all their equipment in place. Phillip had decided to bring two photographers so that he could hopefully spend as much time with Sable as possible. He was completely aware that she could come accompanied and that it was equally as likely that she wouldn't give him the time of day, but he was still hopeful. Oh so very hopeful. He had wanted to give himself the most time available if she was willing to spend it with him. He still didn't know what he was going to say to her initially; he would just have to speak from the heart.

About an hour and a half later, Sable walked in with Diane and Toni. They all looked radiant and happy to be there. They made quite an impression as the three beauties walked in without dates and started hugging and chatting with old friends. They immediately found themselves in a group of friends and were thoroughly enjoying themselves reminiscing and laughing about high school silliness.

Phillip had seen her almost immediately. He stood near the photography stations, but from his angle, he saw her as she walked in with her friends. They looked vaguely familiar to him, but he couldn't remember their names. She was breathtaking. She wore navy and white like himself and he couldn't help but feel a pang of excitement that they were wearing matching outfits.

He couldn't stop looking at her. She was absolutely gorgeous. She was a woman now. He had loved her as a girl, but she was all woman now and he yearned to touch her. She laughed out loud often as she talked to her friends and her eyes twinkled with happiness. Phillip noticed that she was not wearing a ring on her left hand and he wanted to jump with joy. He thought to himself, that even if she was in a very serious relationship, *she wasn't married*, which meant that he had a possible chance of trying to win her love back. The way they had completely and utterly adored each other, surely, could not have disappeared completely on her part, could it? He felt so hopeful at the absence of that ring. Deep in his heart, he knew he had at least an inkling of a chance.

Suddenly, he felt insecure. She was so damn good looking, how would he seem to her? She was still in full conversation and he obviously would have to wait for some chance when he could approach her. His heart beat wildly in his chest. He couldn't believe how nervous he was feeling. Surely, that's not what he was like usually. His heart constricted with the knowledge that if Sable walked away from him this evening uninterested, he would regret it for the rest of his life.

At that moment, Phillip was about to look away and go for a short walk to collect his thoughts, when he saw her turn toward him and look straight into his eyes. Her eyes grew wide with confusion then softened with obvious familiarity. They stared at each other for a few moments, neither one knowing what to do.

Sable's heart had literally stopped. She could not believe she was seeing him here at her reunion, since he was three years older. What was he doing here? And why was he looking at her lovingly? He left her. He stopped loving her. He never looked back or rethought his decision to leave her. She would never forgive him for that.

Sable decided to be friendly. To say hello and get it over with. Obviously, he was someone's date tonight and she was ready to get the awkwardness out of the way. She was glad that she looked her best tonight and that they hadn't seen each other at a drycleaners or at the movies, but at a gathering where she had taken care of her appearance and where she had her dear friends Diane and Toni to lean on.

They started walking towards each other, each with their gaze glued on the other's. They couldn't look away. They each wore a soft smile and they both felt nervous and excited.

Phillip reached her and took her hand and pulled her into him as he kissed her cheek. They pulled apart slightly but didn't release each other's hand.

"Sable, you look absolutely wonderful. I never thought you could get more beautiful, but you have."

"Thank you Phillip. You look wonderful as well." They paused and kept smiling at each other, and Sable let go of his hand.

"What are you doing here? Your reunion must've been a few years ago."

"Yes, it was, but ironically I missed it. I'm here because I own the photography studio that was contracted to shoot the photos tonight."

"Wow, that's terrific. I'm proud that you're such a successful businessman. Do you live around here as well?"

"Yes, I live in El Toro. Do you live around here? What do you do? Where did you go to college? Catch me up, I wanna hear everything."

They decided to walk outside to the garden. She felt juvenile as she stopped to whisper to Diane and Toni that she was stepping outside, while they quietly squealed in her ear and gave her a silly thumbs up.

Outside, sitting on a garden bench, Sable answered him, "I went to UC Santa Barbara. Had a great time there actually. I now live in Manhattan Beach and I own a restaurant in Los Angeles not far from my home. My restaurant's name is *Amor Mio*."

"Love," Phillip said.

"Yes, it means 'my love.' I wanted to honor my Spanish heritage with words that meant something to me."

"It's lovely. It suits you."

"What's the name of your photography studio?"

"Its name is *Enchanting*."

"Funny that we're both business owners with romantic names…What did you do after Princeton?"

"I traveled with Sinclair around Europe and the Caribbean for awhile. I also lived with my parents for a bit in Texas, but felt drawn to return to California. How are your parents and Olivia doing?"

"My parents are doing well. Sadly, my grandmother died quite a few years back. I still miss her very much, but she lived a long life and was a happy woman to her last day."

They spoke comfortably for a few more minutes, but then Sable wanted to cut it short. She wanted to end the conversation on her terms. She knew it was silly, but she didn't want to be "left" again.

She stood up and said, "Well, it's been great catching up. I'm so glad to have seen you again."

"Wait, Sable, don't go yet. I would love to talk to you some more. Maybe dance with you a little later, exchange phone numbers."

"I don't think so Phillip. But thank you for offering. Like I said, it's been great seeing you." She bent down and this time, it was she who kissed his cheek. She quickly walked away, hoping that she'd stay poised the whole time, in case he was watching her.

She quickly went into the bathroom and locked herself into a stall. To her surprise, she leaned against the wall and started to cry. She cried for the fifteen year old girl inside her who was so hurt by him. She cried because she felt that she was incapable of true love because of the wall that she had put around her heart over a decade before. She cried because without a doubt, she knew she had just walked away from the love of her life. She wouldn't let him back in because she couldn't survive losing him again.

While Sable was in the bathroom, Phillip took a walk outside. He couldn't believe that she had walked away. Had he said something wrong? It seemed like they had a great rapport. God, she was scrumptious. She was everything he remembered and so, so much more. He wanted her back, he couldn't deny it. He had to win her back and declare his love for her. To tell her, he never stopped loving her. That their future was meant to be together. He couldn't lose her again. If he did, he knew he would never forgive himself.

About an hour later, after Phillip was tired of stalling for time with his two employees, he decided to ask Sable to dance. He was aware that she had said goodbye, but he just couldn't leave it at that. So he approached the DJ and gave him $50 to play three love songs in a row as soon as he stepped on the dance floor. He told him that one song should be a Beatles song, the other two he didn't care what was played.

Phillip approached Sable and asked her to dance. She hesitated, but then offered him her hand.

"Thanks for giving me a second chance," Phillip said to her.

She smiled at him and said, "I don't know that you deserve one."

"Ouch," and they both laughed. As soon as they set foot on the dance floor, Norah Jones' "Don't Know Why" came on.

They held each other while they danced and they looked and smiled at each other throughout the song. At one point, she leaned her forehead against his chin and the moment was dreamlike for her. She felt her body melting a little bit and it scared her. She wanted to run away, grab her car keys and drive away. Simultaneously, however, she thought to herself, "enjoy the moment." As soon as she told herself those words, he kissed her forehead and brought her in a little closer.

When the song was over, Sable dropped her arms and had every intention of holding on to her resolve and rejoin her group.

But the Beatles song came on next, "And I Love Her." They both looked at each other remembering their first date. How they had manipulated Sable's dad's love for the Beatles to allow them permission to go on their first date. They smiled because they knew the other remembered as well. Phillip took her hand and led her deeper onto the dance floor and he held her so gingerly. He hummed the song softly and Sable tried to concentrate on keeping her composure. The moment was so sweet, it took all her strength to stay strong and a little distant. Although she was enjoying herself, she wanted to guard her heart. He dropped her right hand down by his and he interlocked his fingers with hers. She felt a rush of desire wash over her and it scared her. She could not fall in love with him again. He was dangerous. She had a safe life. A pretty home. Wonderful parents. A successful restaurant. She didn't need him hurting her again. Still, being in his arms felt magical. Breathing into his skin, smelling him, could be intoxicating if she let it. The song was almost over and she readied herself to leave him. She swayed with him for a few more moments, admittedly loving his strong arms around her.

He could feel her resist him. He didn't want to overwhelm her, but he wanted to cocoon her with his love. He didn't know her well anymore, but he knew that those were just details. She was the one for him. He knew it. Now, he just had to communicate that to her.

When the song ended, he knew she was going to try to dart to her friends again, so he tried to preempt her escape. So he said to her, when the song started to wind down. "Just one more please and I'll walk you back to your friends."

"Okay," she said. She felt better that the end was near. He couldn't hold her captive on the dance floor for much longer, and a song is usually 3 minutes long.

Extreme's "More than Words" came on and she leaned into him and his arm encircled her waist. She let her head rest on his shoulder for a moment and he whispered in her ear, "I'm so glad we're here together." She nodded her head but couldn't affirm his comment with her own. Her legs were starting to lose stability and she knew that her strength was slipping. She tried to remember the million tears she shed for him. She tried to remember how she had waited for him, hoping that he'd reconsider and call her or write to her. She also remembered how she used to obsess over all the girls he was probably meeting at Princeton. How painful that had been. And yet, here she was, at *her* reunion, dancing with her first love. The song was magical for her, she knew every word and had sung it countless times.

"Phillip, it's been really nice seeing you. I notice you're not doing the photography yourself....are you here because you thought you'd see me?"

"Absolutely, Sable. I've thought about it quite a bit in the last two months."

"I have a boyfriend Phillip. A serious boyfriend. He's not here because he had to travel. But it's probably not appropriate that I continue to dance all these slow songs with you."

"Oh. I didn't know. Have you dated long?"

"No, but it's serious."

"Are you close to being engaged Sable?"

"Well, I don't know Phillip. I'm just beginning in the restaurant world and that takes up virtually all my time. But yes, we're serious."

"Yes, I know, you keep mentioning that."

Sable felt flustered for a moment, as if he was teasing her. She had to be in control. She had to make all the decisions.

"Phillip, I want to thank you for dancing with me. It was truly memorable."

"Sable, I don't want to ruin your relationship. But I have to be honest with you. I have missed you for years. I have never been in love again. You're all I've thought about in the last few months. Tonight's reunion has rekindled more love in my heart than I thought was capable. I would love to take you to dinner just once. And if it isn't special for you, I promise, I'll never bother you again. But having you in my arms for the past ten minutes has had more meaning than anything I can remember."

Sable's mouth hung open. Every time she wanted to say something, she couldn't form the words. She stared deeply into his handsome face and willed herself to say, "I'm sorry Phillip. It's too late for us. I can't go out to dinner with you. We were kids, it didn't mean anything."

She walked back to her table, quickly said goodbye to Diane and Toni and the rest of the friends there and decided to leave the reunion.

She was practically running through the parking lot and couldn't get to her car quickly enough. She turned on the ignition and rested her head against the steering wheel where she cried for a very long time.

Ten

Phillip was devastated. He knew very well before he went to the reunion, that there was only a slight chance that she'd feel the same way. But seeing her was unbelievable. She was so sexy, her body so flawless. He was drawn to her like no other woman he'd ever met. When his arms were around her, he felt whole. He longed for moments when they would watch movies on her couch for hours, go kayaking in the river, walk in a garden hand in hand, go shopping for diamond rings together, have a loving wedding day, the kids, the house, the dog, EVERYTHING. Dammit, he wanted everything with her. He realized that he hadn't seen her in thirteen years, yet it felt like the core of who they were, was the same as they'd always been: in love and made for one another.

He was hurt beyond belief by her indifference. Even though he understood before going to the reunion, that she might be otherwise committed, he felt deep within himself, that she would want him just as much as he wanted her.

Dancing with her was amazing. Kissing her forehead, holding her hand, humming in her ear, those moments had been special. So innocent, yet so seductive in its simplicity that Phillip was surprised at how much it had moved him both physically and emotionally.

Phillip decided that she was worth fighting for. He was going to find her restaurant in Los Angeles and visit. But before he did that, he was going to try to romance her a little bit. Make her think of him. So that when he went to visit her, she would be open to the opportunity of loving him again.

He didn't know if he wanted to believe that she had a serious boyfriend. What kind of a man in his late twenties or thirties, didn't propose to a woman like Sable and make her his right away? An eighteen year old moron, sure, but, a full grown man? There must be something certainly wrong with him. Sable was everything: intelligent, attractive, successful, loving, tender….how could a "serious boyfriend" not have married her? It was inconceivable to him.

Two days after the reunion, he sent two dozen red roses to her restaurant. On the card, he wrote, "Sable, you are the loveliest woman I've ever seen. I can't stop thinking of you. Love, Phillip"

Sable had received them and was blown away by the love she felt in her heart for him. It angered her actually. She didn't want to love him anymore. That phase in her life had ended. She couldn't experience that kind of rejection again. The roses were sweet, but she would make herself see them only as a friendly gesture. She put the lovely roses on her desk at the restaurant and put the card in her wallet.

Two days later, Phillip reached out to her again. He found her email on the restaurant's website and he decided to write to her.

"Dear Sable,

I have to tell you what my life was like after we separated. I know I hurt you beyond belief when I broke up with you. It hurts me now to think of the pain I caused you. At the time, I thought I was being a gentleman. I didn't want to be the kind of guy to have a "girl back home" stringing her along for years. I kept myself busy with the demands of school life. I thought of you often, but willed myself not to reach out to you and hurt you further.

After graduation, I assumed love would find me again. I was always surprised that anyone I met wouldn't stir in me one-tenth of what I felt for you. I soon realized after that, that you were not only my first love, but the love of my life.

By that point I was in my mid twenties and you were probably finishing college around that time, and I didn't want to disturb your life. I had assumed that you'd moved on and probably very happy with someone else. You're so damn beautiful, how could you not ensnare dozens of young guys?

As I got older, I missed you even more. I actually felt jealous of my younger self because "he" had had the best love, but was too young and naïve to possibly understand that. I tried to feel attachments to others, but I couldn't muster much of anything.

So when I got the contract for the reunion for Madison High, I thought it was kismet, destiny, fate, whatever you want to call it, that was bringing us together again. I might be sounding like a fool to you right now, but I have to try. Because having you in my arms for those minutes of slow dancing, has been the happiest I've been in years. And if I don't say all this to you, I'll regret it, babe.

Please, think about it.

I love you, *te amo*, Phillip"

"Oh my God, Toni, what do I do?" Sable cried after she read the note to Toni over the phone.

"That is the nicest, heartfelt note I've ever heard. The way he looked at you on the dance floor, Sable, it was unreal."

"I don't trust him, Ton. He hurt me. He never sent me a birthday card or Christmas card. He simply erased me from his life. And just because he hasn't found anyone else, I'm supposed to love him again or at least, entertain the thought of letting him back in?"

"Sable, what is the difference between giving it a go with him again or a new guy? He might be perfect, just as much as the next person. You're not going anywhere with Rick, we all know that. What is the difference between letting yourself *feel* with him, like you would a new boyfriend?"

"When you say it that way, no, there's no difference. I suppose a new boyfriend can either hurt me or love me to pieces …the chance taken is the same. However, HE hurt me. I don't think I can forgive him for that."

"Will you be able to forgive yourself if you walk away from this opportunity?"

☙☙ ☙☙ ☙☙

The following Monday, which was 9 days after the reunion......7 days after the roses and 5 days after the email, Phillip pulled up to *Amor Mio* restaurant. It was 9:30 pm and he knew that the restaurant would be closing soon. He wanted to catch her still there and he wanted to talk to her with hopefully few or no customers in the restaurant.

He parked his car and admired the restaurant from the outside. He could see the extra large windows and the numerous chandeliers. The place definitely looked romantic. The romance was in the soft glow of the candles, the small vases of clustered red roses at every table, the ornate ironwork between the main dining room and the kitchen, the sparkles that ricocheted in the lighting from the many chandeliers. Was Sable living out romance through the restaurant? It was an interesting thought. Maybe she wasn't as serious with her boyfriend as she led him to believe.

He walked in and immediately loved the restaurant. It exuded love and passion. How appropriate, he smiled to himself. Phillip thought that maybe Sable was ripe for love. If she was, he was going to be the one to collect it.

"Sorry, sir, we'll be closing in a few moments."

"Actually, I'd like to see the owner, Sable Franco. My name is Phillip McNeil."

"One moment," the waitress said.

"Sable, there is a Phillip McNeil to see you," Whitney, who walked in her office, announced.

"What? He's here? I wasn't expecting him!"

"Well, he's gorgeous Boss. What shall I tell him?"

"Tell him, I'll be out in a few minutes."

Sable leaned back in her chair and massaged her temples. She didn't know how long she could resist him. At the reunion, he had unlocked some old feelings that she had put away years ago. Then, the gesture of the roses and its card had really been splendid. The email had left her speechless for days. He was saying everything she would've wanted to hear, but she felt nervous about ever trusting him again. Now he was outside and she had to face him.

She went into her small bathroom and ran her fingers through her hair. She quickly brushed her teeth and added some fresh lipstick. She took a deep breath and walked out to meet him.

"Phillip, what are you doing in Los Angeles?"

"Hello Sable, you look great. I drove in hoping to catch you."

"Yes, I'm usually here this late. We'll be closing any minute. Would you like a glass of wine?"

"I would love some, yes." Sable led him to a corner table away from the few customers who were still dining and left him for a moment while she grabbed two wine glasses and a bottle of wine.

She sat down at the table and started to pour. She looked up at him and smiled.

"Thank you Phillip for the roses. They were incredible. They were the biggest roses I have ever seen. They're on my desk right now."

"I'm glad you enjoyed them Sable. Your restaurant is impressive. All of these chandeliers really have quite an effect on the room."

"Yes, I really love the glow they give the restaurant and the ambiance. It's been my baby now for over the past year."

"I can see how much of yourself you've put into it."

They were silent for a moment and Sable thought about how she was going to let him down.

"Look, Phillip, the effort you're making is appreciated. It really is. But I'm involved with someone and it really isn't appropriate to be receiving flowers from someone else."

"I'm sorry, I didn't mean to make you feel uncomfortable. I just really had to make a gesture and roses seemed like the natural message for what I was trying to convey."

"Thank you Phillip. Which leads me to the next thing. Your email was heartwarming. You said things that I've probably always wanted to hear. And I was glad that you said those things and I'll always hold your words dear. But I can't reciprocate."

"You can't reciprocate because you're so in love with your boyfriend? Or because you're incapable of caring for me? Or because you hate me too much?"

"I've never hated you Phillip. I can't reciprocate because I just can't. I'm not fifteen anymore."

"Sable, I don't think you're that serious with your boyfriend. If you were, you two would've already married. No one in his right mind would make you wait."

Sable exhaled sharply. She felt exhausted. It was time just to tell him the truth.

"Phillip, you're right. Rick and I will never walk down the aisle. We've been dating for six months and we don't see each other as much as couples should. The problem, however, is not with Rick, it's with you. I will never love you like that again. So I'm afraid you're wasting your time."

"Is it because you're not interested in me at all or is there another reason? Because when I saw you at the reunion, I felt like we had stepped back in time."

Whitney approached the table and told Sable that the last of the customers had paid and left. Only two chefs and a dishwasher were left in the kitchen. Sable gave Whitney a few last minute directions and wished her a good night. She then excused herself from Phillip and went to the front door and locked up. She walked to the kitchen and picked up some bread rolls and filled two soup bowls of lobster bisque and brought those to their table.

She half smiled to Phillip and said, "I haven't had dinner yet and assumed you still wanted to stay awhile."

Phillip smiled at her warmly. "You're absolutely right. I definitely want to stay a while, as long as you'll have me."

Sable knew that he was sending her a message with a subtle second meaning, *a double entendre,* but she decided to speak in literal terms.

"You can probably stay an hour, that's when the kitchen will probably be ready to close down and then I'll have to do a couple of things in my office before I head home myself."

Phillip was not going to be greedy. If she was giving him an hour, he'd gladly take it. He had less time dancing with her and it had filled him with more intensity than he'd had in years, possibly even enough years back since he'd been a kid. Yes, a kid *with her.*

He decided not to continue talking of love, but talk of general topics so that she'd learn to trust him again.

"Sable, this lobster bisque is spectacular. And I can't get over how sophisticated and charming your restaurant is. Will you tell me what led you to become its owner?"

Sable could feel herself relax, "Well, after majoring in business at UCSB, my first professional job was for a company that did advertising for restaurants, *Cuisine Ads*. I worked for them for four years and actually learned a lot about the restaurant world. Later, for my 26th birthday, my parents gave me a ten week cooking class course. I loved it. Not so much the cooking per se, although that was a lot of fun too, but the whole world of restaurant life kind of molded itself into a realistic dream.

"After my grandmother passed away, she had left me $25,000 and my parents invested it for me. I didn't need to pay for college because my parents paid for that. And I had already bought my home from my *Cuisine Ads* earnings, so I decided to invest all the money she left me, plus its invested earnings, plus a little I had saved on the side and an idea was born. I would honor my grandmother's memory and culture from the Canary Islands and call it *Amor Mio*."

For the next hour, they also talked of his business, *Enchanting*, and his travels with his brother Sinclair. They caught each other up on their parents, and Sable even spoke a little about her cousin Desiree, who was probably seven the last time Phillip saw her. They also talked of both of their homes, Sable's in Manhattan Beach and Phillip's in El Toro. They both talked about how they had fallen in love with their homes and how they had decorated them. Phillip also talked lovingly of his dog Joey.

By this time, both chefs and the dishwasher had long gone home and Sable and Phillip had probably been alone in the restaurant for at least half an hour.

Sable let her eyes roam over to the red velvet heavy drapes that framed the windows and she thought that they looked a lot like the roses that were on her desk. Thinking of her desk made her remember that she still had some last minute details to do before she went home.

At the exact same time, Sable was going to bid Phillip good night, Phillip asked if Sable would give him a tour of the restaurant. They had already finished a bottle of wine and Sable was feeling relaxed. After talking so much about issues that were more neutral than rehashing their past, she was feeling more comfortable with him.

She relented and they both got up for the tour. She automatically picked up their empty soup bowls and he picked up their wine glasses, empty wine bottle and basket of bread and followed her into the kitchen. Phillip was impressed at how large the kitchen was with multiple ranges, prep stations, a wall of ovens and several huge, industrial size refrigerators. She also had a walk in refrigerator, the size of a small bedroom. There were several islands in the middle of the kitchen that were red in color and made of distressed wood. There was open shelving on the walls filled with tin canisters. Also, along the back wall, were a few iron baker's racks that housed big baskets of linens, candles and table decor. The whole area seemed reminiscent of a grandmother's kitchen. It seemed quaint and rustic. He loved it immediately. Phillip remembered Olivia very much, was even afraid of her a few times, and thought she would feel very comfortable in this space.

Sable also led him through the main dining space that he had already seen, but she began describing details such as her beloved drapes that were overpriced, but that she had to buy. She described the seven crystal chandeliers that gave the room its rich glow and even spoke of the twinkle lights around the big front window and the smaller side windows that always made her feel happy. Only sparkling lights that bounce off crystal china on one's dinner table could make one feel so enchanted. Funny, she thought, "enchanting" is the name of *his* business.

"Well, the only thing left to see is my office, I'm sure you don't care about that."

"Of course I do. I would love to see where you spend your days and nights."

Sable smiled and led the way. It was furnished with antique black furniture: a desk, an old credenza for her files and a side table for her photographs and laptop. Her desk chair was upholstered in black and white damask and her drapes were of course, the same red velvet that was hanging in the dining room. The only art piece was of a Spanish bull fighter in full Spanish costume in the middle of a bull ring. In the stands behind him, there was a woman standing wearing a long flowing white dress and a large, floppy white hat. Her hands were poised together as if she were either praying or applauding. Sable had always loved that piece of art. Not only because it seemed romantic to her, but because it seemed very Spanish in both décor and passion.

Phillip said, "Everything's elegant in here Sable. Seems old, but strangely current as well. Only you can make an office seem romantic as well as efficient."

Sable laughed at his description and looked up at him and held his gaze. Ever so slowly, he moved towards her and embraced her. She let it happen. She breathed him in and embraced him back. They were hugging so tight and so sweetly that she couldn't tell if they were hugging goodbye or hugging hello.

He melted into that hug and felt his heart constrict. He bent down and kissed her jaw line and felt her skin prickle by his touch. He moved upward just a bit and kissed her cheek and then found her mouth. He kissed her slowly, tenderly, not wanting to scare her off. But she wasn't moving, which he thought was better than pushing him away. He opened up his mouth and swallowed her up with everything he had to give. He gave and she gave. She was reciprocating his every move. They were kissing so passionately that he never wanted it to stop. They were touching each other's faces and embracing all the while and it was the hottest sensation either had ever felt.

Their love was here. It wasn't a love of yesteryear, it was *here*. It was alive and it was now. They weren't remembering old kisses, but enjoying and creating new ones. Slowly, ever so slowly, he dared to unbutton her blouse, awaiting her complaint, but there was none. She slowly brought up her own hands and unbuttoned his shirt as well. His whole body tingled with anticipation for what was about to happen.

Their kissing was so intense that Phillip didn't think he could wait a moment longer. But for her, he would. He would only follow her lead. He wanted her to feel respected, yet he wanted her to feel desired as well. It was in that delicate balance, that he concentrated—not on his passion, but on her needs.

For Sable, she hadn't felt this kind of intensity since…..since she was a fifteen year old girl. She wanted Phillip, she wanted him with her whole body. She was tired of analyzing what had happened to them or what was possibly happening now. All she knew was that her body was heating up beyond anything she could compare it to and she would not stop this explosion of desire.

She lowered her own skirt and kicked off her high heeled sandals. Phillip followed her lead and took off his slacks and dropped his shirt off his shoulders. They kissed for a few more moments, heavily, hungrily, both knowing that there were very little clothes, just their undergarments, separating the consummation of their lust.

After what seemed an eternity of the most seductive kissing either had ever had, Sable pushed some things off of the corner of the desk and perched herself. With her eyes, she invited him to continue. He unhooked her bra and kissed her again and again as she arched her back. In the next moment, they were as one and it was delicious. They whole heartedly gave of themselves. The passion was so intense that their senses were on overload. They tried to concentrate on their hands, on their mouths, on their skin, but there was too much sensation to focus on. And when Phillip thrust in her, it was exquisite for Sable. It was incomparable to anything and she felt whole. For years, she had feared that she would never enjoy intimacy again, but that was not true. For she was loving every single touch and her whole body was ablaze with heat. They kissed and they rocked and they clutched each other. And even as it was slowing back down, the intensity was still overwhelming, but now it was gentle, eyes focused on each other, soft sweet kisses cherishing each other. Their hands treasured every inch of each other. And as it stopped, they just kept smiling at each other. Smiles that held promise. A promise of love, of future, of commitment, of each other. Sable reached out and put both her arms around his neck and hugged him tightly. He in turn, hugged her with all his being, all his love and whispered in her ear, "I love you Sable, I've never stopped. Please love me back."

With tears in her eyes, although he couldn't see them, he knew they were there. She held him tighter to her and encircled her arms even closer to him, skin to skin, soul to soul and nodded her head.

" *S* able, is it true? Can we start again?"
"You asked if I would love you back and I answered yes. I don't know however, if we could enter a relationship."

"I don't understand Sable. I love you and I think you love me. What in the hell would hold us back? We're adults, we live in the same area, and we never forgot each other."

"The problem Phillip," as she put her clothes back on, "is that I simply, repeat, simply cannot live with the pain of losing you again. You broke my heart completely. Everything I had after you was always mediocre and blasé. It was never special. The only thing I ever had that was special was YOU. And if you leave me again, I don't know how I'd overcome that. I have to protect my heart."

Phillip was already dressed by then as well and pulled Sable close. "Sable, I promise you I will never hurt you again. I thought I was being adult and kind with that decision. By God, I've missed you, I swear it. I feel like if we don't take this opportunity right now, *right now*, we will never be who we were supposed to be. I believe you're my destiny. I want to be with you forever, Sable. Please give me the chance of proving that to you."

Sable wanted to believe him. She so desperately wanted to trust again.

Sable shook her head. "Do you know what hurt me the most? You didn't even want to try the long distance. I would've rather that we fell apart, that you would've met someone else, that I would've gotten sick of five-minute phone calls because you were busy studying, that we would have had a big fight, *anything*. But that wasn't the case. You simply decided what was best for both of us and you walked away. You threw me away. And-"

Phillip interrupted her. "I hear you Sable. And I understand what you're saying and what I did to you. Maybe you're right, we should have tried it out and seen what happened. But the reality is I'm here in front of you and I want you so badly. I don't want a fling Sable, I want us."

Sable breathed deeply and looked into his eyes. Her stamina was melting and she knew it. No one would ever compare to Phillip. If she let him go, she would possibly not date again for years. She was afraid depression would set in and she wouldn't be the person she was destined to be at his side.

"Phillip, I need a few things. I need time. I also need to talk to Rick and let him go. I also need for you to be painfully sincere; I can't be romanced and then dropped."

"Baby, I will romance you, but only because I want us together. Guys don't talk like this, but I believe, you and I are meant to be. You make me a better man. I only want to be yours."

They hugged and kissed a bit more in her office and they held hands out to her car, a cute red Jeep.

Sable knew that he'd been trying with her with the roses, the email, and his visit and knew she should extend an invitation to him. "Would you like to come over on Saturday evening? I can cook you dinner and we can walk on the beach. Then, on Sunday morning, we can go for a drive and go eat onion rings at that silly old diner where you first wooed me."

"Are you asking me to spend the night Sable? We never have done that. I would love to, I would simply love to. Would it be okay if I brought Joey? I've never left him alone overnight."

"That would be great. Here's my address. What do you think about 6?"

"I can't wait, babe. I can't wait."

☙❧ ☙❧ ☙❧

The next day, Sable was happy. She was truly, irrevocably happy. She was going to allow herself this happiness. He loved her, he was gorgeous, they had a history, he made her body come alive in passion and she felt safe with him. Granted, he had hurt her as no one else ever had, but she wanted to believe that it was part of adolescence. He had never forgotten her, nor she him. She had decided to open her heart to the possibility.

She would see him Saturday, but today she would have to make a few phone calls. One to Rick, to respectfully say goodbye, and one to her mother, Leslie. She wasn't ready to tell her best friends or her cousin Desiree. But she wanted to tell her mother Leslie and picked up the phone.

"Mom, I've seen Phillip."

"I can't believe it! Where?" Sable filled her in on the reunion, his business, the roses, the email and even his visit to the restaurant. She, of course, didn't tell her about their lovemaking, but she did tell her mother that she was going to see him Saturday.

"Honey, I think this is so sensational. This is a blessing. It's not often that your first love comes back to reclaim lost feelings. This is a gift dear. Don't be afraid of it, embrace it. Take a chance. At the very worst, you'll be alone—but you already have been all these years. At the very best, and I suspect this is what will happen, you'll have him for the rest of your days. Take a chance Sable, welcome it."

"Thanks Mom. That was exactly what I wanted to hear. And Mom, please don't tell Dad. I don't want him to worry just yet. I'll tell him soon."

"I understand dear. You want to make sure everything is a little more stable before your Dad puts in his two cents."

"Exactly."

ᘒᘓ ᘒᘓ ᘒᘓ

On Saturday afternoon, Sable was excited for his arrival. She put miniature white roses in a vase on her table and was washing the shrimp and setting out the cocktail sauce. She had made him pork chops and baked potato and a Caesar salad. She was wearing jeans and a green halter top shirt. She was barefoot and felt very at ease in her clothes and her home and especially comfortable in waiting for his arrival. She wasn't nervous at all, she looked forward to it.

At 5:18 the doorbell rang, and Phillip was at her door. She laughed at his boyish smile and bent down to pet Joey. Joey was a handsome Golden Retriever and loved the attention. Sable stood up and gave Phillip a quick hug and a kiss on the lips.

"I'm sorry I'm so early, but I was eager to see you the whole day. I didn't know how traffic would be, so I guess I just left plain too early."

Sable laughed and said, "I think it's great that you're early. I hope you're hungry and I hope it's okay with you if we eat outside looking at the waves."

"I would absolutely love that! But first, may I kiss you?"

He drew her in and kissed her so intently that she wondered if they'd make it through dinner at all. The kiss lasted for endless minutes and she loved every moment of it.

While she stood in the kitchen and put the shrimp on a platter, he stood behind her and encircled her waist with his arms. He whispered in her ear, "I'm so happy Sable. Tell me that you are too."

"I am. Forgive me if I look dreamy sometimes. I think my heart knows you're here, but my brain hasn't quite processed it all."

He winked at her. "I'm here Sable, I promise."

Once outside, they ate their shrimp cocktails and their Caesar salads. After they ate that, they decided to take a quick walk before eating their main dinner. They walked hand in hand with Joey at their sides. They were both barefoot and were walking in the water and Sable felt a lifetime of happiness in that moment. She looked beyond the waves and closed her eyes for a moment. She saw herself as a young girl in love, she saw herself in her navy and white dress at the reunion, she saw Phillip in his elegant suit, she saw Phillip in his car parked along the curb giving her their first kiss, she saw them nude at her office desk, and then she saw her grandmother Olivia. Yes, she saw her face in the distance, and she was smiling at her! She nodded slightly and smiled again. Sable opened her eyes and Olivia was gone, but she felt her presence and she understood the message. Her grandmother's message was clear: go on, be happy, this is what your life is destined to have.

Sable felt warm all over and happy that the sensation washed over her a sense of validation. Yes, she was making the right choice in giving Phillip a second chance. She would be alright. It was safe to love him again.

Back at her front porch, she refilled their wine glasses and brought out their plates of pork chops, baked potato and garlic bread. Phillip leaned back and rubbed his hands together.

"Is this your idea of spoiling me? I usually eat a sandwich standing up over my kitchen sink."

Sable laughed, "Yeah, I've done that plenty times myself. Let's enjoy the calories."

"Ahh yes, let's! But first, a toast: To new beginnings."

"To new beginnings," Sable echoed and they both reached over the table to give each other a kiss.

☯ ☯ ☯

Later, in bed, Phillip and Sable were holding each other and Phillip asked if she'd spoken to Rick.

"Yes, I told him that he and I weren't moving forward. I told him that he was a very nice person, but that we had no future together."

"Was it hard for you to tell him that?"

"Yes and no. I didn't want to hurt him, but we would've ended eventually at some point. We didn't have the kind of compatibility that endures time. Six months seemed about right."

"Thank you Sable. That's the first part of us being closer and together. Now, I have a question for you."

"Okay, I'm ready."

"At the reunion, you said that 'we didn't mean anything' is that how you truly felt?"

"No Phillip, I lied. I wanted you to dismiss me at that moment. I assumed you were infatuated with me because you ran into me. I never thought I'd see you again and I probably wanted to hurt you a little. I'm sorry for that. Our younger relationship meant everything to me. Nothing ever compared."

He reached over and kissed her. She stroked his chest and relaxed into him. They were resting cheek to cheek and it felt magical. Neither of them had ever felt so happy.

☯ ☯ ☯

The next morning, for the first time, they woke up together. Yes, they had dozed off together as teenagers, but this was different. They had spent the whole night together. Phillip had spooned her throughout the night and she loved it. She slept with her back to him as he cuddled her and held her hand. It was so gentle and loving and she knew that she was taking a big risk with her love. They weren't teenagers anymore and love was more complex. However, she felt so genuinely elated to be with him again, that she knew it was worth it.

He could feel her stir a bit and kissed her ear. "Good morning, mi amor," he said.

"Look at you learning Spanish. I suppose you're trying to impress me."

"Always," he smiled. "God, it's good to wake up in your bed. I could get used to this."

"I'm banking on it." Sable turned to kiss him and threw her leg over his. "Wanna take a dip in the ocean?"

"I would love that. But first there's something I really want to do," and he wrapped her in his arms and proved his ardor.

☙☙ ☙☙ ☙☙

After swimming for awhile, they laid out on towels with Joey. It was a pleasant April morning and the sun was shining. Sable read a little bit while Phillip checked his email on his laptop. They were content just sitting next to each other, they didn't even have to speak.

Sable stopped reading for a moment and gazed out onto the waves. She knew this was a moment in time that she'd always remember. No matter what happened to them, she would look back at this exact moment when he had just spent the night, they had kissed in the ocean, and they were content lying next to each other on the sand, and she would remember it as a perfect day. As if he might have sensed her thoughts, "I love you Sable. We're going to be together forever this time you know."

"I love you too," she reached over and kissed him. "Now, let's go get some onion rings." They laughed walking back to her home.

They changed into dry clothes and when Sable came out wearing a cap, leggings, and a fifteen year old sweatshirt, Phillip laughed out loud.

"You still have my old USC sweatshirt? I wondered what had happened to that! God, you look sexy in it!"

"If you only knew how many times I slept in this old thing, haha."

Desiree was going to the doctor that morning. She had decided she was going to keep the baby and had already phoned her parents and told them the news. Since they had retired in Spain, they urged Desiree to move in with them so that they could help in raising the baby. Desiree's parents were in their mid 60s although Desiree was only twenty. She wasn't ready to make a decision about leaving the country. She wasn't ruling it out for the future, but at this point, she was still coming to terms with being a young mother and possibly a college drop out. She didn't want to leave school, but she was trying to be realistic. Her boyfriend, Dane, didn't want to be involved. He was scared and didn't want to tell his parents. Desiree actually didn't hate him for it. She even told him honestly that if she could run away from the problem, she would as well. But obviously, the baby would be with her always. Sable was accompanying her to the doctor's appointment. Desiree had called the Ob Gyn a month ago, but the receptionist had told her that the doctor didn't see patients until the 10ᵗʰ week of pregnancy. Apparently, there were many cases of false-positives and the doctor saw patients only beyond that timeline.

Desiree guessed that she was between 10-12 weeks. She'd also read that doctors started counting from the date of one's last period and not the actual date of conception, so she was a little confused by that. Either way, she was sure that she was keeping her baby and that she needed to start her prenatal care right away.

Sable had asked her own doctor, Dr. Morgan, for a referral for her younger cousin and she and Desiree were seeing Dr. Eileen Jashe this morning. Desiree was nervous and excited and was also anxious to hear the baby's heartbeat. She was sad that Dane wouldn't accompany her, but she had decided not to hate him. Hating him would malign his image and she wanted to keep positive. After all, he was the father of her baby and she wanted her baby's life to be full of love, not trouble.

The two pretty cousins waited in the waiting area and talked about how Desiree's life would change.

"Des, I know you live with roommates now, but you need to start thinking of where you and the baby will live. You can live with me and you know my parents have offered their house as well."

"I know, but there's so much to think about right now. I just want to start the prenatal care and make sure everything is alright. Soon, I'll make a decision about where we'll live. I'm not showing yet and my roommates are more than supportive. I'm going to finish out the year at school; it's only seven weeks away. I might even take a summer course. The more education I have now, the better. When the baby is just a bit older, I'll only have a year and a half of school work to wrap up my Bachelor's Degree in English. I know my parents want me to move to Spain and be with them. But I really want the baby to be born in an American hospital. And with the finishing of my degree in sight, I'd hate to just pack up and leave. The baby needs me to finish my degree sooner than later, so that I can have a career and support us both. I'm so afraid of being a college dropout, cous. That won't help us in the least."

Sable sighed. She knew her younger cousin had so much to think about. She was going to give her full support and be the best Godmother she could be. Sable's parents would also be very supportive. Desiree's parents come twice a year from Spain as it is and would surely come more often once the baby arrived. In the meantime, they would probably send her enough money to live off of monthly while she finished up her degree. Now, Desiree mainly lived off of student loans, but since she was going to have a break in schooling, her student loan package would probably be compromised. Her parents were wonderful people and would support Desiree in any way.

The nurse finally called, "Desiree Castile" and Sable squeezed her cousin's shoulders. "Vamanos," she said, "*let's go.*"

After Desiree was weighed and had her blood pressure taken, they waited in the small room for Dr. Jashe. She came in moments later and smiled at both girls. Desiree held out her hand and introduced herself and her older cousin.

"Will your spouse be joining us later?"

"No, unfortunately my boyfriend and I have broken up and he's not going to be involved."

"Well, I'm very sad to hear that. You'll have to have a strong support system with your family. Having a baby is very hard work and it even tests the strongest of marriages. But babies are a blessing and very worth the cuddly chaos they cause when they enter this world. Now, let me have you lay down and we'll start the exam."

Dr. Jashe gave Desiree a pelvic exam and stated that everything felt normal. Then she proceeded to squeeze a clear jelly on Desiree's stomach and pulled over the ultrasound monitor. Dr. Jashe showed them the bright outline of the baby's body and the pulsating, tiny blob that she explained was the heartbeat. While Sable and Desiree exclaimed with glee about the heartbeat, Dr. Jashe grew quiet and started zooming in on the image and documenting on her chart.

Desiree noticed that the doctor wasn't saying anything and asked, "is there anything wrong Dr. Jashe?"

"Oh no, not at all. But I do have to check here just a little bit more carefully….yes, I'm certain now. Desiree, congratulations, you're not going to have one baby."

"What! What are you talking about?"

"What I mean to say is, that you're going to have two babies! The second amniotic sac was hiding just slightly behind this one and I had to make sure. But yes, I'm certain! You're going to have twins. You are 11 weeks, 2 days along which makes your due date December 18th. Of course, mothers delivering twins almost always deliver a few weeks early."

Sable and Desiree started giggling like little girls and embraced each other.

"Oh my God!" Desiree shouted. "I can't believe it!"

☻☻ ☻☻ ☻☻

Later in the car, Desiree pensively looked out the window in silence. The news of the twins greatly unsettled her.

"Sable, I'm scared. What the hell am I going to do with twins? I'm twenty years old! I was so confident that I could do this. I thought I'd take a semester off while I recuperated and nursed, then I'd go back to school for a year and a half, crank it out, then have a career or at least be on the way of attaining one, while the baby was very little. Now with two, it's going to be that much harder to have everything they need, and the patience to provide it all while balancing work and school. Not to mention the cost of daycare once I do return to college. I'm so overwhelmed!" Desiree started to cry.

Sable felt so bad for her. Everyone had already offered their help: Sable and her parents, Desiree's parents, but ironically, she still felt alone in this experience. Not having Dane for support was really affecting her. Desiree wanted to be strong and mature, but she felt scared for the future.

"Des, it will be alright. You know what Dr. Jashe said, every baby is a blessing. I know you're going through a lot right now, but once you meet those little angels, you'll be so in love, your anxiety will all but almost disappear."

"Sable, what would you do in my place?"

"I thought about that a few weeks ago when you told me about your pregnancy. If the baby would have been

Phillip's I would have kept it. I loved him very much. But if it was someone else's, I honestly just don't know."

The next day, Desiree looked online at adoption agencies. She was shocked to learn so much about the process. She read about so many couples trying to start a family and sometimes, waiting for years to be accepted as a worthwhile couple. In addition, she read that many of those couples often tired of waiting, and instead pursued international adoptions, especially children from South America, China and Romania. Desiree couldn't believe it. The system often allowed babies to grow into toddlers and sometimes small children before they were placed, wasting precious time of their young development. In turn, many of the babies had problematic health concerns such as fetal alcohol syndrome, AIDS, and drug addiction. Many of the babies had little or no prenatal care, and to Desiree's horror, some cash was exchanging hands between the young mothers and the potential adoptive parents. Furthermore, some of those same mothers *still* chose other "parents" at the last minute, forsaking the first parents who had paid for the opportunity of being selected by the mother.

Desiree was so disenchanted with the whole process that it made her feel even more committed to her decision in keeping the babies. For a few self-doubting moments, she thought she might make other choices, but after reading some information, she just couldn't give the babies away. She was so blessed that she was even able to get pregnant. Reading about all the sad infertility problems that some of the couples had shared, just put it into perspective for Desiree that babies are gifts. She would be honored to be their mom.

Another thought that solidified her decision was that she had to remember her own childhood. Her own mother could not conceive until she was forty-five. In an age, where little help was available, Desiree's parents had lost hope of ever becoming parents. They had been married for sixteen years before Desiree was born. She was obviously an only child, and yet her childhood had been fabulous. She was so doted on and cherished by her parents, loved by her cousin Sable and her parents, and finally adored by her grandmother Olivia. How could she even consider giving away her parents' grandchildren after all that they had gone through? It would crush them if Desiree took away their possibility of becoming grandparents, when they almost missed the opportunity of becoming parents in the first place.

Yes, the more she thought about it, Desiree knew that she was making the right decision. She had faltered a bit after learning that she was expecting twins, in that she was so overwhelmed with the challenge. But the more she thought about it, the happier she became in the prospect of becoming a mom. She knew becoming a *single* mom was going to be the hardest thing she would ever do. But, she had a loving family who would help support her emotionally and financially, she was more than half way done with her degree, and she knew that Olivia would be watching over her lending a hand. Those reasons added to her commitment and determination.

Phillip was beyond happy these days. He had never been unhappy per se, but he was always busy trying to keep the void of loneliness out. But now that Sable was back in his life, he couldn't contain his joy. He thought of her every moment of the day. Since the night when he had visited her restaurant and they had become lovers in her office, he hadn't been the same. He knew he couldn't lose her for a second time in his life. Without a shadow of a doubt, he wanted to be hers for all time and start a life together.

Making love to her had been incredible. He hadn't expected it to happen so quickly, although it was all he could think about after seeing her at the reunion. She had looked so alluring there, older, poised, but ever so vulnerable. He wanted to make her feel secure in the knowledge that he would never hurt her again. He had driven to her Los Angeles restaurant in the hope of gaining some of her trust and hopefully opening the door to some romance. He had never let his mind wander to actual passion, he had assumed they were months away from that. But gazing at her over the table as they had talked for that hour had been splendid. By that time, the restaurant had emptied, and it was just the two of them catching up on their lives. Of course that was very important, but even as they spoke, in the back of Phillip's mind, he knew it wasn't their past he was interested in, but their future. Their future *together*. Once they had walked into her office, he had wanted to kiss her so badly. Just one, he had thought to himself. He never imagined that she would allow herself to get carried away in that sort of passion. Surely, not to consummate their passion that very night. He remembered that he had held back at the precise moment when he felt he'd come undone, but it was that moment that Sable had moved forward. It was such a turn on when a woman wanted you. It was incredible to be with her as a man. The last time they had made love, he had been eighteen and she had been fifteen, and although any eighteen year old boy would want to consider himself to be an adult, Phillip knew it was no comparison to making love to her as a man.

It was hard to believe, but they had even topped that intense, passionate lovemaking, at her house last Saturday night. Phillip had never been as satisfied as he had been that night. Falling asleep with her and holding her all night was incomparable. Yes, Phillip knew he was taken with her beyond description. He would never love another woman like he loved Sable. If it was up to him, he would propose tonight, but he didn't want to scare her off. He knew that she was freshly out of a relationship with Rick and he also knew that she still held her guard up.

He would romance her until they were absolutely comfortable with each other, until they could overcome the ghosts of their past. And then he would propose and they would marry and start a family. He was never going to lose her again. Of this he was certain.

He remembered back to the beginning of their young courtship when she had asked why he loved her. They were on his bed watching TV, just having finished some of their homework. He was lying down and she was sitting up resting against his bedroom wall. Her legs were under his and they were holding hands. They had just become lovers for the first time the week before and everything felt so tender and adoring. She looked down at him and sighed softly, love in her eyes, butterflies in her stomach.

"Phillip, why do you love me? And make it good, I know you're studying poetry in advanced lit."

Phillip laughed wholeheartedly and sat up and crossed his legs in front of her. He took both her hands in his and reached over and kissed her cheek, slowly moving his lips to brush against her left eye.

"Let me think.....hmmm...this is hard, but I'll try......

It could be your hands, I love the way they touch me. It could be your eyes, I love the way you look at me. It could be your mouth, I love the way you kiss me. It could be your skin, I love the way it feels against me. It could be your heart, I love the way it draws me in. It could be your voice, I love the way it entices me. Okay, that's all I've got!"

"Phillip, that was great! You are a poet, haha!" She jumped on top of him and started tickling him, until he was begging for mercy! They made so much noise, that Sinclair walked in.

"Hey, hey, what's going on?" He laughed, "Mom says you need to come down for dinner and to invite Sable if she wants to join us."

"Hey Sinclair, do you want to know how romantic your brother is-"

"Don't you dare tell him what I just said! You want to ruin my tough reputation?"

Sinclair made a face while he closed the door. As he left, all he heard was whooping and hollering.

ᘒᘒ ᘒᘒ ᘒᘒ

Phillip laughed at the memory. Those were some sweet times. She was arriving shortly and he was walking around the house making sure everything looked great. He had gone to the store last night and bought some candles to light tonight. He was playing soft music and walked outside to his barbecue to check on the salmon. He was so excited to see her and show her his home. He wanted to assume that she'd be spending a lot of time there from now on and he wanted it to feel welcoming. He even tied a red velvet ribbon around Joey's neck, he was sure she'd love that.

When she knocked on the door, he opened the door, stepped forward and hugged her completely. His whole body was pressed against hers. She sighed against him, loving the moment.

"Hi beautiful."

"Hi there, I love your home. Show me around."

Phillip showed her his four bedroom home and his pride and joy, his stainless steel kitchen. He then walked her outside to his patio, where he had set the table with candles and a small bouquet of miniature white roses.

"This is incredible Phillip, thank you." She reached over and gave him a light kiss on the lips. "What are we having?"

"We're having spinach artichoke dip with French Bread as an appetizer and salmon and rice for dinner. For dessert, all you get is me."

Sable laughed and rewarded him with a kiss again. "Did you do all this cooking yourself? I'm impressed."

"Anything to impress you baby."

They sat down to eat and Sable poured the wine. "Tell me Sable, about your baby cousin Desiree. I remember her with that jet black hair that used to hang down her back. She was always so cute when she'd sit next to us and watch movies with us."

Sable smiled warmly. "Well, she still has that long black hair that flows down her back. But she's no longer a baby. She's twenty now and is in terrible straights."

"Why, what has happened to her?"

"Desiree just had a bad breakup with her boyfriend Dane. So besides being heartbroken, she's now single and pregnant with twins. She's almost three months along."

"Oh my God, Sable, I'm so sorry. What is she going to do? She must be so afraid."

"She is. Her parents live in Spain now. Dane wants nothing to do with the pregnancy. Although, she has me and my parents' support, I know she feels lonely. She's still in school and about 2 years away from getting her degree. She's overwhelmed with having twins. When she decided to keep the baby, she was determined to make it work. But when the doctor said that she was expecting two, she was overwhelmed with daycare, nursing, space, supplies, everything. Her parents want her to move to Spain so that they can help her, but I'm fairly certain, she'll stay. Another thing is that with twins, you often go on bed rest early and they're usually born early as well. She at least wanted to take summer school courses to get ahead a little before she put school on hold. It's a lot for any young girl to take."

"Definitely. I understand. I'm certain she'll be a great mom as soon as the dust settles. But what a challenging next few years she'll have."

"Yes, she will. My heart goes out to her. Children should come into a home that welcomes them. To two parents who are committed to each other and who can financially provide. Well, ideally, at least."

"Do you want children one day Sable?"

"I would love children one day Phillip. But I'm afraid my baby right now is the restaurant. I've put all my time, energy and money into it and I'm determined to make it successful. We've had a great first year, but I need to be realistic that restaurant life is often unpredictable. How about you, do you want children?"

"Yes, Sable, I do. I really want to be a father to three or four kids. I've always known that I would want a big family. A carload of kids laughing or screaming would be fun, call me crazy." Phillip laughed at that and saw that Sable was laughing too. "Since I'm thirty-one, I need to start hustling soon. Being that I'm always shooting weddings and talking to brides, it's a subject that's often on my mind."

They stayed quiet a moment and Phillip gazed in her eyes willing her to love him, to want to marry him one day and have these children they were talking about. In turn, Sable was gazing back into his eyes telling him that she would not be hurt again, that she didn't completely trust him yet.

"Sable, would you consider thinking about your future and mine as one that we could make together?"

"Phillip, I don't know. That is a huge topic to think about. Up until a few weeks ago, I thought I'd never see you again and here I am in your house enjoying a bottle of wine. We've become lovers and you've even spent the night."

"And I hope you spend the night tonight, my love," he said.

"Yes, I'd like to…"

"Sable, I know it's too early to talk about the future….but we're not a regular couple who just met. You were my first love, and actually, you've been my only love. I never met anybody else who even came close. I know, without a doubt, that you're the love of my life and meeting you again is a blessing. We're picking up on a love that never ended for me. So when I talk about the future, it seems like the most normal next step."

Sable's eyes were glistening with tears. She loved what she was hearing, but she was still afraid.

"Phillip, all I can say is that I love what you're saying. I really do. But you hurt me beyond belief. I never thought my heart would heal. It's going to take a while to trust you completely again. I understand your reasons, but when you're fifteen, you're not logical, you're emotional." Sable paused and touched his cheek, "as for our future, let's take it slow. There's no hurry. If we let this new love blossom, it will lead us to wherever we're supposed to be."

They both leaned toward each other and kissed for a few moments, their passion kindling again.

"Don't hurt me again Phillip. That's all I ask."

"I won't. I promise. Come here, love." He led her into his living room and turned on the music. He put on Styx' "Babe" and they danced so slowly, that they were barely moving. It seemed like they were hugging more than anything. They were both thinking of the conversation they just had. Sable hoped that their love could survive a second chance. Phillip desired that with all his soul. He decided to lighten the mood and enjoy the playful side of her. He played the same Beatles song that they had danced to at the reunion, "And I Love Her." He twirled her, turned her in his arms and dipped her several times. They laughed and kissed throughout the song.

"This isn't becoming our song is it?" she laughed.

"Ha, I think it just might be."

They danced for a few more moments in silence.

"I love you, Phillip," she whispered.

Phillip closed his eyes and let his heart squeeze in his chest. "I love you too Sable." He swirled her around a bit and said, "Sable, I have a very important question to ask you."

Sable grew pasty white, "Yes?"

Phillip chuckled to himself, "Will you spend next weekend with me in Santa Barbara?"

Sable laughed and drew up her arms to encircle his neck. "My old stomping grounds eh? Yes, I'd love to spend next weekend with you there."

"That's music to my ears. We'll drive out there Friday night, my love."

Fourteen

$\mathcal{S}$able walked into her parents' home and threw herself on the sofa. They had left her a note on the coffee table that they had taken a walk to the bakery to pick up croissants. For Sable, a few moments of quiet and solitude suited her. She closed her eyes and let the peace overtake her body. She had had so many emotional days lately. Seeing Phillip and falling in love with him again. Internalizing Desiree's anguish. Saying goodbye to Rick. Keeping *Amor Mio* running with efficiency and elegance. She welcomed the silence, the warmth of her parents' home. She decided to get up and curl up in her old bed. Her parents had never redecorated her old room. Being that she was an only child, they couldn't bear to change Sable's space, besides the fact that they already had an office and a guest room, why change hers? Sable snuggled in the warmth of familiarity and nostalgia. Good times, she thought, being safe in Mom and Dad's care. She must've dozed off for a few minutes before her parents called out to her from the living room.

"Sable, where are you honey? We saw your car parked out front."

"I'm here Mom. I must've dozed off!" She fixed the pillows and walked out to meet them and kiss them.

"Those croissants smell heavenly! Where's the jam?"

They got cozy in the kitchen nook and had a delicious breakfast along with hot chocolate.

"I have something to tell you Dad. I don't know how you're going to feel about it." Sable waited for his response, but he stayed quiet in anticipation. "I met Phillip McNeil at my reunion a few weeks ago. He owns the photography company that was taking photographs that night. We've been seeing each other ever since."

"Oh honey," Sable's father, Daniel, said. "That boy broke your heart when you were a young girl. Could you really trust him again? And Leslie, did you know?"

"All I knew, dear, was that Sable had seen him at the reunion and that he made several attempts to reconnect with her." She turned to Sable, "I always agreed with Phillip's decision to terminate your relationship back then, sweetie. Long distance relationships are traumatic and are often ill-fated anyway. What I didn't count on, was you taking it so hard." Leslie said.

"I did take it very hard. He broke my heart and nobody's compared to him in these last thirteen years. I have my reservations, but I'm going to take a chance."

"What's to say he doesn't hurt you again?" Daniel asked.

"I don't know. I'm very afraid of that. But I'm more afraid of ignoring his advances and regretting it for the rest of my life."

They all sat back and all took sips from the hot chocolate, soaking in Sable's admission.

Her mother spoke first, "What happened to Rick? We thought he was a fine young man."

"He is Mom. But he doesn't drive me crazy. We were lukewarm. He's very nice, but neither of us made much of an effort to reduce our work time and spend time with each other. We didn't have high expectations of the other, nor did either of us ever get upset over broken dates or postponed plans. Let's face it, we didn't have a future and if we had, it would've been pretty empty."

Daniel said, "Yes, he was a nice fellow, but either the timing wasn't right or more specifically, you two weren't right for each other."

"So what does Phillip say? What has he been doing all these years?" Leslie asked.

"He finished Princeton in four years, Mom. Then he traveled with his brother Sinclair who is in the Navy. They went all through Europe and part of the Caribbean. After that, he moved back in with his parents who still live in Dallas. During all that time, he developed a love for photography and started selling some of his work to magazines. Shortly after, he decided that Texas wasn't for him and moved back to California. He still does magazine work, but his studio mostly does wedding photography. Recently, they picked up a contract with a Reunion company and basically, that's how he and I met again, at my reunion. Both his studio and his home are in El Toro."

"I'm very glad he's successful dear," Leslie said, "but, what does he say about the two of you reuniting?"

"Mom, he's been trying so sweetly to win me back. Roses, sweet notes, surprise visits to my restaurant. He says that not only was I his first love, but his only love. He hasn't dated with much success through the years. He says that we're each other's destiny. I know he'd like to get married one day and have a large family. He's also smart enough to not be too pushy with me right now." Sable laughed.

"Do you love him Sable?" her father asked.

"I do Dad. I'd be lying if I told you that I don't love that he's back in my life. I love him. I think his return was meant to be. However, I'm afraid to get hurt, my fifteen year old heart feels very vulnerable. But I gotta take a chance on him. I've never been happier." She wiped at her eye and smiled brightly at her parents.

They got up from the kitchen table and hugged their daughter warmly. "We are so happy for you honey, we really are."

They all hugged again and returned to the table where Sable had to tell them about Dr. Morgan.

"Mom and Dad, I have to tell you something else. I'm going in for an ultrasound a week from Friday."

"What do you mean? Aren't ultrasounds just for babies?" her father asked.

"Well, I guess they're used mostly for babies, but they are also used to investigate problem areas. I've been having some issues lately. Some pelvic pain, lower back pain and bladder problems. Besides, keeping off my feet a bit more, eating more regularly and taking iron, my doctor wants to do an ultrasound to rule out anything such as cysts."

"Oh, honey, are you okay?"

"I'm fine Mom. But I want to take care of it of course."

"Of course, of course baby. I'll go with you."

"Thanks, Mom. I would love for you to go with me."

ෙ ෙ ෙ

Sable was packing her bags and was so excited to be going away for the weekend with Phillip. She had never done that with anyone and she also hadn't visited the Santa Barbara area since her graduation six years before. She had always meant to, it was a quaint town, but she had always been too busy and had never gone. Now, she was to go with Phillip and have a glorious weekend. She packed three bathing suits, her red one, her flowered one and her orange and white one. She also packed the prettiest of her sun dresses, strappy sandals, her favorite tight jeans, some t-shirts and a red cocktail dress if they should go out to a fancy restaurant. She happily looked at her clothes and knew that she had over packed, but didn't care. This was going to be a weekend that she'd always remember. Sable also picked out some of her prettiest panties, grabbed her make up bag and finally dug in her closet for her pink UCSB hat. There, she thought to herself, I'm ready.

Phillip arrived about ten minutes later and didn't even say hello to Sable, he just smiled at her and swept her up in his arms and whirled about a few times and then whispered in her ear, "Hi, babe."

"Hi, you sure know how to make an entrance."

"I'll take that as a compliment. Sorry I was a few minutes late, I had to drop off Joey at my buddy Vince's place for the weekend."

"No problem, I just finished getting ready myself. Give me a kiss, love."

"No time, Sable, we have to get on the road!"

"Come here and kiss me or else."

They laughed together and kissed for awhile before Sable locked up the house and walked towards Phillip's car. As Sable was getting in the car, Phillip took out a very small camera from his coat pocket. "Smile baby, I'm recording everything this weekend."

"Phillip, what a great idea, I didn't even think of bringing a camera. Thank you for that. But hey, I want one of us together. Stretch your arm out as far as you can, ready, 1, 2, 3." On three, instead of smiling into the lens, Sable kissed Phillip's cheek. They checked the photo on the screen a moment later, and the picture was adorable. Phillip's smile couldn't be bigger.

"Oh yes, doll, we're going to record this weekend through and through, I know we're gonna have the best time."

Later, after they had driven a bit, Phillip asked, "So Sable, I know we're heading back towards your old university. Tell me about all the boys who vied for your attention."

"You'll never know about all the boys who fell at my feet in adoration."

"I bet, you're a knockout!"

"I wish I could play the part of the campus seductress, but I pretty much kept to myself and my studies. No one rocked my boat. I made some great friendships and went to plenty of parties, but it was all platonic."

"That's hard to believe Sable. You are so cute and you're such a doll. How could you not have half the student body pursue you?"

"It's nice that you would think so but I guess I just didn't release that kind of vibe. I was friendly to everyone and had a blast in the dorms and later on in my apartment, but no significant other to speak of. How about you? How many Princeton ladies did you make swoon?"

"Can I plea the fifth on that one, babe?"

"Yeah, that's what I thought!"

"No, seriously, it wasn't like that for me I was just kidding. I met a lot of nice people as you said, but no one really left a lasting impression. My freshman year I missed you so very much Sable. I wanted to write you or call you countless times, but I thought it would be cruel after the way things ended with us." Phillip looked into Sable's eyes apologetically.

"Really? Phillip, had you done that, it would've lessened the pain I felt back then. I knew the logic you were following. But what hurt me the most was that I felt so disposable to you. Had our breakup lingered for a few months into your arrival at Princeton, maybe it would have felt a little more normal, as if it were tapering off. The fact that our relationship was cut off so drastically, felt almost like a death to me. Yes, that's exactly what it was because I mourned the loss of it for years." Sable reached out and touched Phillip's hand and then looked out the window remembering how hurt she had been back then.

"I felt the same way. I thought about it so often. I'd see kids on campus holding hands and I longed for you. But in my young mind, calling you or writing to you would have been cruel, no matter how much I wanted to as well."

Sable turned and faced him and said, "It makes me feel better to know that you missed me too."

"Oh babe, I did. I promise. I will spend the rest of my life making up for it if you'd like." He reached over and held her hand for a moment and then brought it up to his cheek. The gesture was nostalgic of a time he did that at the beginning of their relationship when they were younger, and Sable's heart melted a bit and she smiled at him.

"Yes, you can definitely spend the rest of your life making it up to me."

An hour later they reached their hotel and it was welcoming. It was decorated as a Spanish hacienda and the lobby had red and yellow tiles and ornate, black ironwork. Since Santa Barbara was the site of one of California's 21 missions, most of the town had a historical or rustic feeling reminiscent of the Spanish influence that prevailed in the region. Sable held Phillip's hand as he checked them in and a truly romantic feeling washed over her. It felt as if they were honeymooning. He looked down at her while he was signing and winked at her. She felt sheer happiness in that moment. She felt a foreshadowing of what she imagined it would feel like to be his wife. She felt secure and taken care of. She trusted him.

They had the hotel attendant take a few pictures of them in the elegant front lobby. They were having fun knowing that they were memorializing this weekend forever. They walked to their room and it was splendid. They had ocean front views and the bed was a King size bed with a white duvet and red pillows. Opposite the bed was a grand fireplace with an oversized mantle. The drapes were gold and white and the bathroom had a huge soaker tub with jets and a window over the bathtub also had an ocean view. The room was just precious.

"Oh, Phillip. I just love it here!"

"I do too babe. But we have 7:30 reservations so we should hurry if we're gonna make it."

"Okay, is the place fancy or casual?"

"It's casual hon, tomorrow we're going fancy."

"Great, I'll slip into my jeans."

"Mind if I watch?"

"Okay, if you promise to stand on that side of the room. If you don't, we'll never make it to the reservation and I'm starving!"

"I promise, just indulge me. Please."

Phillip held up the camera and Sable squealed, "don't you dare!"

"I was just kidding Sable, I knew I was seconds away from getting yelled at!"

Sable laughed and tried to act like a vixen although she felt very silly doing it. Thank goodness, she had worn a pretty cream colored panty and bra set that he was about to see, Sable thought to herself. She slipped off her black Capri pants and striped shirt and slipped into her best fitting jeans and a coral colored sweater that did wonders for her auburn hair.

"Sable, you are absolutely scrumptious," he said as he walked across the room to hold her. "Your butt looks amazing! God, I want you," he said huskily.

"Patience, love bug, your girl is starving."

"K…let's start walking or we're never going to leave this room!"

The restaurant was quaint and Phillip ordered her a bottle of wine and a beer for himself.

"A whole bottle of wine! I can't finish that!"

"Sure, you can, let's enjoy ourselves."

They ordered calamari and bruschetta for appetizers and fed each other across the table.

"I like this Sable, maybe you can feed me also when I'm an old man."

"Will you be wearing a bib and will I be wearing polyester, elastic-waisted pants?"

"That sounds great, but don't forget the old lady hairdo…that is such a turn on!"

"Haha, will you walk erect or will you do the bend over, stare-at-your-feet walk?"

"Oh, I'll be erect, I promise!" Phillip's joke made Sable laugh loudly.

The waiter came just then and they decided to share an order of filet mignon and lobster. With all the appetizers, bread and salad they had been consuming, they didn't think they could each finish off a plate. When Sable suggested it, Phillip thought it was an intimate gesture, and he agreed immediately.

"You know, had I suggested sharing a plate, you would have thought I was an incredible cheapskate. But you suggest it, and I think you're a doll. How does that work?"

"I guess that *is* somewhat sexist I have to admit, but sharing a meal with you is special. Regardless of whether its onion rings or lobster. And yes, to answer your earlier question—I'll feed you when you're old if you play your cards right!"

"Sable, I have a question for you and I don't want you to get spooked by it."

Sable smiled, "I'm ready Mr. McNeil, I won't get spooked."

"What kind of wedding do you want?"

"What!"

"Hey, hey settle down," Phillip laughed, "I run a photography studio and shoot three weddings a month usually and I was just curious as to what kind a bride you'd like to be and in what setting."

"To be honest, Phillip, I've never let myself indulge myself in that kind of fantasy."

"Come on, surely you have some ideas or thoughts about it."

She thought a moment, "Well, the loveliest moment would be my father walking me down the aisle and surely Desiree would be my maid of honor. I would like my dress to be nostalgic, but not old fashioned. I think I'd rather wear a creamy ivory, than a bright white. I don't like lace. I think I'd like an outside garden reception and I'd like to wear gloves. How did I do?"

"You did great, love. You would look like an angel. Tell me, would you wear your hair down or up? Tiara or flowers in your hair?"

"Boy, you really are into details. The style of my hair would depend on the style of the dress. No flowers in my hair, since I want to hold bunches of them in my bouquet. A very tiny tiara would be pretty, I suppose. Okay, Mr. Wedding Photographer, since you've attended countless weddings, what do you think about your future day?"

"Do you really want to know?"

"Of course, as long as you don't mention Las Vegas drive-thrus and Elvis Ministers."

Phillip laughed heartedly, "No, my mother the artist, would have my head if I embarrassed her like that!"

They paused to laugh about that and Phillip reached over to kiss her lips gently.

"My dream wedding would entail of you walking down the aisle on Daniel's arm towards me. You'd be wearing a ring that I bought for you with all my love. Your father would meet me at the altar and hand you over to me. We'd say our vows and promise to live out our lives together. We'd kiss and our guests would applaud. Later, during our First Dance, we'd swirl and twirl and kiss promising each other the best of ourselves. The rest, my Sable, are just details."

Sable's eyes welled up and had already spilled over. Phillip reached over and wiped her tears with one hand while kissing the corner of her right eye.

"Oh, Phillip. That was so sweet. But we said we'd take this slow."

"I've known you for over thirteen years, how much slower do we have to take this?"

"You know what I mean!"

"Yes, I do. I'm sorry, I spoke from the heart Sable. One day, we'll profess our love to each other."

At that moment, a young girl with a basket of flowers walked by and Phillip waved her over. He bought Sable 6 white roses and the girl noticed the camera on the edge of the table and asked, "Would you like me to take a picture of the two of you?"

"Yes," Phillip answered, "but, how about if you take two?"

In the first picture they smiled grandly at the camera and for the second picture, Phillip gingerly bit Sable's ear, while she squealed loudly in surprise. As they viewed this picture, Phillip said, "Your surprise laugh is darling. I think this might be my favorite picture of all time, and you know I've taken a few."

Sable gave him a quick smooch and said, "Let's finish this meal and this bottle of wine and rush back to the hotel, I'm feeling frisky."

"Now, you're talking!"

👓 👓 👓

The next morning, Phillip was spooning her and Sable was sleeping very comfortably. He started kissing her ear and her shoulders and she felt him stir.

"Don't even think about it. I'm exhausted."

"Ha! You're sounding like a wife already!"

"Oh I am, am I?" Sable laughed. "How about you go get me a cup of coffee, while I take a shower?"

"I got a counter-offer-"

"Oh, you're an attorney now?"

"Very funny, Chuckles. No, I was just going to say that, how about we take a quick shower together and we'll head on down to the café for breakfast on the corner?"

"I like your dimples, so I'll take that offer."

Sable ran into the bathroom, while Phillip playfully made purring noises and ran in after her.

At the café, Sable sipped her coffee and breathed in the salt air. Although she lived by the beach, its beauty never ceased to amaze her. She sipped some more coffee and gazed at the water.

He surprised her gaze across the water, by the sound of the camera's click. He shrugged in apology and winked at her. Phillip was the first to speak, "I'd love to walk the UCSB campus with you today."

"You would? That is so sweet. I could show you my dorm, the commons and the bookstore, and for a special treat, I could show you my favorite library alcove."

"You're making it sound so tedious! I really want to see your school and where you lived as a young girl. With that cap you're wearing, you'd still pass for a student! I promise to show you my old stomping grounds if we ever make it back to Jersey."

"Okay, then we will. Actually, it's a great campus and I loved attending it. If you want, we can walk it from here. It's probably two miles but it would do us some good after the big breakfast we just ordered."

"I'd love to do that, great idea."

An hour later, they were standing in front of Sable's dorm and Sable was smiling from ear to ear. Phillip took a picture of the dorm name and of Sable looking up at its front entrance. "Wow, I didn't think I'd be so happy to see this old place. Let's see if we can go on in."

As luck would have it there was a worker replacing a window in the exact dorm room where she used to live! She could see him from across the bushes and rushed over there to ask him if they could enter.

"Excuse me sir, but could I trouble you to let us in? I used to live in that exact room ten years ago and it would mean the world to me to see it again."

"Listen, little lady, I could get in real trouble over that –liability and all that, you understand. But, I could see how much it means to you, so I'll tell you what. I'm going to my work truck now to get a tool and I should probably be back within 5 minutes. Do you understand what I'm trying to say?"

"Oh yes sir, I do! Thanks so much!"

They waited for the man to exit the door and could see that he was shaking his head.

"Looks like he probably gets that request a lot, Sable. Let's hurry, before he comes back."

"Follow me, Batman."

"I'm right behind you Robin."

They reached Sable's room quickly and Sable opened the door. She threw out her arms and did a spin, "Wow, this place looks identical! The two beds and desks are even in the same position as my old roommate Sabrina and I had them in!"

"It's a cute room, I wish I could've snuck in here while you were a freshman and did sinful things to you under the covers."

"Phillip! Is that all you think about?"

"With you? Yes! I love you and I can't get enough of you! Come here I'm going to kiss you."

"Kiss me baby, it will be the first and only kiss I ever have had in this room!"

"Then let me make it a good one! Pucker up!"

A few minutes later, they were on their way out the dorm and were walking towards the Food Court.

"Sable, you look so proud of yourself. What we did back there wasn't exactly high tech espionage."

"Haha, yes I know it wasn't, but it made me feel good to be in my old space. And giving you a smooch there was practically surreal."

"I'm glad you enjoyed that. How about we get a scoop of ice cream and walk back to the hotel?"

"That would be great, it's almost noon and I'd love to spend the day sunbathing on the beach, how does that sound to you?"

"Nothing could make me happier, let's do it!"

ⓒ⊙ ⓒ⊙ ⓒ⊙

"So now, the real question is which suit do you like best, the red one, the flowered, or the orange and white?"

"Are you sure, you really have to wear one?"

"Yes, the last time I checked, there were no nudie beaches in Santa Barbara."

"Dang it. Hmmmm, tough choice m'lady. But I think I'm going to go with the orange and white one. Would you like to know why?"

"I'm afraid to ask, but let's hear it."

"The orange and white one reminds me of a cream-sicle. Remember those from when we were kids?"

"Yes, I do. Only you would connect swimwear to ice cream. Orange and white it is!"

As Sable was changing in the bathroom, she looked at herself in the mirror. There was something different about her appearance. She knew what it was. She was completely in love and it showed. "Please Grandmother Olivia," she prayed, "please let this time be for real. I couldn't endure another heartbreak. *Please*, let this be for real. Gracias, Abuela."

As they walked to the beach, Sable couldn't keep from chuckling. It was her turn to grab the camera and take photos of the photographer. He was an absolute sight to see! Phillip was holding a grocery bag filled with countless magazines, chips and water bottles. He was also holding a beach bag full of towels and sunscreen bottles and a beach umbrella. Sitting high up on his shoulders were two beach chairs that had straps for easy carrying. He was wearing a huge straw hat similar to what her father used for gardening and he had big white stripes of sunblock across his nose and cheeks. He was a sight to behold. "Phillip, you sure brought a lot of supplies for hanging on the beach for a few hours. You look like we're going to be out here until Tuesday!"

"Preparation is everything, my dear. You should know that. You run a successful restaurant."

"Yes, but I think of a trip to the beach as spontaneous, not so utterly efficient."

"I'd like to think that I have everything you need right here in my arms."

"Silly, the only thing I do need *are* your arms, everything else is fluff."

"Shhh, don't mess with my process."

"Good God, Phillip, you remind me of that scene in *I Love Lucy* when they packed their whole apartment in their convertible on their road trip to California. Ricky only had a 6 inch opening to see through as he drove!"

"Oh, I see what you're saying! You're calling me Fred! You're comparing me to that ridiculous old man!"

"Well, yes, now that you say it, yes! But thank goodness, we're here. Throw all that stuff down, let's run into the water."

"Anything you say, Ethel!"

There's nothing better than taking a nap for a couple of hours on the beach. Sable and Phillip felt relaxed and refreshed. What a great swim they had. But between going to bed late last night, all the heavy meals they'd been eating and the long walk to and from UCSB, the nap was the best indulgence.

"Sable, we skipped lunch, is that ok?"

"Of course, I can't imagine eating again and another big dinner tonight at seven. What time is it anyway?"

"It's 4:15 actually. My, Sable you really tan beautifully. I hope I don't look too red."

"Thanks Phillip. No, you must have lathered on plenty of sunscreen because your skin doesn't look red at all. As for me, I decided to take a walk on the wild side because I didn't put on any at all today. Complete Vitamin D, just this once. The sun felt great today and I really wanted to get some color."

"Well, you sure did. We better start thinking about heading back. We have two hours to get ready."

"That's plenty of time to wash up and blow-dry my hair. Is that enough time for you too, my handsome man?"

"Absolutely," he laughed, "let's start heading back."

"Let me help you this time please, with all this cargo."

☙☙ ☙☙ ☙☙

Stepping out of the bathroom, Sable let her mouth drop open, "Phillip, you look delicious! Let me look at you!" Sable playfully walked around him like a hungry lioness.

"Stop it, some more!" they both laughed at that and hugged each other tightly. He truly looked seductive to her. He had dark black slacks and a cream button down shirt, but it was his black velvet blazer that made him look like a model. His facial stubble was just too irresistible. "Baby, truly, you are a beautiful man, I'm so happy to be seen with you tonight!"

"But look at you, Sable, in that red strapless dress. What it does to your hair and eyes. I'm truly blessed to have you as mine again."

They walked to each other and hugged and kissed in front of the fireplace. They knew this weekend was the most loving either had ever had. It was to be unforgettable.

Phillip said, "I really like this spot, holding you here. What do you say that after dinner, we build a fire and ....." the rest he whispered in her ear and she blushed.

"Yes, that's exactly what I'd like you to do to me. Let's go, before we throw dinner out the window."

Holding hands, they walked out the door excited about the rest of their evening.

At the restaurant, several couples turned to stare at Phillip and Sable as they entered. They were so striking together and they exuded all the love that they had for each other. Phillip and Sable weren't aware of their admiring stares; they only had eyes for each other.

They skipped the appetizers tonight and went straight to ordering their hearty meals. Sable ordered her favorite, Chilean Sea Bass, and Phillip ordered London Broil. They were both sipping wine and reminiscing on some old stories when their dinners arrived.

"Remember the time your grandmother walked into the family room when I was trying to unbutton your blouse? I don't think I'd ever been that scared."

"Yes, lucky for you she walked into that room looking for her glasses. She didn't see a thing!" They laughed. "Or how about the time Sinclair caught us kissing in the

Jacuzzi at your parents' house? I was truly embarrassed for weeks!"

"I remember that! That clown used a bull horn or banged pots and pans every time he entered a room when you were there for months after that episode."

"Yes! Yes, he did. I'd forgotten about that. Ah, the joys of having a little brother," Sable remembered. "You know," Sable continued, "after you left for Princeton, your brother was very nice to me."

"Really? How so? I don't know anything about that."

"When we started school that fall, he was a senior at Madison and he always made a point to come over and ask me how I was doing every few days. He'd either give me a few words of encouragement, or sometimes he'd just give me a hug. Other times, he'd squeeze my cheeks or even grab my nose. He knew I was hurting and it was the simplest gesture every time, but it just gave me hope and perhaps a little bit of you. He never lingered for long, but its simplicity always made me smile and remember the good instead of how much I was missing you. He did it for the whole year."

Phillip sat back in his chair and stared at her.

"What, what's wrong with that?" she asked.

"There's nothing wrong. On the one hand, it hurts me that he was the one comforting you and not me and on the other hand, it fills me with pride that my brother was a good man, even at such a young age."

"Yes, he's great. Does he know we're together again?"

"I haven't told him myself, but I'm guessing my mother must've told him. How about we call him from the hotel and surprise him? I'd like to tell him how much I love you and while I'm at it, I'd like to tell him how much I love him as well."

"Sounds wonderful. I can't wait to see him again."

"He'd like that. Hopefully, he'll be home from Puerto Rico soon. You know yesterday, you'd said that Desiree would be your maid of honor. Well, Sinclair will definitely be my best man. But be warned, he would give me a hell of a naughty Bachelor Party."

"Absolutely! But since Sinclair has a funny sense of humor and because he likes me so much, he would probably hire *me* to jump out of the cake!"

Later, back in their room, Phillip was putting some logs into the fire and Sable had kicked off her shoes and was sitting at the bay window with a glass of wine in her hand. She was taking in the moment and knew that she was very fortunate to have him in her life again. She thought it was funny that in all the years that they'd been apart, no one had come to mean very much to her in comparison. She knew that if they were not successful in their relationship this time around, she probably wouldn't ever bother with men again. For what? She'd always compare their imperfections and flaws to the wonder of this very weekend. She knew her heart and this moment in her life was just everything she had ever wanted: Phillip and all the love and tenderness he brought her, the beauty of the restaurant, her comfortable home. She wished she could freeze time and just enjoy this phase in her life forever. She was so elated with life. She knew her Grandmother Olivia was blessing her life with goodness.

"Hey, why so pensive over there? We're supposed to be having fun."

"This weekend has been more than I could have dreamed of. I was just thinking that I'd like to freeze time and preserve this forever."

"It has been a perfect weekend. I'll remember it forever. But we'll have countless of weekends together. Even the ones that are the most commonplace will be special because we'll be together."

"Yes, you're right. This hotel, you, our time together, it's just overwhelmingly special."

"Hold on, right there." She went back to sipping her wine and looking into the fire and he snapped a photo of her. "Okay, now that's spectacular. You should see how the flames are dancing in the reflection of your glass."

"You're such a romantic Phillip."

"Come over here in front of the fireplace and I'll show you romance."

They swayed together in front of the fireplace hugging each other for a few moments. Sable was the first to start undressing Phillip and he breathed in her scent. He couldn't believe that she was back in his life. He was so grateful. He loved her so much. He was blessed with her goodness and love.

They were kissing so deeply and as the clothes were flinging away in all directions, they were both eager to make love, but they stopped to laugh.

"We're acting like we used to as kids."

"You affect me in the same way, it's no wonder."

They slowed down to completely enjoy the moment of making love in Santa Barbara on the rug in front of a crackling fireplace with the windows open. They could hear the waves crashing in the background. The lights of the embers danced around the room and they joined as one in a heightened passion. They couldn't get enough of each other. Their mouths were everywhere and their hands explored each other's bodies until they were both satiated and spent with exhaustion. They fell asleep in front of the fireplace with their fingers inter-locked, Sable's head on Phillip's arm knowing their love would be for all time.

On their drive home the next day, they chatted about their upcoming busy week and Sable promised to visit him on Wednesday night and spend the night in El Toro. They were relaxed with each other and often reached out to each other for a quick kiss while Phillip drove.

They had been through a lot together, tears, joy, lovemaking, reconciliation, desire, heartbreak…but all those experiences had led them to this exact mo-ment in their lives. Santa Barbara was symbolic of all the love, romance and goodness that was to come. Phillip reached out to hold her hand and brought it up to his lips to kiss it.

"Hey, one of my favorite songs! Bee Gee's "How Deep is Your Love." Want to sing it with me?"

Sable laughed, "You're such a softie!– Okay, 'I know your eyes in the morning sun, I feel you touch me in the pouring rain and the moment that you wander far from me, I wanna feel you in my arms again…' "

Fifteen

The following Friday, Sable and her mother went to Dr. Morgan's office. Sable was a bit nervous, but since taking Dr. Morgan's advice from her last visit, her lower back pain had subsided from reducing her hours at work.

"Sable, good to see you again."

"Dr. Morgan, this is my mother, Leslie Franco."

"Good to meet you Mrs. Franco. Now let's see what we can find out today. Tell me about your last menstrual cycle."

"It was a week ago and it lasted four days like usual."

"Did you have excessive bleeding?"

"Now that you mention it, I was a little heavier than I typically am. I usually taper off on day three and this time, I was heavy for the whole four day duration."

Dr. Morgan noted something on her chart. "Have you had any bladder problems Sable?"

"Well, I often feel the need to go to the bathroom immediately. I haven't been able to hold it very long at all. And then, there's very little urine to speak of."

"Okay, Sable I have a few ideas. Let's see if this ultrasound will give us more information. Now, lay back and try to relax as I get you ready."

Leslie Franco moved forward and sat on a stool adjacent to the examining table and held her daughter's hand.

After a few minutes of the ultrasound procedure, Sable and Leslie looked at each other and smiled. Sable was trying to be hopeful, but all of a sudden, she felt afraid. She had never really thought about her health, she imagined most twenty-eight year olds seldom do, but now she felt a little concerned. She had so much to live for, she certainly didn't want to endure any of this.

Dr. Morgan looked up and tried to smile warmly at Sable, but Sable sensed imminent concerns in her eyes.

"Sable, Mrs. Franco, I'm afraid I have some bad news. I see two issues that we must take care of right away. You have uterine fibroids which are small nodules that grow on the wall of the uterus. They are benign tumors that live in the female pelvis. This is probably the real reason for your lower back pain and small bladder problem."

Mrs. Franco bent over and kissed her daughter's temple. "You said there were *two* concerns, Dr. Morgan."

"Yes, I also see uterine polyps. These are an overgrowth of tissue in the endometrium. They account for your heavier period cycle this past month. Typically, they cause excessive or severe menstrual bleeding and since you don't have that yet, that might be very hopeful that we've caught this in time before it causes more harm to your system."

"So Doctor, given that I have both uterine polyps and uterine fibroids, does that mean that my case is more severe than if I just had one or the other?"

"Yes, Sable it is. You see although uterine fibroids are benign tumors, they are tumors nonetheless. And if we don't take care of the uterine polyps right away, the overgrowth of tissue would ultimately develop into endometrial cancer. Given that we're fighting two areas, although very close to each other in proximity, makes me feel that we need to be proactive immediately."

Sable swallowed and looked quickly at her mother. She didn't want to panic in front of her mother, but she was nervous. "Where do we go from here Dr. Morgan?"

"I think we need to schedule surgery. I need to try to remove the fibroids and the polyps as soon as possible. We are going to thoroughly check your ovaries, fallopian tubes, cervix and the rest of your uterus to make sure there are no more nodules, cysts or polyps that would concern us."

"When do you think this surgery would take place?"

"I believe we can schedule the surgery by Thursday."

"Six days? That doesn't give me much time to get the restaurant ready for my absence."

"That is frankly all the time I would dare risk taking Sable. We need to be proactive. You should probably also plan to be home resting for two weeks after the procedure."

Sable sighed deeply. She even hated to take off one day occasionally; she didn't know how she'd manage

with a two week absence. But she knew this was important, so very important.

Her mother spoke first, "Dr. Morgan, tell me, what is
the worst case scenario?"

"I'm afraid worst case scenario, Mrs. Franco, is a partial hysterectomy which is the removal of the uterus."

Leslie and her daughter stared at each other. Neither
could tell who had more tears in their eyes.

⚭ ⚭ ⚭

Toni was walking at the mall during her lunch hour.
She was enjoying her break and sipping at her coffee.
She was thinking of going to the jewelry store and buying a watch or a locket for her mother whose birthday
was next week. She took the escalator down to the first
floor and by the time she had reached the jewelry store
had decided on a locket.

As soon as she walked in, her heart started beating. There, in front of her, talking to a salesperson, was
Phillip McNeil.

"Phillip, is that you?"

"Toni! It's great to see you!" They hugged and gave
each other a kiss on the cheek.

"We didn't get to talk very much during the
reunion."

Toni laughed, "I would say not. You were pretty busy
romancing my friend as I recall."

"Ahh, guilty as charged I'm afraid."

"Well, what are you doing here? This isn't really a
guy hangout you know."

"Of that, I am certain. I uh, was shopping a little."

They took a moment and stared at each other. Phillip knew that she knew. And Toni knew that he knew that she knew.

"Phillip, it's much too soon. You guys just got back together."

"I know Toni, I really do. If another friend were doing this, I would call him crazy. But truly, I know it's so right. It's all I think about. Us getting married and having a carload of kids. Don't worry, I wouldn't ask her right away. I was thinking more about the holiday season. But I must admit, I just wanted to buy the ring and have it at my house to occasionally look at." He actually blushed as he said it.

"Why Phillip, you *are* a romantic," she looked around at the display counter behind him. "Well, I certainly agree that you shouldn't ask her now, it might seem too soon for our conservative Sable. But since you and I are both here, let me help you. I can tell you right now, you're looking at the wrong type."

"I am? Oh Toni, you're an angel! Sit down and help me out. If she doesn't accept my proposal, then I'll blame it on you!"

"Ha! With what I'm about to select for you, there's no way she'll refuse you!" They hugged again and he sat down beside her.

"First of all, you're looking at yellow gold and she wouldn't wear that. She likes white gold like her mother wears. You're also looking at round stones and she loves pear shape diamonds. They're a lot less common than some of the other types, and she loves the unique. Besides, she already has pear shape diamond earrings that her grandmother gave her years ago and I swear to you, if you do white gold in a simple band and pear, she'll accept in a second!"

Phillip laughed. "Boy, I was so far away from where I needed to be! Thank goodness, you're here to help me Toni. This is wonderful. I like the way it brings in a little of both Leslie and Olivia in the choice."

"Yes, she'll love that connection. Phillip, what size are you thinking of?"

"Definitely, two carats."

"Two carats! That's too big!"

"No, it's not. She's worth it. And besides, this is our second time in love, so the two is very symbolic."

"Oh my God, Phillip. How about you marry me instead?"

Phillip laughed heartedly at her joke and then asked the salesperson to show them what he had with the criteria Phillip wanted.

"Sir, I have this one and it's 2.6 carats."

Phillip looked at it and held it in his hands. He nodded enthusiastically. "Great, let's go with it! Oh Toni, I think this one is the one."

"It is absolutely the one. It's huge! She'll adore it Phillip!"

esiree called her cousin and was very concerned for her. They talked every few days but she had not known about Sable's surgery. It was her Aunt Leslie, the night before, who had told Desiree about the procedure. She was heartbroken for her cousin. It seemed so unfair that Sable would have these issues when she was in such good health. It also seemed unfair that Sable's female reproductive system was in peril, while hers was so damn fertile. It sickened her heart to know that her cousin was suffering. This should be such a joyous time in her life, now that Phillip was back and obviously as in love with her, as Sable always had been with him.

Sable didn't answer the phone, so she left a message instead, "Hey prima, it's me. Your mom told me what's going on and I want you to know that I'm thinking about you. I have faith that everything will work out fine. She told me that the surgery will be Friday morning and I will be there, no doubt about it. I'm praying for you and love you. And if by chance, you're sitting on the couch ignoring my call, it's ok, I forgive you."

From her plush white couches, Sable chuckled at her cousin. She knew her too well. Desiree knew that she was on her couch watching the waves roll in surrounded by a box of tissues, feeling sorry for herself. It wasn't often that Sable allowed herself to be pitiful, but the timing of this really overwhelmed her. Her restaurant was only a year old and her relationship with Phillip was just becoming strong again. She had ceased to feel insecure about his intentions and felt that he too wanted to love her again. Now, with a fairly new business and love in her life, she was going to be taking time off for health issues. Or worse, what if….she refused to think about that.

Dr. Morgan had checked with the hospital and the first available appointment had been Friday. It was a day after Dr. Morgan had hoped, but Sable saw it as an extra day at *Amor Mio*. It would be a day that would be cram filled with directions for Miles to prepare him to take over. As her executive chef, he would be the one to instruct the rest of the staff with all the decisions and possible situations that would come up. She called her purveyors and let them know that Miles would be her replacement for a few weeks. She sighed. She felt overwhelmed and sad.

Last night, she had broken her date with Phillip. She had lied to him and told him that she wasn't feeling well. Always the gentleman, he had offered to bring her soup and an assortment of over-the-counter meds, but she had begged off. She didn't know what she was now going to do with her fledging relationship. She was panicking about the possibility Dr. Morgan had spoken to her about, the partial hysterectomy. She had said that it was unlikely that in removing the fibroids and the polyps, that there would be a need for anything more radical than just their removal. But still, Sable was panicking. She had never really thought about her fertility before. She had assumed that she would have children exactly when she wanted them. Since she had been an only child, she knew that she wanted a medium sized family. The fact that there was the slightest chance that this decision would be taken from her, horrified her.

She couldn't see Phillip last night and tell him about her doctor's appointment. She just couldn't articulate her fear to him, while still trying to protect him of the possibility that she might soon appear damaged. Her own body cringed at the word *damaged* and she reached for another tissue and brought her throw blanket closer around her shoulders. How could she tell Phillip, her lover of just a few weeks, that she might not be the person who could provide him with a future? It killed her to think of that. She would need a few days just to process this in her mind. She decided that she'd tell him in two days when they were set to see each other again on Monday night. She sighed again. She leaned over and put her head on the pillow, letting sleep take over and rest her tearful eyes.

☜☞ ☜☞ ☜☞

The phone woke her up and she picked up on the third ring. "Hi honey," he said.

"Phillip, hi, how are you?"

"I'm missing you very much. How are you feeling?"

"I'm really tired. The phone just woke me up. I'm glad you called. "

"It's great to hear your voice. But, I'm sorry I woke you Sable."

"No, not at all. And it's great to hear your voice as soon as I wake up of course." Sable smiled.

"Well, hon, I'd like to see to it that you hear my voice everyday when you wake up."

"Are you flirting with me?"

Phillip laughed out loud, "There's nothing more fun than flirting with you, Sable! I just wish you'd feel well enough to let me come visit you. I hate to be without you on the weekends."

"Oh Phillip, I'm just not myself today. I really think I need to rest and concentrate on getting better. We're going to see each other Monday night. How about you spend the night?"

"Are you suggesting I spend the night and fight horrible traffic from Manhattan Beach to El Toro Tuesday morning? I would love to do that! Soon, I want us to be so addicted to each other that we're spending the night in each other's home, every night baby."

Sable stayed quiet and choked back a sob. His sheer delight at spending the night on a Monday, lovingly surprised her and saddened her as well. What was she doing? She might be leading him on to thinking he had a future with her, when the potential of their future could be cut short on Friday on the operating table. Suddenly, she felt angry at herself for becoming so negative and pessimistic. In short, it was her chaotic fluctuations of emotions that were making her crazy. Phillip deserved better. And until Dr. Morgan gave her more concrete answers, Sable thought she wasn't going to worry Phillip. Their love had been blossoming and strengthening in the last couple of weeks and she didn't want to ruin their joy.

"Of course, I'd love that too. Santa Barbara was only a small taste of what I imagine life with you to be like. You're addicting, babe. But I look very forward to Monday. Bring Joey if you'd like."

"Ok, Sable. Thank you for inviting Joey, he'd love to come. But I do have one request. Maybe you can indulge me with one little fantasy, that I must admit, I've had for years."

"Really? I'm scared to ask, but I'll do my best in indulging you. What is it?"

Phillip laughed, "Well, I'd like to bring bubble bath and I'll leave the rest to your imagination."

"Hmmmm, I couldn't think of a better indulgence. It looks like we've got one hell of a date Monday night."

ෙ෨ ෙ෨ ෙ෨

On Sunday morning, Sable went to *Amor Mio* and worked at her desk for four hours. She wanted to make sure that she was up to date with her ordering, her billing, her payroll and the employee work schedule. She was hoping to leave the restaurant in as an efficient manner as possible. Of course she was still working through Thursday, but she felt better organizing some files and completing paperwork to assist Miles. She worked for another hour at her computer catching up on emails, before she drove home.

It was 2pm by the time she got home. She felt restless. She decided to take a walk on the beach and let the wind ease her tension. She could feel herself relax the further she walked. She thought of the restaurant and she thought of her grandmother. What advice would she give her if she were here? Besides smothering her with hugs and filling her tummy with comfort food, what would Olivia say of this medical procedure? She sighed.

She let her mind wander to Desiree and her heart squeezed. How could a single twenty year old adequately deal with the emotional upheaval of raising two babies while trying to finish college? She knew her baby cousin was about to have a very challenging year. She couldn't begin to imagine the fear and insecurity she must feel at facing this alone without Dane. Not even Dane's family would know about the babies, since he didn't want to inform them of Desiree's pregnancy. Sable disagreed with this as she believed that Dane's parents should know that they were about to become grandparents. However, Desiree had already agreed that she would not inform his parents against his wishes. She felt that her cousin was acting honorably, although Dane surely wasn't. Sable wasn't going to judge nor push her cousin on this issue. Desiree deserved the respect of the family and she had their full support as well.

Sable smiled and walked back to her beach house with an idea in her mind. She was determined to go to the mall and do some much needed shopping to release some of her frustration. It wasn't often that she shopped emotionally, but she suddenly felt great and wanted to spoil herself and Desiree. She grabbed her purse from the couch and walked to her red Jeep.

At the mall, the first thing she did was pick out some sexy pajamas for herself for the next evening. She wasn't one for lingerie but she wanted to buy herself something alluring to feel pretty for Phillip the next night. She decided on a silky hot pink set with black polka dots. They were very short shorts and a short sleeved button down top. It was pricey at $70, but it was luscious and she had to have it!

Next, she walked into a baby boutique. She knew that her cousin would do most of her bulk shopping for the twins at big wholesale baby stores to make it cost effective. But Sable wanted to spoil her new baby cousins and with a determined step, walked into the most heavenly of baby boutiques. The pieces were delightful and it was hard not to select at least twenty-five items. She lightly fingered some of the textures of chenille and soft cottons and knew that no matter how hard it was for Desiree, she would be there to help whole heartedly no matter how busy she was at *Amor Mio's* or with Phillip. After looking around and easing the tension that she had had in her heart the whole weekend, Sable started selecting the sweetest of pieces. She knew she had to be gender neutral so she picked pieces in creams, mint, red, and yellows. She bought onesies, hats, blankets, bibs, shoes, burp cloths, shirts, pants, socks, rattles, books and even CDs with lullabies on them. She bought several bibs and onesies with funny sayings on them that she knew Desiree would just love. She bought for beauty not for practicality and she felt so much joy in her heart because of it. After all, she would be the babies' Godmother and she wanted to spoil them.

After such a tense and depressing few days full of medical worry, this shopping spree had done Sable so much good. She was always so efficient with everything she did, that it was fun to step out of character and be playful and carefree.

☙ ☙ ☙

That evening when Phillip called, Sable told him that she had a surprise for him. He loved that she was feeling better and that they'd be together the next day. He couldn't wait to propose to her and make her his wife for all time, but as he had promised Toni, he knew that he had to give Sable some time. He told her he loved her and counted the minutes until he'd see her the next evening.

When he did come over on Monday evening, Sable was taking out the Chinese food she had purchased out of their containers and setting the table. He came right over to her and embraced her strongly and nuzzled at her ear. She loved his warmth and kissed him twice.

Phillip pulled back and started laughing, "Hey, is this my surprise? There must be 8 shopping bags here! And all baby stuff? Hey, are you trying to tell me something? I know we've been careful…"

Sable laughed back, "Of course we've been careful! Those aren't for us, they're all for Desiree and the babies. I had an incredible urge to spoil them yesterday and had the best time at a little boutique as you can well see."

"I would say so! You must've made the salesperson's week with all this stuff. Show me what you got the little angels."

So they sat for half an hour going over the babies' layette enjoying themselves. It was a very precious time and the knowledge of that didn't escape either one of them.

"You know, love, one day, we'll be shopping for our own little ones," and he kissed her sweetly.

Sable couldn't stop herself, but her tears easily flowed down her face. She still didn't want to tell Phillip about her procedure, but it hurt her to know that there was a chance that her own fertility would be compromised, however much Dr. Morgan tried to be careful.

"Oh baby, don't cry," Phillip said, "did I upset you? Don't you want to have children?"

Sable tried to will herself to be strong, "Of course, I want children. It's just that this is a very sweet moment, here, us two, enjoying bags and bags of baby items. And…"

Sable's words hung in the air. She knew this was the perfect opportunity to tell him about her procedure on Friday, but she just couldn't utter the words yet. She wanted to enjoy dinner with him and their romantic evening before she told him.

Instead of letting him know, she said, "Phillip, our food's getting cold. Let's eat the Chinese food before we plunge in the bath with Mr. Bubbles."

Phillip laughed, "Now, you're talking!"

All through dinner, Phillip's comment about wanting children danced in her mind. She knew she had to tell him about Friday, but she was enjoying the evening so much. When he reached over and fed her chow mein, she thought she'd melt. It seemed innocent, but it felt so romantic and tender. She could feel his love radiate through her. He often stopped and kissed her through dinner, or sometimes just touched her hand or her knee. His attention amazed her. She was so swept up with her love for him. She often thought that she should follow her own advice with taking it slow, but her heart simply did not allow it. She'd loved him since she was a teenager, and had never, ever stopped thinking about him. The fact that life had brought him back to her, was the biggest gift of her life. She knew it was better than anything.

After dinner, they stacked the dishwasher together. He was standing behind her, while her hands were still in the suds, and his arms encircled her waist. Ever so discreetly, he started rubbing himself against her. He started kissing her neck and she tilted her head up so that he could reach all of it. She tried to move her arms, but he gently kept them at her sides. She closed her eyes and let the moment take her. He was kissing her shoulders by now and unbuttoning her blouse. By the time he started kissing her earlobe and her collarbone, she was beyond ready for him.

He turned her around and started kissing her deeply. She was so turned on, she could barely think. Sable was following Phillip's every lead. By the time she knew it, they were making love standing up by the kitchen sink. They were very much in tune with one another and it felt so natural and so *good*.

Phillip giggled into her ear, "Have you ever made love in a kitchen?"

Sable muffled her response, "Absolutely not, have you?"

"No, baby. First time. With you. I love that."

"Me too. Let's get into that bubble bath now, my legs are getting weak."

"No problem, darling, that's why you have me," and with that he swept her up in his arms and carried her into the bathroom as she giggled down the hallway.

"I don't suppose Mr. Bubbles is in your pocket, Phillip. Where is it?"

"Patience, Sable! Start running the water and I'll run out to the car and get it with my overnight bag."

Sable smiled. Her life was so perfect now. A cozy home. A thriving restaurant. A hunk of a man. Why did she have to have this procedure on Friday? She had her stomach in knots over it. Sable thought she would have less apprehension if Phillip was not in her life. But now that he was, she felt that she was going to let him down with her health concerns. If the procedure became problematic, and if they indeed had a future together, then his future would be affected as well.

She made a silent prayer for strength. Strength to be able to tell Phillip about it tonight while he was there with her. And strength that she would overcome these obstacles that were about to challenge her life. Please, she prayed, I've been lonely for almost half my life, please let me have some happiness with this man. I love him so. More than I ever thought possible.

She quickly wiped away a betraying tear because she didn't want Phillip to see her sad. At least, not yet. If he had a fantasy about a bubble bath, then she was going to darn well fulfill it.

∾ ∾ ∾

The bubble bath was just what she needed. She was able to relax and let the tension run from her body. She still had anxiety over talking to him, but her mind let

her subside that feeling for an hour, and she was grateful. She eased her back on his chest and rested her weary
soul. He wrapped his arms around her again and soaked
herself into his being. They rested together there for a
long time, just holding each other, he holding her waist,
and she holding his arms in front of her. It felt so sweet
and safe. She didn't feel fifteen again, but she did feel
like their love was *new*. It was new because they were
adults now and ready. She felt him stir and she turned
around and knelt in front of him and kissed him completely. He moaned and she knew he was happy. She
straddled him and looked deeply into his eyes.

"Is this what you had in mind?" she asked
innocently.

"Oh yes, oh yes!"

ᏇᎧ ᏇᎧ ᏇᎧ

"Go sit on the couch. I need a few minutes by
myself."

"Sable, we've just made love twice and taken a bath
together and now you ask for privacy?" he chuckled.

"Just do what you're told young man! A woman
needs a few minutes! Geez!"

He laughed all the way down the hallway back into
the living room. He opened up the striped curtains to
fully enjoy the view of the ocean in front of him. Her
house was precious. It looked like her. Beautiful and
sun-kissed. He felt so happy to be with her. He glanced
over at her bookshelves and saw a few wide-based, navy
colored candles and decided to rummage through the
kitchen drawers for some matches. After he found them,
he came back and lit the three candles. He really liked

the effect it had on the room. The soft glow was cozy and pleasant. He hoped she'd enjoy the lighting.

When she came out a few minutes later, she said, "Oh Phillip. What a nice touch. Thank you for this. The waves look very dazzling by candlelight." She smiled as she looked around the room and let her eyes rest on his.

"You're welcome. But I think it's me who needs to thank you. You look sexy in those pink PJs." Phillip's gaze was loving towards her.

She laughed, "I was hoping you'd like them."

"Yes, I do. I love them. Come sit next to me."

They snuggled for a few minutes watching the waves crash. Sable gathered up her courage and faced Phillip.

"There's something I have to tell you."

Phillip smiled at her, "I'm all ears, doll."

Sable momentarily closed her eyes, willing herself to just blurt it out. She breathed in air and opened her eyes and saw that Phillip was looking at her questioningly.

"Phillip, I've been having some health concerns lately. I've had back pains and pelvic pain and I've even had bladder problems. I recently went to see my doctor with my mother and they did an ultrasound and found that I have a few issues." Sable paused for strength and Phillip kissed her cheek and squeezed her hand. His kindness actually unsettled her. She looked down and panicked that she would cry, but she drew back her shoulders and continued.

"They have found that I have uterine fibroids which are benign tumors that grow in clusters on the wall of the uterus. In addition, they have also found that I have uterine polyps which are an overgrowth of tissue in the

endometrium and this is what has probably been causing my pain. The fibroids are benign which is great I
guess, but if the polyps aren't taken care of, they would
ultimately someday develop into endometrial cancer.
The fact that I have both simultaneously overwhelms
me."

"Oh baby, come here." Phillip held her and the
strength she had been mustering, gave way to her tears.
She found comfort in his arms and the floodway of emotions drained her, leaving her lifeless and very tired.
She always tried to be strong in front of her family and
friends. But it felt comforting to just be held. She felt
safe in his arms and allowed herself to be vulnerable.

"We'll get through this Sable, we will. I am here for
you and I always will. I'm not going anywhere. I'll help
you in anything you need and I'll support you. I want to
be there for you while you're ill, babe."

"Thank you, Phillip. You don't know what that means
to me."

"What is worst case scenario, baby?"

"I don't think I'll develop cancer because they've
caught these issues in time."

"Thank goodness for that. It's a blessing that they've
found all this in time, Sable. It truly is."

"Yes, but I haven't told you what worst case scenario
is. I have this impending doom that Dr. Morgan will find
my uterus even more problematic than the ultrasound
has shown and that I'll need a partial hysterectomy to
remove my uterus."

"Oh Sable, I'm so sorry. I really am. I love you,
Sable."

He held her close and kissed her forehead and cheek
over and over again.

What Sable didn't tell him, was that if she did require a partial hysterectomy, she would have to leave him forever. There was no way that she was going to be selfish and hold on to him while sabotaging his dream of becoming a father someday. She just couldn't even bear to lose Phillip again in her life. But she knew she would, if her health warranted it. God forbid.

On Thursday evening, Phillip showed up at *Amor Mio* with a dozen red roses looking for Sable. He found her in her office overlooking the last of the details she wanted to tend to.

"Phillip! I didn't know you were coming here. I thought we were going to see each other at the hospital tomorrow morning."

"There was no way I could leave you alone tonight. You're sleeping in my arms tonight and if you're nervous, I'll be there. If you want to talk or scream, I'll be there. And if you want to get frisky, I'll be there as well."

Sable had to laugh, although it was a serious matter. She was lucky to have him, she knew. She walked over to him and placed both her hands on his face and put her forehead against his.

She whispered to him, "How can I resist you? Thank you, hon."

When they got back to her house, Sable spent a lot of time on the phone. She kept mouthing apologies to Phillip who was relaxing on her couch with a beer in his hand watching old reruns of *Seinfeld*. He shook his head and smiled telling her that he was fine and to take her time. By the time she talked on the phone to both her parents, her cousin Desiree, her friends Diane and Toni and even her aunt in Spain, a few hours had passed.

"Oh hon, you drove all the way down here and I've barely had time to give you a minute. I'm so sorry."

"Don't worry about that. I'm relaxing and I'm with the woman I love. Please. I wanted to be here with you tonight."

"Thank you for that. I'm not hungry since I have so many butterflies in my stomach. But I think I'll have some soup. What can I get for you?"

Phillip suddenly looked like a cat that swallowed a canary.

"What aren't you telling me Phillip?"

"Well, I thoroughly enjoyed a Big Mac on the way down. Sorry hon, I was starving. But I'll sit with you while you have your soup."

Sable laughed. "How could I ever be grumpy with you? After all, it was a surprise that you even came down. If I could, I'd enjoy McDonalds myself right now. No hard feelings lover boy."

After they sat down, and Sable had finished most of her clam chowder, they held hands at the table and didn't talk very much. Phillip knew that she was afraid, and frankly, he was too. He didn't want her to experience any sadness, but he knew that tomorrow would be an emotionally charged day. He hated that he couldn't take her problem away.

"Can I do anything for you?"

"I'm gonna take a two-minute shower, I'm so tired. Will you lower my USC sweatshirt for me from the closet? I want to wear it tonight."

Phillip smiled, "You don't need to snuggle with an old sweatshirt, when you have me."

"Well, I guess I'll be snuggling with both of you tonight. And don't argue with a nervous woman, McNeil. I might just have to hurt you."

"Sure baby. You take your shower. Ill get the sweatshirt and the candles. And Sable?"

"Yes?"

"I love you. More than anything. We'll get through this, I promise."

⊙⊙ ⊙⊙ ⊙⊙

The next morning, Phillip drove Sable to the hospital for the removal of the polyps and the fibroids. She was anxious on the way there and they didn't speak at all. They just looked at each other occasionally and smiled. Once Sable saw her parents, however, she started crying.

"Oh Daddy, I'm so scared. I don't have a good feeling about this."

"You'll be fine, love. Be positive in there, that often means a lot. We love you and we'll be right here when you come out."

Her mother also hugged her and said, "Thank goodness, they have found this early baby. The consequences could have been untreatable."

Sable quietly nodded. Phillip hadn't seen Sable's parents in thirteen years, but he moved forward and shook both of their hands.

"Great to see both of you again after all these years, Mr. and Mrs. Franco. I just wish it was under happier circumstances."

"It's wonderful to see you Phillip," Daniel Franco said as the men shook hands, "You being here means a lot to the family."

Actually, that remark meant a lot to Phillip. He was nervous about seeing them after so many years and had assumed that they felt resentment towards him.

Leslie added, "It especially means a lot to Sable. Your presence is a gift." She hugged Phillip and Phillip squeezed his eyes shut, surprised at the sentimentality that was rising up inside of him.

These were such good people, he thought to himself, I want so badly to be a part of their family.

"Hey, what's all the sappiness about?" a young voice said from down the corridor. "Sable will be just fine!"

They all looked over and smiled at Desiree. It was just like her to bring in some sunshine to such a bleak morning. They all took turns hugging her and Sable kissed her cheek. And then Desiree and Phillip looked at each other.

"I've missed you so much little Desiree. You are as adorable now as you were when you were seven!" Phillip picked her up and gave her a quick hug, wanting to be careful with her bulging tummy.

"And you're just as hunky, Phillip, as I remember you! Try not to run away again, will ya?" They all laughed as Desiree gently berated Phillip.

"I promise, I'm not going anywhere." Sable and her father locked eyes as Phillip said this. Sable was glad that her father felt good again about his presence in her life. In that look that they shared, Sable knew that her father felt comforted by Phillip's words.

Sable sat down to fill out a clipboard's worth of paperwork and ten minutes later, a nurse came to pick her up. Sable stood and hugged her family and they all whispered that they loved her and wished her good luck. Her hug with Phillip lingered just a bit longer than the others.

"I love you babe. So much. You're my whole life again. No matter what happens, I'm here for you."

Sable tried to be strong and merely replied, "thank you" before releasing her hold on him and following the nurse through the double doors.

ꚉꚉ ꚉꚉ ꚉꚉ

Three hours later, they were allowed into the recovery room to see Sable. She was still groggy but felt good. Her parents were holding each of her hands and Desiree and Phillip were sitting in the room's chairs. Dr. Morgan came in and greeted the family. Sable immediately heard her voice and opened her eyes and asked her father to fix the bed's controlling buttons so that she could sit up and talk to the doctor.

Dr. Morgan asked the family to step out so that she could speak to Sable in private.

But Sable said, "It's okay, Dr. Morgan. They can hear anything you have to say. I trust them completely." Sable mentally braced herself. She knew that if the news were good, the Doctor wouldn't have asked for privacy.

"Well, Sable, I'm afraid the ultrasound only showed us a portion of the problems in your uterus. Both your polyps and fibroids were quite extensive. One of the fibroids was especially large, the size of a lime. I did the best job I could, but I'm afraid that your uterus is so compromised in that the fibroids and polyps would more than likely reappear in the near future. I would highly recommend that we consult a specialist and move forward in talking about a partial hysterectomy. We need to be proactive to avoid future complications in the uterus such as the endometrial cancer that is often seen in cases such as these."

Leslie Franco spoke first, "Are you suggesting a specialist because you're not sure of the diagnosis or because you don't do partial hysterectomies yourself?"

"Neither, Mrs. Franco. Your daughter and I didn't speak at length about the possibilities of a hysterectomy and it would have been in very poor judgment if I would have simply removed it without your daughter's consent. I have a lot of experience in such procedures, but once again, I needed Sable to permit me in doing so. The only time a doctor continues in surgery without the patient's consent is when their immediate life is threatened. I suggested a specialist because I feel that in situations such as these, women feel better once a few doctors agree on the same course of action."

Sable was trying to take this all in. She said, "Dr. Morgan, how much time do I have before such a decision needs to be made?"

"I wouldn't want to schedule it past a month's time Sable. You will be on ten days' disability after today's procedure, but once a patient has a hysterectomy, even a partial one, the recuperation time is six weeks. You need to see a specialist within that time and hopefully, we could all coordinate the timing sooner than later."

The room was quiet for a moment and it was Phillip who spoke next and surprised everyone with his question.

"What would happen if Sable were to get pregnant immediately?"

Sable's parents looked at him, as did Sable, Desiree and the doctor.

"I'm afraid young man, that *that* would be a mute point. The lining in Sable's uterus wouldn't sustain the attachment of a fertilized egg. A pregnancy would result in a miscarriage."

Phillip put his face down and felt the sadness wash over him. It seemed so unfair that after all the years of hoping for love, he would find the love of his life again, but wouldn't be able to start a family with her. He had always longed to be a father, but the possibility of becoming a father with anyone else eluded him. All he wanted out of life was Sable. Of this, he was certain.

Sable started to cry as soon as Dr. Morgan excused herself and Desiree was the first to cry with her. Desiree started to really feel the anguish of the irony that plagued the room.

"How could it be, that I'm expecting twins because I was careless? With a person who wants nothing to do with me? At an age, where I can barely take care of myself? And you, the most perfect cousin, will not be able to have babies now. The irony is killing me. I hate this! I hate myself!"

Desiree was crying so hard that it was Sable who was trying to comfort her.

"Please don't hate me Sable. Please, I couldn't bear it! I wish it were me! I wish it was me who couldn't conceive, I'm so, so sorry!"

"I could never hate you, Desiree. I love you so much, like a sister. You didn't do this to me. I would never blame you for my health. Please don't think that. The idea simply never even entered my head. I guess there is irony in all this, but there's no one to blame little prima." Sable's tears kept running down her face.

With that, all of Sable's strength was spent and she reached for the tissue box. She couldn't stop the steady stream of tears no matter what her loved ones said to try to make her feel better. She was beyond disappointment and rage. She was so brutally sad that she wouldn't become a mother one day. She was only twenty-eight years old and she felt that she had just been given a death sentence. She loved her life at the restaurant and her cute beach home, but she had always assumed that there would be more. The realization that there wouldn't be was a heavy weight on her chest. The pain, that she was indeed *damaged*, overwhelmed her.

Sensing that Phillip really wanted to be alone with Sable, Leslie suggested to her husband and niece that they step out for a cup of coffee in the hospital cafeteria.

As they walked out the door, Phillip and Sable embraced with a fierce need. He wanted to protect her and love her. He wanted her to understand that it didn't matter to him. He just needed her. The rest, his job, the photography…. all of his life, were just details. She was the essence of his life.

Sable was the first to speak, "I've been such a planner my whole life. It gave me peace and it grounded me. There have been only three events in my life that I couldn't control. My grandmother's death. Your breakup with me. And now, this. I'm overwhelmed with sadness. I had always assumed that I'd have children the moment I wanted them. I never questioned my fertility, and now I feel like such a fool. Could I have prevented the fibroids and the polyps? I don't know, I guess I'll have to ask Dr. Morgan that." Sable stopped speaking and looked out the window and ran her hands through her hair in frustration.

"I'm just so sad that my parents will never be grandparents. They've talked about that phase of their lives, for as long as I could remember. In fact, when other people had talked about extensive vacations during their retirement, my parents only spoke of helping me raise my children, as Olivia had lovingly helped them in raising me. They said it was giving back for the next generation."

Sable's voice cracked and when she spoke again, it was barely a whisper, "But now there won't be any future Francos. Oh my God, I just can't believe it. I feel so empty." Sable cried again, this time until her body gave out and she fell asleep.

Phillip put his head down on the side of her body, delicate not to hurt her side and stroked her arm. He also felt a deep sadness in his heart. He wasn't able to tell Sable that it didn't matter to him, that she was all that he wanted out of life, because she had fallen asleep in pure exhaustion, both emotional and physical. Slow, silent tears ran down his cheeks. He loved her so. They had wasted so many years apart! If he would've looked for her, say, five years ago, they would've been married by now and possibly had a child or two. It crushed him to think that they had missed out on the opportunity of having children *together*.

He must have fallen asleep along side of her at some point because he woke up and noticed that it was 2 pm. He was surprised that her parents had not returned, or if they had, they hadn't woken him up to spend some time alone with their daughter. He knew how much they loved her. That, they all had in common.

He quickly wrote Sable a note,

"Sweetie, I had to leave because I have an evening wedding tonight that I'm shooting at 6. I love you so, so much and will call you tonight around midnight. Love, Phillip"

*L*ate that night, after Sable had gotten home, she was resting on the couch with Diane. Her mother had just left and although Leslie had wanted her daughter to spend the night at her house, Sable really wanted to stay in her own home. Diane had offered to spend the night and nurse Sable since her husband, Clark, was spending the night at his brother's home in Las Vegas.

"Okay girlfriend, the only way you're staying the night is if you don't ask me how I'm feeling about today's procedure, the hysterectomy or future babies. If you do, out you go!"

"Feisty, feisty. What the heck Sable? That's okay, I agree with those terms. You could even beat me up, if you want to!"

"That's another thing that's not allowed: sympathy, empathy, pity, whatever you want to call it!"

Diane had to laugh, "Okay, Sable. We're just two girls spending the night and one of them happens to have one hell of a stomach ache."

"Okay, that I can handle, Diane." Sable put her head back on the pillows and reached for the remote. Diane went into the kitchen to find the tray and grab her friend some saltine crackers and diluted apple juice.

"Have a little Sable. You need something in your stomach."

They waged an eye to eye silent debate, but Diane won. Sable propped herself up a bit, put the tray in her lap, and started to nibble a bit.

Sable wanted to speak of neutral subjects so she asked Diane about Clark. "How's Clark doing now that he's finally off crutches?"

"Good Lord Sable, that man is acting like he's just been let out of prison. Even though the doctors have told him to take it easy in the beginning of his recuperation time, he just can't sit still. It's awfully cute. He's up making breakfast early, even doing the dishes. He's visiting all his friends. He has the biggest zest for work, even going into the office extra early. This weekend, his brother from Vegas, invited him down to spend the weekend with him. He flew out this afternoon. I'm sure they'll even hit a few nudie bars in celebration. I don't even mind, he deserves some laughs. I'm also pretty sure he'll come back a few hundred dollars poorer from all the slot machine game time, those two are sure to put in."

Sable laughed heartedly. She could only imagine how caged up Clark must've felt after months of nursing a broken leg. She was glad he was having a fun weekend with his brother, he surely deserved it.

Sable finished the crackers and juice and tried to extend the tray to the coffee table, but the pain in her abdomen stopped her from doing so. Diane quickly got up and helped Sable set the tray aside.

"Wow, even that little exertion tired me out. How am I supposed to go to work in a week? I'm a mess."

"You'll be fine, Sable. Even women who have c-sections are up and around pretty quickly. I'm sure you'll be fine by tomorrow. Dr. Morgan said the first day would be the worst."

"I told you not to mention babies."

"Oh, sorry. Let's get you another painkiller."

"Now, you're talking Diane, now you're talking."

ΘΘ ΘΘ ΘΘ

About a quarter after midnight, the phone rang. Sable had dozed off finally and Diane answered the phone.

"Hi, this is Phillip."

"Hello there, Phillip. This is Diane."

"Hi Diane, how's our patient doing?"

"Well, she was in some discomfort earlier and took another Percocet. She ate a little and is now dozing. Her mom left around nine and said that she'd be back around ten in the morning."

"I'm glad she has all of you there to take care of her. Please tell her that I have to go to the studio in the morning to do some editing on tonight's wedding shoot and that I'll be there tomorrow around three. I'll bring an overnight bag and will take care of her for the evening shift."

They both laughed softly at the image of Sable as a patient, she was so strong and independent, it seemed incongruous to think of her as needing all their help.

"And Diane, please tell her that I love her."

"I will, Phillip."

☙☙ ☙☙ ☙☙

Sable slept through the night, in her USC sweatshirt of course, and woke up feeling weak, but definitely better. Diane was sleeping in the big arm chair next to her bedroom window, sprawled out and looking as they did in high school.

"Diane, you don't look a day older than sixteen. You wear pigtails to bed? Are you kidding?"

"Well, good morning to you too sunshine. I sleep in pigtails because if I don't, my hair is wild in the morning. This is the only thing that I've found that keeps my hairstyle manageable for the next day."

"Wow, Clark must think that's super sexy," Sable laughed.

"Ha, when he met me in college, I was still sleeping with my retainer and rubber bands on my braces. Pigtails are nothing compared to all that."

Sable laughed at that a little too hard and had to hold her abdomen.

"Ouch, I think you hurt me. Cut out the comedy."

"My pigtails aren't comedy Sable, they're a hairstyling solution, trust me." She threw her feet off the chair's ottoman, and walked over to Sable's bed.

"How can I help you?"

"Just help me heave myself out of this bed. I think I want to take a bath."

"No problem. I'll go run some water for you while I'm brushing my teeth."

By the time Leslie arrived, Sable had bathed and dressed in sweatpants and a tank top. She wore her hair in a loose ponytail at the top of her head and was just finishing up eating half a bagel with milk.

"Hi Honey. You look really good. Your color is back in your cheeks." She walked over and hugged and kissed her daughter.

"Thanks Mom. You just missed Diane. She left a couple of minutes ago."

"No Sable, I caught her outside. We talked for a few minutes. She told me Phillip called last night and that he'll be here later."

"Yes."

"That's all you're going to say about that?"

"Yes."

"Sable, that boy is in love with you. You know that right?"

"Yes, Mom. I do." Sable sighed with great exasperation. "I really don't want to talk about it."

"I'm sensing a problem. Sable, what is it?"

"Mom, back off please. I said I don't want to talk about it. Let's go for a walk, I need to stretch my legs and attempt to feel normal."

They walked for about five minutes on the sand before Sable was tired and wanted to head back home. Later, she laid down on the couch, while her mother made her a sandwich. She was only able to eat about half of it, before she was exhausted again.

"Mom, can you go into my bedroom and get me another Percocet? It's been twelve hours since I took one and I'm hoping this will be the last one I ever take. I feel so much better than I did yesterday, but I feel like I need one right now, I have a lot of cramps."

"Of course hon. But don't try to be so strong Sable. You were just in the hospital yesterday. Dr. Morgan says most women take these for 5-7 days."

"Well, I really don't think I'll need to go that far Mom. But I do need one right now. And how about my navy throw? It's a bit chilly all of a sudden."

Leslie Franco came back with the medication and the navy throw that was in Sable's bedroom, the one Diane had used last night on the chair. Leslie also closed the sliding glass door so that her daughter wouldn't feel cold.

"Take a nap honey. I'll be in the kitchen preparing dinner in case you need anything."

☙❧ ☙❧ ☙❧

It was almost two-thirty when Leslie woke up her daughter.

"Hi hon. How are you feeling? You've been sleeping for four hours. I thought you might want to freshen up before Phillip gets here in half an hour."

"Yeah, thanks Mom. I do."

She walked to the bathroom and washed her face and brushed her teeth. She felt groggy, but stronger and more like herself.

Her mother was getting ready to leave. She hugged and kissed her daughter.

"Okay honey, I made you Arroz con Pollo and it's on the stove top. You don't even have to heat it up because I just turned off the burner. There's bread you can slice up on the cutting board. I want to head out before your father comes home and before Phillip arrives here. I want to be able to give you two some privacy."

"Thanks, Mom. You know that's my favorite dish. Makes me think about Grandmother Olivia. I'll call you if I need anything. But I promise you, I'll be fine. That nap was really what I needed, I think."

"I'm glad honey. Take care of yourself tonight. You said you felt chilled earlier. I don't want you coming down with a fever."

Sable giggled. "Thanks Mom, for everything. Especially for making me feel like I'm still ten."

They hugged again and Leslie left. Sable was just folding her blue throw when Phillip walked in.

"Hey babe," he said.

"You just missed my mom," Sable said.

"No, I just saw her outside."

"That's funny. This morning, as Diane was leaving, my mother found her outside as well. You guys are a regular relay team," she laughed.

Phillip had reached her by then and bundled her up in the softest bear hug he could muster. He held her so tight, but was careful not to hurt her. He hugged her completely and lovingly. Sable was stretched against the length of him and she felt so good in his arms.

She too thought he felt fabulous. She breathed in his scent and hugged him back with all the strength she had. She nuzzled her face in his neck and felt protected and loved. She sighed and broke the embrace.

"It's good to see you. Sorry we didn't talk last night, Diane told me you called."

"It's fine Sable. I know you needed your rest. I just wanted to check in after I got home from the wedding."

"Thank you for that. Do you want to eat? My mother just made us dinner. Arroz con pollo, which if I remember correctly, you used to love."

"Mmmm, you remember correctly sweetheart. You sit down. I'll get us everything."

An hour later, they both sat back at the table and massaged their bellies. Phillip had talked mostly of last night's wedding details during dinner. He sensed correctly that Sable wasn't ready to talk about what Dr. Morgan had talked to them about. So he talked about the romantic wedding and answered her questions with many details. He was dying to tell her that their wedding would even be more splendid, but he knew that it wasn't the right time for that yet.

"I can't believe I ate that much! I had two helpings! I haven't eaten that well in a week!"

"Well, don't look at me Sable, I had three helpings! I'm ready to roll over to the couch."

"Me too….it's so good to have you here Phillip. It really comforts me."

"Thanks babe, I love being here."

Sable looked at him like she wanted to say something else and then changed her mind. Instead, she asked him if he wanted to watch a movie.

"Oh no, the last two movies I remember us watching were *Gone with the Wind* and *Terms of Endearment.*"

Sable really laughed at the memory. "I thought you enjoyed those!"

"Ha! I enjoyed holding your hand and kissing you in between all of your dad's walk-thrus of the living room. It was as if at any moment, he was going to come in and sit between us!"

"That's true, I remember that. He was a nervous wreck the first few months we were dating. He thought dating a senior would be bad for me."

"Was it?"

"No, it was the best thing I ever did."

They kissed softly a few times. Phillip would have loved to kiss her senseless, but he knew that Sable was sore and that this wasn't the time for romance.

Sable also stopped kissing him at that precise moment and asked. "I'm in the mood for a classic. How about *Pulp Fiction*?"

"Can't ever say no to Travolta. You sure you don't want to watch *Grease* instead?"

"No silly. *Pulp Fiction* is one of my favorites. Put it in, it's in the top drawer of the entertainment center. I'll get a few extra pillows from the bed so we can snuggle on the couch."

Phillip wanted to talk about the procedure, and ask her a dozen questions about her thoughts and concerns, but again, he sensed that she was steering them away from that topic completely. He wanted to indulge her by keeping the evening's mood light and sweet. He noticed that she laughed at the movie whole heartedly and that she didn't take any further pain medication that day. Her mother had told him outside that she had taken one that morning. She sat between his legs on the couch resting her back on his chest. He loved their closeness. He constantly kissed her cheek or her ear and occasionally, softly rubbed her tummy. He didn't want to annoy her with too much affection during the movie, but he couldn't seem to let a five minute interval pass, before he needed to touch or kiss her in some way. Sable loved his tenderness very much and vowed to remember this night forever. She had already made her decision, but tonight was theirs.

Later that night, in bed, Sable acted clingy; she kept asking him to hug her longer or tighter. He spooned her the whole night and if he shifted at all, she molded her body to his so that she'd have complete contact with him. At some point, in the middle of the night, Phillip thought she was trying to make this night last forever. He became insecure about it.

👀 👀 👀

The next morning, Phillip couldn't contain himself any longer and rolled himself on top of Sable and tried to feel her completely under him. He knew they couldn't make love, but he just wanted to lay like that for a moment. It seemed she knew exactly what he was doing because she wrapped her legs around his ankles and drew him in a bit closer. If it had been any other time, they would have already been ripping off their clothes, but they knew that it just wasn't permissible. She might have internal complications if they did.

So instead of heating things up any further, they hugged and walked into the bathroom together to take a shower. It was sweet and gentle and Sable took in every moment of it.

Over breakfast, Phillip made a comment about last night.

"Babe, I felt that I just couldn't love you enough last night. You didn't let go of me for a second."

"A little clingy huh?"

"Yeah, maybe, but I liked it."

Sable smiled at that genuinely and then paused as her eyes welled up.

Phillip saw it immediately. "Baby, what's wrong?"

Sable shook her head and stood up to put her plate and coffee mug in the sink. She stood there a minute trying to brace herself for the inevitable.

"Phillip, I love you. I have loved you since I was practically a child. I thought that when we broke up, I was going to die. After a few weeks of that, I realized that my demeanor was tormenting my sweet parents, and I decided to steel myself through it in silence in my bedroom at night. I tried to date at UCSB, but no one seemed to be a fraction of the person you are. I tried dating afterwards, while I was starting my career—usually a client or two or a friend of a colleague, but no one measured up. You met me while I was dating Rick, and although he is a very nice person, I was galaxies away from ever falling for him. You are the love of my life and always will be. Last night, if I acted like I was literally holding on to you for dear life, it was because I was. You see, I will have to relive last night again and again in my head. It was the last night you and I will be able to share. Phillip, I'm letting you go."

*D*esiree walked around the block trying to control her thoughts. The irony that she was unwed and pregnant with twins, while her cousin was suffering an unjust medical situation, made her sick to her stomach.

She had just called her mother this morning to give her an update on Sable and she cried so hard on the phone, that she thought her mother might be flying to see her right now. She tried to reassure her mother that she was fine, but the pain of it all overwhelmed her. She had no boyfriend, no college degree, no nearby parents and yet she was about to be given the biggest responsibility of her life in the care of two precious innocents who would depend on her for their everything. Compare that to Sable who had a career, a special man, a home, and she was punished with those damn polyps and fibroids that had ripped her life apart. Why couldn't it have been her with the medical issues? Realistically, she hadn't imagined herself becoming a mother for another decade anyway. She just wasn't prepared. The unfairness of it, broke her heart. She was lucky that Sable loved her enough to not despise her for this situation. She knew Sable would love her little ones to pieces, but it wouldn't be the same as her own children with Phillip.

By the time she walked back to her apartment, Desiree felt a little better, but the guilt hadn't lessened. Although Sable was a good hearted person and didn't blame her, Desiree felt like the worst possible being. Maybe she would go to church on Sunday and pray about this. She sighed and walked up her steps.

Inside, she called her Aunt Leslie and asked if she would go with her to her ultrasound on Tuesday. Sable had gone with her to her last one, but she didn't have the heart to ask her to go again. Not only because she was recuperating, but because it was in bad taste obviously. Leslie said that she would love to go with her.

"Have you looked at the baby book of names that I got you?"

"No, I just haven't done that yet. Do you suppose I should pick out several names now and see which ones grow on me over the next few months?"

"Well, Des, you need at least two boy names and two girl names. Some people make a list and decide at the hospital which name they believe suits the baby the best. Other people have the names selected well before the baby arrives. You'll have to see what feels right for you.

Maybe since both you and Dane share the D initial, you would want to select D names."

"No way! Definitely not. He's not here to help me, I'm certainly not going to play homage to him in that way."

"Well, alright dear. Some people pick cultural names to honor their past, others pick virtues such as Hope, others love floral names, the possibilities are endless. You really should pore over the book Desiree."

"Okay, I promise I will tonight. I need some cheering up and that might just do the trick. Can I ask you for a favor?"

"Yes of course Desiree, whatever you need."

"I was wondering if it was ok with you and Uncle Daniel that the babies call you Grandma and Grandpa. Well, more specifically, *Abuelo* and *Abuela*. Since Dane's folks won't be in the picture, I'd like the babies to still feel like they have four grandparents."

Leslie swallowed the lump in her throat and said, "I would really love that."

Leslie hung up the phone after talking to her niece and instantly tears overtook her. She was trying so hard to be strong for her daughter and her niece, but the anguish washed over her. She was never one to be pitiful, but she cried out at the disappointment she felt at being robbed of the chance of being a grandmother. Sable had always been such a healthy woman, had always made wise choices and now this happened. As Desiree said, it was completely unfair.

For years, she and Daniel had been traveling all around the world on their summer vacations. They would save $500 a month all through the school year, so that they could enjoy a 2-3 week vacation during the summer. Sometimes they would take Sable, sometimes even Olivia, but often they would go off by themselves to rekindle their love. They had always wanted to get all their traveling dreams out of the way, so by the time Sable had children, they would be able to help her with babysitting, carpools, etc. Olivia had helped them so much when they were fresh out of college and starting a family themselves, that they wanted to lovingly reciprocate and help raise their future grandchildren. Now, it seemed so futile.

Leslie cried a little harder. Now Desiree was saying that her twins would call *her* "Abuela," or grandmother, in Spanish. She couldn't believe that it would be her grand-nephews or grand-nieces who would take that place in her heart, and not Sable's children. It pained her so much. She sat up and wiped her tears away and decided to call her daughter to see how she was feeling.

ᘛᘚ ᘛᘚ ᘛᘚ

"The hell you're NOT letting me go, Sable! What are you talking about?"

"You're destined to be a father. I cannot make you one. I am in love with you. But I love you enough to let you fulfill your dream of a true marriage, of children and grandchildren. I won't *ever* stand in your way of that. My problems will not ruin your chance at fatherhood. I will not let you convince me otherwise."

"Don't be a martyr, Sable! I don't want anyone else. I've been away from you for years and no one even mattered a bit. You are the love of my life! Only you! If you leave me, I wouldn't marry anyone else anyway! We'd both be lonely and miserable. And *alone. Apart.* Listen to me Sable, I would not marry anyone else and therefore wouldn't have children anyway."

"You feel that way right now Phillip. But in time, your feelings will change and you'd grow to resent me. You'd see your friends being soccer coaches to cute little boys or escorting their daughters to school, and you'd feel robbed of the opportunity. I would not forgive myself to have taken that from you."

"Sable, would you love me if I had cancer?"

"Yes."

"Would you love me if I were blind?"

"Yes."

"How about if I was in a car accident and lost the use of my legs and had to sit in a wheelchair?"

"Of course."

"Then, what is the damn difference? You'd love me if I had health problems. Why won't you trust me to love you with your health issues?"

At this Sable yelled at him for the first time, "Because all those scenarios still have the ability to conceive! To have a family! For posterity! I cannot strip that of you! I will not and you need to start understanding that Phillip!"

After a few minutes' pause, Phillip said, "Sable, honey. Please don't make choices for me. I respect and love you that you're worried about my future. But listen clearly, YOU are my future, baby. I will not marry anyone else, I want my whole life to be beside yours. I can't lose you again, I can't." He sank into the sofa in weariness.

"You didn't lose me Phillip. You walked away from me."

Phillip looked up at her, surprised that she would say that, and answered, "You're right. I did. I was eighteen and a fool. But I'm not a boy anymore and I won't let you do this to us. I want to love you all the way to our 90s Sable. We found each other again, it's bigger than us. It's more than love. It's what we're meant to be honey, together. I will not be half the man I'm supposed to be without you in my life. You are endless, Sable. My love for you is endless. Please don't throw me away. I couldn't bear it."

Sable saw that Phillip had tears going down his cheeks and that his hands were shaking. She felt herself becoming vulnerable and weak. She stood up straighter, forcing her determined conviction. She breathed in and looked at him sternly.

"My heart is breaking Phillip over the loss of my opportunity at motherhood. It really is. In fact, I feel like the totality of it hasn't even hit me yet. But there is no way that I will sabotage your future. No way! So please, take this breakup as a man. I will not change my mind. I love you Phillip and God knows I always have, but I will not share my life with you. I want you to leave please."

"Sable, you are breaking my heart. Please don't leave me. I couldn't bear it. Let's give this a few months, we'll talk about it again. I just can't be without you. Think of our weekend two weeks ago in Santa Barbara. That's just a glimpse of how perfect our lives can be." He walked over to her and took her hands. "These are the hands I first held in that car ride to the movies when we were kids. These are the hands that I want to hold when I dance with you at our wedding. I also want to hold your hand when we're old and feeble. Please don't leave me."

"Phillip, I will not change my mind. I have thought about it. Extensively. You once told me you want a car-load of kids, I cannot give them to you! Did you hear what I just said? I cannot give them to you! I will not stand in the way of what you want!"

"You're what I want Sable. Listen to me! If you leave me, I will not marry anyone else, therefore there will be no children! I would much rather be with you, the love of my life, than live a lonely existence without you!"

"I wish that were possible Phillip, but it wouldn't be like that. You are a darling man. You are so damn handsome and you are so good. You will inevitably meet someone else who can give you a quality life. I'm so exhausted Phillip. I'm asking you to go."

"Sable, I'll leave now. But I do not accept that we're breaking up. I do not accept it. I will marry you one day and we'll either adopt or who knows what, but I'm not losing you." He walked over to his bag and took something out that had a ribbon wrapped around it and set it on the coffee table. Then he walked to her and kissed her hard. He held on to her as if, he held her *long* enough, her decision would change. His shoulders shook as he openly started to cry. He cried for her health, he cried for the years they had wasted, and he cried about the fact that it was so easy for her to give up on their love.

The next day Phillip woke up sick to his stomach. He couldn't believe the anguish he was feeling. He thought back to the pain he must have caused Sable in high school. Her tears, her pleas to reconsider, were just sitting in the pit of his being right now. To be in her shoes right now, so many years later, seemed to put perspective on what he had caused her. Her pain at fifteen had seemed so juvenile and young. He had known that he had hurt her, but it wasn't until now that he felt how poignant that rejection was. He loved her and wanted to marry her. And now he would be alone. A life without Sable seemed incomprehensible to him. But ironically, so deserving, as he had once left her. But he wasn't a teenager and they weren't living on opposite sides of the country. They lived within an hour's drive from one another and their future was within their grasp. Their happiness was attainable. Yet, Sable had let him go.

He swallowed a lump in his throat and got up to clear his mind. He put the leash on Joey and decided to take him for a morning walk.

ඖ ඖ ඖ

Leslie knocked on her daughter's door and entered without waiting to be let in since she could see her daughter resting on the couch through the screen door.

Sable was resting with her right arm thrown over her eyes and her left arm gripped a book. Without looking up, she said, "Hi Mom."

"How did you know it was me?"

"I know the jingle jangle of your purse, Mom. Hooking your keys on the side of your bag is a dead give away."

"Oh, I didn't know I had upgraded to old lady sounds and habits."

"Yup, jingle jangling makes you an official old lady."

"How are you feeling?"

"Physically, the cramps and discomfort are gone. But my insides are killing me. I'm nervous and afraid about my decision about Phillip. I miss him so much Mom. The tears won't stop flowing. It's killing me. I prayed for him to return to me all through my youth. And in the recent years, he constantly drifted into my thoughts. And now, after just a couple of months of bliss, I had to let him go. It's so unfair!"

"Sable, perhaps you decided this too impulsively. You should have given it more time like you told me he suggested. Look at you, your eyes are sunken in and your face is blotchy. You need to talk to him; this decision was just made too hastily."

"All I think about is calling him Mom. But I can't. I miss him so much, I'd crumble in a second. He told me he wants three or four kids, Mom! I can't give him any! Although painful, I know I did the right thing. After all, I'm in the same position I was months ago: an owner of a romantic restaurant living vicariously through the lovers who dine there." Sable paused and handed her mother the photo album that Phillip had laid on the coffee table before he left. "These are the pictures we took in Santa Barbara two weeks ago Mom. The photos are stunning and yet, so sweet....and I've looked at that album about one hundred times since he's left… and I just can't bear to look at it right now. My heart physically hurts over it. Please take it Mom. Hide it if you must."

"Sable, I'm proud of you for being selfless and considerate to Phillip's future. But I must admit, I'm afraid you're going to regret this decision for the rest of your life."

"I am too Mom, believe me, I am too."

ᘓ ᘓ ᘓ

It was four days later, when Phillip found himself knocking on the Francos' door.

"Phillip, what a surprise to see you, young man. Please come in."

"Thank you Mr. Franco. I really need your help."

As Phillip walked in, the two men shook hands. Leslie was just coming into the living room when she saw Phillip and immediately walked over to hug him. The gesture made Phillip silently choke up. He sensed that Leslie knew about her daughter's decision and felt sorry for him—for both of them.

As they all sat down, Leslie was the first to speak, "Phillip, before you tell us why you're here, I just want to tell you that Sable is beside herself with grief. She said she keeps reliving the last moments you two shared together and she's utterly distraught."

"She's distraught? She's the one who ended our relationship! I don't care if she can't have children. I told her that if I wasn't with her, I wouldn't have children in my life anyway. I said that it was a mute point that we'd both be alone and apart. It makes no sense. I just don't want to be without her. All my dreams are wrapped into the idea of us."

Daniel said, "Perhaps if you gave her some time. She feels like she's losing a part of herself. Part of her femininity and womanhood. Plus, she fears that you'd feel resentment towards her in 5 or 10 years when your buddies are doing activities with children."

"Resentment towards her would just never happen. Mr. and Mrs. Franco, I came here for help. I need you two to help me convince her that she's all I want. I'm 31, I'm not a boy. It will be a bigger tragedy to lose the love of my life than to lose children I might never have had anyway! I love your daughter completely. We can adopt or do foster care or surrogacy—whatever she wants. But please help me before it's too late." Phillip's voice cracked just slightly at the end of his words.

"Phillip, thirteen years ago when the two of you broke up, I knew it was a young heart's first pain. But when I saw my daughter recently cry for you, it was devastating. A mother doesn't want to see her child in that way. I know she's stubborn, that's the Española in her. But I promise you Phillip, I will use all my influence to try to help the both of you. In the meantime, please have patience and don't give up on her."

"I will never give up on her, please tell her that."

Ten days later, Sable called the specialist. "Yes, I'm calling about the referral from Dr. Morgan to your office. I need to see Dr. St. Francis about a possible partial hysterectomy. Yes, I'm free tomorrow at 9. Thank you for accommodating me so quickly."

Sable hung up the phone and sighed. She couldn't believe this was truly her fate. To be alone, without Phillip and a family. She would not take away his chance of being a father, she just couldn't. Love was about respecting the other person's needs above one's own. His words the other day were just so passionate, yet so pained. And when he cried on her sofa right before leaving, it took all her strength, all her being to not rush to him and comfort him. She hated herself at that moment, how could she hurt him so? But she forced herself to stand rigid in her spot and watch him walk out her door minutes later. She watched him walk to his car and held her breath when he turned around. Would he return? No, he just kissed his fingertips and blew a kiss in her direction. She wasn't sure if he could see her as the distance between them was quite far, but the tenderness of the gesture cut her deeply and brought her down to her knees. She laid on the carpet in the same spot until the next morning, completely ripped inside out and weakened by her endless tears.

Today, she missed him so much that she almost dialed his number a hundred times, but her strong will always won the battle against her weak heart. She knew she was doing the right thing ultimately.

*S*able drove to Dr. St. Francis' office feeling weary and sad. She missed Phillip so much. The short time they'd been together had been so loving and she cherished it. She would treasure that time for the rest of her life. The comment that Phillip made about not ever marrying anyone else and therefore not having children anyway haunted her. Her biggest fear was both of them reaching old age alone, having wasted their lives. She loved him enough, however, to take a risk that he *would* indeed find someone else who could bear his children someday.

She sighed as she parked the car. Phillip was all she thought about. She chastised herself for not resting more to improve her health….but her mind always lingered back to Phillip. When he had asked Dr. Morgan in front of her whole family about the possibility of getting pregnant immediately, her heart had swelled. The intensity of his love had filled the room at that moment and she still got chills every time she relived it.

Sable checked in with the receptionist and took a seat. Minutes later, a forty-something year old woman came in and sat across from her. She was wearing a hat on her head to cover the absence of hair and Sable noticed that she had no eyebrows. Her face was graceful and kind. She spoke first.

"I haven't seen you around here before. A person gets to know the regulars. My name is Camille."

"Hello. My name is Sable. I've never been here before. I'm here for a second opinion."

"You'll love Dr. St. Francis. I've been coming to him for fourteen years."

"Fourteen years? That's incredible. That must mean that you really love him."

"Yes, Dr. St. Francis is both an oncologist and an Ob Gyn and that appealed to me greatly. I've been battling cervical cancer for all these years and I truly believe that I'm alive today because of him. I still have a lot to do in my life, so I come here faithfully for my screenings and treatments."

"I'm sorry to hear about your illness. Your attitude is inspiring. You have a lovely aura about you."

"Thank you. I'm comfortable with it and that takes time. I can tell that there's sadness in your eyes. Everything is a process of the heart."

"Yes, I feel like I've been processing a lot lately."

"I understand completely. I'm 44 and I'm still learning a lot too. But one thing that being sick teaches us is appreciation for life, family, friends, lovers."

Sable put her head down at the reference of lovers.

Sable said, "I'm new to thinking about my health so much. I've been naïve and busy with life, my house, my business. Seems sort of selfish when you streamline it to such simplistic terms."

"I think it's perfectly natural to forget about health in our fast paced lives. It's only when our health is compromised or questioned, that we are forced to focus on it. I was thirty when I first felt betrayed by my own body."

"I'm 28."

"I would love to be your age again, I would do many things differently."

"Really? Can you tell me what you would do differently? I mean, if it's not too much of an imposition into your privacy."

"Well, I have great parents, siblings and friends. During my 20s, I never wanted to date much because I was too busy working on my career. Then at 30, I started chemo and radiation and I was on my journey to save my own life. If I had to do it again, I would have actively pursued love. On my headstone, I might have been able to put loving wife or mother. Now I feel like I've let that time run its course. I've never been in love and that's the one regret I have in life. Have you ever been in love?"

"Oh yes. I love someone very much. I loved him as a young girl and I recently found him again. He's undoubtedly the love of my life."

"How wonderful for you. You are blessed then."

Sable smiled at that, then frowned.

"What's wrong?"

"I've let my boyfriend go. It's been over two weeks now. My health won't allow me to have children and he wants to be a father one day."

"What does he say about that?"

"He says he doesn't care."

"Then, you have your answer. Love him. Let him love you. That's what life's all about. It's not about careers and real estate. It's about hugs, passion, dinners for two. Don't keep him on the outside. His place is *in* your life."

Sable's name was called just then and Sable stood up.

"Thank you Camille. You don't know what your words have meant to me."

"Well then, today was a good day. Best of luck to you."

On impulse, Sable hugged Camille and rushed off to follow the nurse down the corridor.

಄಄ ಄಄ ಄಄

Desiree was really starting to show. She was already wearing maternity clothes to her dismay. Having two little bundles was sure taking a toll on her body. She was tired all the time and nauseous in the mornings. She knew she should be experiencing huge bouts of love and excitement, but she had such a heavy heart.

First of all, she was worried about moving. Her apartment was a three bedroom that she shared with two roommates and she knew that she wouldn't be able to fit two cribs in her room with her. Of course, the babies could share a crib for the first few months, in fact, that was even encouraged for twins, but eventually she would need more space. So her anxiety came with the decision of whether to move now when she was tired all the time and still trying to finish out her last semester of school.

Or later, when the babies would be here and consuming her every moment. Of course, disturbing her roommates' studies was another problem.

Secondly, the fact that Dane had not called to at least ask how she was feeling, consumed her mind. She realized that he didn't want to be their father, but they were a couple until just recently and Desiree felt that she deserved at least an occasional phone call from him to be polite as any random friend would do. The fact that he could dismiss her and their babies so readily hurt her beyond belief. It would have been such a blessing to talk to him about her fears or dreams or even laugh at her disgusting cravings of pickles and mayonnaise. It would have been loving of him to rub her tummy or ease her anxiety.

Her heart was heaviest, however, with concern for her cousin Sable. The irony continued to crush her that her cousin would not be able to have babies and she was having them without a boyfriend or a future to speak of. It weighed on her soul that however wonderful Sable would be as the babies' Godmother, she would never have the privilege to carry her own. She sighed with the comfort that Sable didn't have any animosity towards her. She knew that in another family, this delicate situation would have proven to be a very strained problem. Instead, Sable had gone on shopping sprees for her babies and assured her of the love that she felt for her and her little ones to come.

ଡ଼ଡ ଡ଼ଡ ଡ଼ଡ

Shane rushed to the phone and answered, "*Enchanting Studios*, how may I help you?"

"Shane, it's me Phillip. I'm calling to say I won't be in the office today and perhaps tomorrow either."

"What's wrong? You've never missed work before."

"I know, but I have a deadly migraine that I just can't shake off and plus, I have insomnia. I need a couple of days to recuperate or I'm going to be a zombie for Friday's photo shoot. Being that today is Tuesday, I think I can spare a few days and have you and Vince man the ship."

"Sure, sure. There's a potential bride coming in at noon today and another at 9 in the morning and I'll speak to both of them for you and hopefully sign them on."

"Thanks. Vince will probably have to call back the Turner Group for the marketing meeting. I remember they left a message at the end of the day yesterday. Tell Vince anytime next week for a consultation should be fine, just to check the appointment book of course."

"Will do. I think we can manage. We'll call you if we have any questions but it all seems easy enough."

"Thanks. Hey, how is Marli feeling with the baby?"

"She's feeling great. When we were expecting Audrey, Marli was an emotional mess. Probably due to all the anxiety we felt prior to conceiving. But this pregnancy is going very well. We're very happy. Thanks for asking."

"Anytime, Shane. I'm happy that you're going to be a second-time father. Pretty exciting time for you I'm sure."

"Yes it is. Scary, but exciting. But Marli's positive and she calms *me* down!"

After they hung up, Phillip felt a pang of jealousy. Shane had everything Phillip wanted out of life. His jealousy was not about the baby, however, but about Shane's relationship with Marli. They had gone through their problems and stress with conceiving and had made it together. If Sable were here, she would argue however, that they made it *with a baby—no, two children.*

Phillip sighed and ran a hand through his hair and then leaned back in his chair rubbing his eyes. "Dammit, I miss her. I can't believe this is what the rest of my life is going to be like."

He got up and walked to his bedroom and opened up the top drawer to his dresser. He opened up the jewelry box and withdrew the two and a half carat pear diamond ring. He had wanted to propose so badly. He wanted to be her man for all time. Sable was so stubborn in her decision to let him go to seek out a more perfect woman. Phillip knew however, that she was his idea of perfection. He gazed at the ring for a few more moments before he put it back in his top drawer.

"Phillip, why don't you come over here at 8? We can watch a movie and my parents won't be back until 11. Of course, my Grandmother Olivia will be checking in from time to time, but she usually crashes by 9 since she's such an early riser."

"I don't know, I have to finish reading Canterbury Tales by tomorrow and I have eight chapters to go. But, I'd love to see you. How about if I come over and read, while you wear those huge, sexy headphones of yours while you watch your movie?"

"Sounds wonderful. But don't make fun of my headphones! My dad paid a pretty penny for those!"

When Phillip came over, Sable was looking sassy in a red tube top and jeans and was already wearing the headphones! Phillip laughed heartedly and picked her up and swung her around in his arms a few times.

"You are too freakin' adorable, do you know that?"

"What! What? I can't hear you? You need to speak up!"

He laughed again and set her down and kissed her soundly. They were laughing between their kisses and she led him to the family room.

He plopped down on the sofa and took out his novel. Sable put in the movie and plugged in her headphones as promised.

"You look like Princess Leila."

"What?"

"Oh no, not that again!" and they pealed off another round of laughter.

"What movie are you going to watch?"

"My favorite, Terms of Endearment."

"Not that one again! You made me watch it last month!"

"Listen, Loverboy, you need to study. I had to select a movie that you wouldn't watch while you're trying to read."

"Okay, fair enough. I know I won't be watching that girlie movie again!"

She playfully punched him in the arm and lay on his chest, while he opened Canterbury Tales. He took the headphone off her right ear and whispered, "I love you Sable Franco." She turned around and kissed him softly and said "I love you too."

Phillip leaned back in his chair and smiled. The innocence and wonder of those years. How he made fun of those ridiculous headphones. He chuckled and then was pained on how much he missed her. Dammit, sixteen days without her and he couldn't bear another one. And he decided that if he wouldn't be in her life as a boyfriend, he'd wedge his way back into her heart in another way.

🦉 🦉 🦉

"Very nice to meet you Ms. Franco, I'm Dr. St. Francis. I've already read over your file, gone over all your medical assessments and have spoken to Dr. Morgan."

"Thank you for being so thorough. What do you think of my prognosis?"

"Before I answer that, I'd like to use my ultrasound on you and see with my own eyes."

Sable lay on the table as he proceeded to evaluate her himself. After a few moments, she sat up and they talked at length about her options.

"First of all, Ms. Franco, I believe that Dr. Morgan's evaluations and course of actions were exactly what I would have done. You already know that your uterine fibroids are benign tumors. However, yours were quite large. I counted five in Dr. Morgan's surgery report and one was the size of a golf ball. As for the polyps, you still have numerous clusters of them on the wall of your uterus. The polyps are normal tissues that grow in abnormal formations. We can attribute these two conditions to causing your pelvic pain, excessive menstrual bleeding, bladder problems and lower back pain. Most women do develop fibroids or polyps at some time in their life, but I generally see it in women past 45. Given that you have both and that you are only 28, gives you more years for the polyps and fibroids to worsen, so it is imperative that we proceed with the partial hysterectomy and remove your uterus."

"Dr. St. Francis, I completely understand. However, I'm saddened to hear that you substantiate everything Dr. Morgan has already explained to me. I was hoping that you would have offered other alternatives."

"No, I'm afraid not. But have you and Dr. Morgan discussed the freezing of your ova?"

"No, we have not. Please tell me about it. I only have a vague idea of what that would entail. Besides, I assumed that because I had multiple concerns that the ovaries would have been compromised in some way as well."

"Your ova and ovaries are fine. Women are born with all the ova they are to have for the rest of their lives. They do not self-produce like a man does sperm. It would be an appropriate decision if you want to think about ova retrieval. However, it would be my medical advice to perform such a procedure immediately."

"Can you tell me what it would all entail?"

"Certainly. We would have you ingest fertility drugs to ripen your eggs for removal. We need to time it just right with your monthly cycle. Most doctors recommend up to four stimulations in order to retrieve enough eggs. But I don't feel comfortable delaying your partial hysterectomy up to four months' time."

"So, how long can the eggs stay frozen?"

"For years. Women have used their ova from a decade before. Later, the eggs are fertilized with sperm and injected into the uterus of a surrogate."

"And of course, the baby conceived would be genetically all mine..."

"Yes, the surrogate would have no genetic linking to the baby whatsoever."

"I have a lot to think about. Would you be the doctor to retrieve the ova?"

"I would send you to a fertility specialist for that. If you decide to do so, I would think about it immediately. I would like to schedule your hysterectomy within 8-10 weeks."

"Thank you doctor. I feel like I have been given a second chance today. Thank you so much." Sable impulsively hugged Dr. St. Francis and rushed out the door feeling like a new woman.

Twenty-One

$\mathcal{S}$ able walked in to *Amor Mio* and let the atmosphere wash over her. She'd been gone two weeks and she had missed her restaurant so much. Although she did work on her computer and spoke to Miles daily, it was wonderful to step into *Amor Mio*. She promised herself that she'd only work five hours. She wanted to take it easy and not push herself excessively. She told herself that she'd also limit the rest of the week to five-six hours a day. She walked around the tables and peered up at the impressive chandeliers. She slowly and thoughtfully walked over to the big windows with the twinkle lights and peered out at the sidewalk. She loved the ambience and knew it was the perfect time to return to *Amor Mio*. She lightly touched the velvet drapes and turned to find Miles in the kitchen.

"Ms. Franco! How wonderful to see you! I wasn't expecting you until tomorrow!"

"Thanks Miles, it's great to see you too! I felt strong enough this morning and longed to be here. I know we've been emailing, but fill me in on the particulars."

After half an hour of talking to Miles and a few of the waitresses, Sable walked into her office and at once, the image of her and Phillip making love on her desk, washed over her. The image was so strong that she actually closed her eyes and lifted her hand to her heart. What an intoxicating, passionate liaison that had been. She exhaled deeply, opened her eyes and walked around to her desk and started looking through her files, invoices, emails and phone messages.

True to her word, she left after a few minutes past five hours. She was proud of herself for getting through the day. She was afraid that after being at work, she'd have to regress to taking a Percocet pain killer, but she felt great—at least physically she did. Emotionally, she was a mess. But tonight, she would call her parents and Phillip to discuss what Dr. St. Francis had said. That brought her excitement; perhaps true happiness was finally on the horizon.

@@ @@ @@

Phillip was determined to stay in Sable's life. He understood her stubborn decision to "save" him from her destiny without children, but he had an idea to stay in her life forever, while both of them got what they truly wanted from each other.

Phillip drove over to her house and picked up some large sunflowers on the way there. He decided against romantic roses and instead, decided on something cheerful and bright. He had thought about having the conversation over the phone, but he missed her so much, he just wanted to see her precious face. He hadn't seen her in two and a half weeks and what a desolate time it had been. He was sure he had lost weight as he had barely eaten or slept out of anguish and anger. This was his second day staying home from work and with new energy pumping in his veins, he parked the car, picked up the flowers and directly walked to her door.

"Phillip, what a surprise," she said as she saw him. She smiled brightly at him, but Phillip looked serious.

"Sable, I have to talk to you."

"Of course, come in. I was going to call you tonight."

That completely surprised Phillip as just two weeks ago she had wanted to be alone forever, it had seemed. "You were Sable?"

"Yes, I was. Thank you for the sunflowers. I love them. I'll put them in a vase in a second. But first, tell me what you wanted to talk to me about."

They both walked over to the white couches and sank in. Phillip was aware that this was the first time since the reunion that they had seen each other and not touched, hugged or kissed in anyway. Phillip thought to himself that this is what their future probably had in store, chaste meetings.

"Now listen Sable, I would like you to hear me out before you argue with me."

Sable couldn't help but chuckle at that. "Am I that argumentative Phillip?"

"Last time you were and I drove all the way over here to be heard and I really just want to say it all at once."

"I will respectfully hear you out, Phillip."

"I completely disagree with your decision to break up with me. Knowing you again, spending the night here, making love to you, bathing together, our weekend getaway, wearing practically matching outfits at the reunion tells me in my heart that you are the love of my life. You were my first love, my true love and you will be my last love. I will not marry somebody else, I don't care how damn fertile she could be.

"But I understand that there's something inside of you that feels like you're holding me back. I can only wait it out with you as a friend. And that's what I came here to tell you. If you won't have me as a lover, and a future husband as I would want to be, I'm going to be here as your best friend. I'm going to be there at the procedure and I'm going to hold your hand when you wake up. When you come home, I'm gonna carry you into the house. When you're recuperating, I'll wash your hair and bring you soup and wrap your legs in your favorite navy throw. I'll even watch those sappy girl movies with you and hand you tissue at all the appropriate spots. I'll do this as a best friend and as someone who adores you. As best friends, we can be here for each other for the rest of our lives. I was without you for thirteen years and it was practically lifeless. But these past few weeks were pathetic. I love you Sable and if friendship is all you'll allow, I'm here for the long haul."

"Phillip, I don't want to be your best friend. I want to be your girlfriend." Sable sat a little closer to Phillip on the couch and gently put her hand on his knee.

His eyes searched hers and he raised his eyebrows. "What? I'm confused, Sable." Last time I was here, you broke my heart and were very adamant about your decision. I went to speak to your parents and laid it all out for them to see as well."

Sable touched his face and took his hands in hers. "Baby, I'm so sorry. I truly am. Believe me, these days without you have been hell for me too. I wanted to drive out to you countless times, but I wanted to be fair to you too." She wanted to explain further, but she *had* to hug him at that moment. Their hug was fierce and the reconciliation was heavenly. Her heart was bursting with happiness and love. She kissed him three times before she drew away and wanted to continue talking.

"Today, two things happened to me that I believe changed my outlook and my perspective on my health. It's a long shot, but it's a chance and a chance is all we need."

"What happened, babe?"

"First, I met a woman at the doctor's office. She's very pretty, forty-four and bald. Her name is Camille. She's one of the loveliest people I've ever met. She's been battling cancer for the past fourteen years and her attitude was inspirational. But the one thing that stayed with me the whole day, is that she told me she's never been in love. Never. Could you imagine? Her whole life without someone to love and whisper her fears to. I fell in love at fifteen and I knew it was a gift beyond comparison. And after finding you again recently, I know that I don't want to live without you. And if that makes me selfish, then so be it. I can't live without you Phillip. Please forgive me."

She moved forward again and they hugged sweetly. "I want to be with you forever Phillip McNeil, please believe me."

"Sable, we will never be apart again. 13 years and a couple of weeks is too much. I couldn't bear it again."

"I know. But I have so much more to tell you."

"More than just Camille? I swear I'm sending her a dozen bottles of wine tomorrow to thank her!"

Sable laughed at that. "I think she'd love the spontaneity of the gesture."

"So what else happened today, love?" he held her hand as he asked.

"I went to see the specialist that Dr. Morgan referred me to. They had already spoken about me and Dr. St. Francis had already seen all my assessments and medical file. In Dr. Morgan's reports he read I had several fibroids, 5 to be exact—one being the size of a golf ball. He did an ultrasound and was able to confirm the severity of my uterine polyps and he concurred that the partial hysterectomy is the right course of action."

Sable paused, and Phillip kissed her cheek and asked, "What else did he say to change your perspective on all this?"

"What he said was that I should consider freezing my ova. I could do it later on in life, but if I were to have further complications in the future, we might unknowingly compromise my ovaries as well. As of right now, my ovaries are clean and healthy. He considers it a good idea to freeze my ova so that you and I can have *our* children in the future through a surrogate."

"Our children," Phillip echoed. "Oh Sable, I'm so happy. I am beyond words."

"It might take two months to collect as many ova as they can. Most women do it over the course of four months, but Dr. St. Francis doesn't want to delay my hysterectomy beyond that."

"I'm sending your doctor a dozen bottles of wine too! He inspired you to give us a second chance. I'm so happy! What does freezing ova entail?"

"I need to take a few drugs to ripen the eggs. The actual procedure, is I believe, like a pap smear….the patient is awake and it's done in a lab. However, they say the procedure is very expensive."

"I don't care how much it costs, Sable." It's on me. Anything to try to have a child together. But how would you feel about the fact that you'd never be pregnant yourself? And have you thought about the possibility of the implantation not working in the body of a surrogate?"

"I have Phillip. The fact that I'll never be pregnant is sad, but it's not heartbreaking. And the possibility of failed implantations is a reality. However, the knowledge I gained today that I'd even be able to freeze my ova is a gift beyond words. I had assumed my *whole* female anatomy was destroyed, and now that I know my ova are healthy, I feel like I've been given a second chance at motherhood. If it doesn't work, I will die a happy woman that we had tried all that science allowed us to try. In that event, I'll give my whole heart to the possibility of adopting. But we've been given this chance for us to have a baby together. It's an unbelievable second chance."

"Sable, I'm the happiest man. I have you in my life and in my future. I love you so much."

Sable held his two cheeks in her palms and they rested their foreheads together for a long, sweet time.

July and August were a whirlwind of activity. Sable felt that she had never been so busy. She put in eight to nine hour days at *Amor Mio*, she would have loved to stay longer, but she kept promising her parents and Phillip that she wouldn't push her system too far. Even on days when she felt particularly energetic, she went home as promised and wrote down meticulous lists of what to do the following day to be as efficient with her time as possible.

Her parents had also become a Godsend. She would be at home recuperating soon and her parents had offered to help at the restaurant a couple of days each to minimize her workload. Miles, was amazingly detailed but already had so many other responsibilities.

So Sable spent the first part of July training each of her parents. Leslie would be taking over all the ordering. Sable introduced her to all the purveyors she would be working with and taught her how to analyze the stockroom and kitchen so that Miles and his staff would not be low on any of their necessities. Sable also taught her mom how to inventory the supplies and how to input all the information on spreadsheets and in addition, run bi-weekly reports. Sable and her mom agreed that Leslie would work at the restaurant about ten hours a week, spread between two or three days. Sable was impressed at how quickly her mother learned and how efficient she had become.

Her father, Daniel, was similarly working about ten hours a week, but he was helping with all the finances. He was learning from his daughter how to run the employee weekly payroll and do all the record keeping and billing of the steady stream of invoices that came in. He would also do any kind trouble shooting and he'd reconcile the restaurant ledger. Finally, he would run the deposits to the bank.

With so much help from her parents, namely twenty hours a week combined, Sable's workload was significantly reduced which allowed her more time to do her egg harvesting and more importantly, her parents would say, rest. In addition, because her parents insisted wholeheartedly to work for free, Sable was able to afford to give Miles a five percent raise to accommodate all his extra hours as well. Miles had really stepped up to his added responsibilities and Sable wanted him to feel appreciated and well compensated. The last thing she needed was for Miles to feel too overworked and leave to another restaurant.

By the second week of July, Dr. St. Francis had or-ganized Sable's treatment at the fertility clinic. Sable was being injected daily with FSH to stimulate her ovaries and egg production. The clinic told her that if they weren't successful with FSH injections, they would move on to HCG, but so far, Sable was doing well with the treatments. Once a month, the overly stimulated ovaries would hopefully produce a batch of eggs that would then be removed by an ultrasound guided needle while Sable was under a mild sedative. The eggs would then be drained of any excess fluid that could form ice crystals and ultimately damage the eggs. Finally, the eggs could be frozen and stored in liquid nitrogen.

Later, when the time would come when Sable and Phillip decide that they're ready to move on with a sur-rogate of their choice, the eggs would be thawed and placed in a dish with a single sperm. Hopefully, embryos would develop and the embryos would be implanted in the uterus of the surrogate with a catheter.

Although everything seemed somewhat overwhelm-ing at first, Sable felt at peace with her decision for the partial hysterectomy and the course of action that she was undergoing to hopefully become a mother some day. She knew it wasn't a perfect plan, but she was grateful that she'd been given a second chance at maternity.

The clinic would extract her batch of eggs both at the end of July and the end of August. Her hysterecto-my was already scheduled for the 6th of September, right after Labor Day. Dr. St. Francis and Dr. Morgan, both, had wanted for Sable to have her procedure done in mid-August, but her menstruation cycles wouldn't have

allowed it given that Sable was very adamant about doing at least *two* egg retrievals. Sable felt that the delay in
scheduling would well be worth the wait.

The daily FSH injections left her tired and lethargic
for a few hours. At times, she was irritable or she developed a slight headache on occasion. But it was all very
tolerable. She let herself daydream of the day she really
would have children and that always lifted her spirits.
She read at length about surrogacy and she also read a
lot about adoptions. She knew that adoption might be
the route that she and Phillip ultimately take and she
wanted to mentally prepare herself. There were times
when she was alone that she felt afraid or–even allowed
herself to feel a few minutes of self-pity, but those occa-
sions were rare. Luckily, she hadn't suffered from the
erratic emotional bouts that she read that other women
sometimes faced. Overall, she knew that the egg harvesting, was a glorious second chance and her heart
warmed at the possibility.

Desiree, on the other hand, wasn't having an easy
time with her pregnancy. She was due in four months
now and her stomach was so pronounced! Given that
she was carrying two and that her frame was so small,
made Desiree look further along than she was.

The family had just learned that she was carrying
both a boy and a girl and everyone couldn't be happier!
Her parents were set to fly to California in two months'
time. Desiree's two roommates had assured her that it
was no problem with them about the approaching chaos that the two babies would bring once they were born;
and that she should take her time in deciding when and
where to move later. Desiree agreed that she would worry about the decision about moving once her parents

arrived. She had just finished a very hectic summer session at the university and was exhausted. She was proud of herself for finishing out the two summer classes and was now just a mere year and a half from graduating. But between carrying two kicking babies, being single and studying hard, Desiree had pushed herself to her limits. During her last conversation with Sable, she had joked that she would sleep two weeks' straight without a moment's guilt!

As of lately, the whole family had been giving Desiree too much advice on the babies' names. She had been a good sport the first few months, but recently she had told everybody to cease with the recommendations!

She called Sable and said, "Okay prima, I have the names!"

"Wow, Desiree that's great! Congratulations, I know you were struggling with the names for quite awhile now. So tell me, what are my little cousins' names?"

"After a lot of consideration and baby book searching, and even some searching in the white pages for inspiration, I have them: I'm naming my son Beau, which means handsome and beautiful. And I'm naming my daughter Farrah which means lovely and happiness. I'm so happy Sable, I've grown tired of calling them 'the babies,' I wanted so much to start thinking of them as my little beauties and funny enough, both of their names mean 'beauty' in some way, so it's all perfect. I love their names!"

"Beau and Farrah, both meaning beautiful. Oh Desiree, how clever! I love it. You chose excellent names little cous!"

"Yes, I feel that in naming them, I'm even more of a mom, if that makes any sense. Oh Sable, my anxiety and fears are lessening and I'm really coming to love the idea of motherhood finally. I can't wait to meet them!"

"I've read that it takes most women time to bond with their babies, sometimes even after their birth. I'm happy for you Desiree. Enjoy the moment, they are a gift."

"Yes, they are. You, more than anyone, have taught me that."

"I'll take that as a compliment. No one is gonna love them more than their crazy Godmother!"

"Amen!"

"So tell me Desiree, how are you feeling?"

"Now that those two classes are done, I'm finally relaxing! But to tell you the truth, I've been having migraines lately. At first, I thought it was just the stress of finishing up the summer coursework, but now that classes have been done for over a week, I've still had two recently."

"Have you talked to Dr. Jashe about it?"

"Well, I see her on Friday, so I'll just mention it to her then."

"Yes, do that. Well, I'd better let you go, Phillip will be here in an hour and I look a mess."

"Okay, you tell *Loverboy* I said hello."

"Will do!"

😊　😊　😊

"Phillip, I spoke to my mom today and we've decided to give Desiree her baby shower the first weekend of October."

"Why so early? Her due date is not until mid December."

"Well, if we do it in November or December, the surprise might be on us since most twins arrive around four-six weeks early. Desiree's parents are arriving the first of October from Spain and my aunt can't miss the party of course! Besides, that will put me at a month's recovery time from the procedure, and hopefully I should be as good as new by then."

"What kind of party do you have in mind?"

"I thought my cousin might enjoy a shower in my parents' backyard. My parents' garden and koi pond are so lovely and their patio easily sits fifty. I could have the meal catered from *Amor Mio* easily and I already found the sweetest blue striped ribbons and pink polka dot ribbons for the invitations. About a hundred balloons would make the yard festive and colorful for her. I'll rent chair covers in pastels and order big floral arrangements for the tables. Desire loves tulips, they're so sweet. The only thing I don't know about yet is the cake."

"Wow, you have a lot of that planned already! Would you like a handsome photographer to come and record the delightful day for all time?"

"Oh Phillip, would you? That would be great! Desiree would love that."

"It would be my pleasure to photograph our little squirt!"

"I'm glad you love her so much because we're working on her invitations tonight. With only four and a half weeks' time, I'm running short on time for the RSVPs."

"But, this is our last weekend before Tuesday's procedure. I was hoping to go out to a nice dinner and come back home and cuddle and," he stopped and wiggled his eyebrows ridiculously.

"Phillip, please stop that! You don't look provocative, you look crazy!" Sable laughed so hard, her sides ached.

"But Babe, do the invites really have to go out so soon? Truly, I want to spend the evening with you–"

"Yes, they do! You *will* be spending the evening with me. You'll be working on the address labels, while I print the invitations and run all that ribbon through them. Then we need to stamp and lick the envelo–"

"Did you say 'lick'?"

"Oh no! Stop wiggling those eyebrows!"

👁👁 👁👁 👁👁

Desiree had to lie down. Today's migraine was unbearable. Tomorrow, she had an appointment to see Dr. Jashe and she had to get something to ease the pain. Her head felt like it was going to explode. She wished her mother was here already to help her, but she wouldn't be here for another month. Now, that school was over, she was doing her best to relax and finally enjoy the pregnancy. And now it was the migraines. She had lost count, but she thought this was her fourth or fifth this week.

She tried to distract herself with watching TV and when that didn't work she soaked in the tub. After soaking for almost an hour, she massaged her temples and although her headache had lessened, it was still strong. She dressed warmly and decided to take a long walk to tire herself, and hopefully fall into a deep sleep where the migraine would be dulled.

During her walk, she couldn't help but wonder what her life would've been like if Dane had decided to stay with her. Granted, their relationship was just budding, but Desiree had thought they had great potential and had assumed they would fall in love eventually. They had similar personalities and they laughed all the time. They were immensely attracted to each other and had all the makings of a great relationship, when her pregnancy had shattered their foundation. Granted, Dane was too young to be a father and was frightened, but the reality, she knew, was that he was weak in character. Even as a young man, he could've been more responsible and supportive. He could've gone to the doctor with her or rubbed her stomach at night. But no, he hightailed it as soon as he found out.

Desiree fantasized what it would have been like if Dane would have asked her to move in with him and try being a family. With the help of their parents, maybe they would have been able to finish college and start their careers and, just maybe, they could have made it. But Dane hadn't even given her or the babies a chance. That was what hurt Desiree the most, that he hadn't cared to try. His blood, *his children.*

Maybe if she would have had an abortion, they would have stayed together. But she doubted it, considering that she had already learned what a cowardly spirit he had. And it wasn't that she was against abortion, but given that she had come so very late into her parents' lives after they had tried to conceive for almost two decades, she just couldn't bear to throw away the opportunity for motherhood so carelessly. Especially since her own mother had longed and struggled for the very same thing all her young life.

Desiree sighed. Yes, what lay ahead would be very hard, but she could do it. Without Dane and without her degree, she would do it. It would be hard, but she had her friends, Sable and her parents, and finally, she had her own wonderful parents. She had support and love and she knew she was strong. She would love Beau and Farrah and she would give them a loving life regardless of Dane's rejection of them.

Desiree had heard a professor say once that one should always have a five year plan. Hers would be to have two healthy babies in a home where they all had enough room. She would also finish her degree by the time the babies were two hopefully. Afterwards, she would soon have a career position. She didn't care so much about top earnings as most of her friends cared about, but she would hope to be comfortable. She knew that she was fortunate that her parents would supplement periodically even without her ever asking.

As she opened her front door, she thought to herself, "Yes, I'll be fine."

ΩΩ ΩΩ ΩΩ

"What are you talking about, Phillip? You haven't even been with her 6 months!" Sinclair yelled in his ear.

"I'm sorry, little man, I need to do this. I've known her almost half my life and I know she's the one. Being apart from her those couple of weeks this summer ate me up alive. I'm going to do it."

"I still think that you're rushing things. She has a lot on her mind right now and if it's for forever, there's no need for forever to start *this* very moment."

"It's precisely because she's going through a lot right now that I want to propose. I want to show her that regardless of whatever comes her way, I'm here for her. Only her. I want her to feel secure that I love her no matter what."

"But who's to say, you can't ask her early next year, when all of this trouble has died down?"

"You're right that it would be more sensible to wait, but I can't. This is the time, I know it is."

"Man, Phillip, you're a goner. I see you're not going to listen to reason."

"No, I'm not. Besides, I already bought the ring."

"You did what? It's too early, I say."

"Then it would surprise you that I've had the ring quite a few months now!"

"You are a crazy man. Well, in that case, I wish you the best. Sable couldn't have loved you more as a kid. I can't imagine the amount of love she exudes now as a woman. I hope your marriage is always happy, big bro."

"The love she gives now is even better than when we were kids, if you can believe that. Thanks Sinclair, your good wishes mean a lot to me. I want you to be my Best Man."

"It would be my honor. When are you going to tell Mom and Dad?"

"Uh, sometime after Sable accepts."

"Good idea, definitely, good idea."

Miles walked into Sable's office and sat down. He and Sable were going over some preliminary cost numbers of a banquet party they were to have in the second week of October. Sable usually didn't do banquet style parties given she didn't have a banquet room and would have to close down the restaurant for the client, but this engagement party was too lucrative to pass up. It was a couple who was eloping in Maui, but wanted to have their engagement party as a would-be pre-reception. They were having the best of both worlds, a private wedding on the beaches of Maui *and* all their loved ones in a private setting at *Amor Mio's*. The only real challenges that Sable and Miles had to figure out was deciding what tables to clear out for the dance floor and DJ and the ordering of extra alcohol. The couple wanted a six hour party for 120 guests and it was going to be magnificent. The bride had already scheduled cake delivery and a floral delivery. Nothing else was needed as the beauty of *Amor Mio* was very romantic and elegant. The restaurant was set to make a $14,000 profit that night and with Sable taking so much time off during the next six weeks, she welcomed the financial security of it.

"Sable, would you mind if I made a suggestion?"

"Yes, Miles of course. I always welcome your ideas."

"I think that perhaps, the restaurant could use an Assistant Manager. Your parents are dedicated and organized and they're helping immensely. And although my wife and I welcomed the generous raise you just gave me, I feel like I'm running at maximum capacity."

Sable sat back in her chair and looked at her talented executive chef. She didn't want to lose him, but really wanted to hear what he was saying from a business perspective.

"Miles, for as much as I'd like to say that I can do everything myself at *Amor Mio,* I know I can't. My health betrayed me this year, but that's life and I know it. I never thought about the prospect of an Assistant Manager, but I will think about it, I really will. I know you have been working on overload, and I appreciate your time and dedication."

"Thank you Sable, I think it would be the healthiest solution to our problems. I would be home a little more as would you. When we're rested, we do a better job and we're really building a name for *Amor Mio*. We need to make sure our first year's success continues."

"I agree with you Miles. We'll touch base on this again, I promise."

Twenty-Three

" $\mathcal{S}$ able dear, what time are you and Phillip coming on Labor Day? Your father has bought enough to barbecue for an army. He's only cooking for ten, but would think that he's cooking for two dozen."

"Oh Mom, Dad is so cute for the holidays. Did he buy a new apron for the occasion?"

"No, he's wearing the Harley Davidson one he's had for a few years."

"Dad's so cute, I love that one," Sable laughed. "I was thinking we'd be there by one, is that okay? Dr. Morgan says I can't eat past ten pm and I certainly want to have my fill of Dad's special ribs."

"They sure are delicious, I must admit. One o'clock is perfect Sable, we'll see you then."

Sable hung up the phone and started to tidy up around the house. She'd been working so many extra hours that week at the restaurant that the house looked unkempt. Sable walked to the CD player and put on a CD of the *Gypsy Kings*. Their loud, flamenco style music always reminded her of Olivia and its sounds always lifted her spirits and made her happy. Sable picked up around the house, straightened the magazines, polished the tables and changed her bed linens. She wiped down the granite in the kitchen and loaded up the dishwasher. After an hour, she looked around and was pleased with her efforts. Phillip was due to arrive in an hour and she wanted to bathe and blow-dry her hair before he and Joey arrived.

She had worked so much this week in anticipation of her six week absence, that she felt pleased with her efforts. Miles did a superb job and now that both her parents were on board helping, she felt she could relax knowing that *Amor Mio* would continue to succeed during her recovery. Besides, her hosting and waiting staffs were excellent and they counted for the majority of the customers' great experience while dining there. Hopefully, her daily phone calls and emails to Miles and the others would lessen the impact of her absence considerably. She wanted to be loyal to her recovery so that her body would be healthy and strong upon her return. She knew that it would be hard to be away for a month and a half, but she prayed this was the last time her health ever took her away from *Amor Mio*.

She felt the tension ease out of her neck and shoulders under the hot steam of the water. Tonight, they were going to order in pizza and chicken wings and walk on the beach. She started chuckling to herself when she thought of Phillip two nights ago on Thursday's fiasco. Phillip had been hilarious working on the baby shower invitations. He had used a business font for the labels and was upset when she asked him to find a more romantic, cursive font. After he was done with that, she asked him for help with threading the tops of the invitations with the ribbons. After he tied a few in knots, she scolded him that she didn't want knots, she wanted bows. He didn't understand the difference! She took him off ribbon duty and put him on stamping the envelopes.

"Phillip stop! You're doing it wrong!"

"What! How do you stamp wrong? Top, right hand corner of course!"

"Love, love, love. Everyone knows that when an invitation is sent with love, the stamp is placed upside down!"

"For the love of God, Sable! That is ludicrous!"

"What is ludicrous is your effort! Get with it McNeil."

He had had a grumpy face for the next hour, but they had indeed finished the thirty-five invitations. Most of the women invited were Desiree's friends of course, but some were old friends of the family and a few were her Aunt Sara's friends who would be so happy to know that she was to become a grandmother of two soon!

Sable continued to chuckle to herself at Phillip's lack of savvy of the invitation world. Funny, he dealt with brides and elegance all the time, but he didn't even know about the upside down stamp! She was still smiling about that nonsense, as she finished blow drying her hair, when she heard the doorbell ring.

She rushed out to unlock the front door and flew into his arms.

"Wow, what a reception! I just saw you two days ago hon, but I can grow to get used to this!"

"It's just that I know this is our last weekend before I become a picky or stubborn patient and you need to remember me for fabulous me."

" 'Fabulous' huh? Maybe I should make that your new nickname…"

"If you insist!" They both laughed over that and Phillip playfully squeezed her nose.

"Well, maybe if you order that pizza pronto, you'll get extra credit points for sure. That traffic was murder to get here and I'm starving."

"You got it! I'll call right away."

"Mind if I take a shower?"

"Sure, go right in. I'll be here when you get out and Phillip….?"

"Yes, Sable?"

"Sorry if I was a little rough on you Thursday during the invitation-"

"No need to apologize drill sergeant! I love you and always will. No matter what." He walked over to her, kissed her forehead and walked into the bathroom.

ை ை ை

Desiree had already re-played the conversation at Dr. Jashe's office half a dozen times in her mind. She had previously guessed that the migraines were probably a sign of a bigger problem, but she had tried to stay hopeful. When Dr. Jashe's examination had informed her that she had pre-eclampsia, Desiree was not ready for such a diagnosis. Now, she sighed heavily as she propped herself against several pillows on her sofa and let the conversation consume her thoughts yet again.

"I can't believe it Dr. Jashe. I'm healthy, I walk every day, I watch my diet, for Pete's sake, I'm *young and healthy*! How does this happen?"

"To be honest Desiree, we don't know what causes pre-eclampsia. Some call it toxemia and it includes high blood pressure and protein in the urine. It's not genetic per se and it usually occurs with first time moms and moms of multiples like yourself. But, it doesn't target a specific type of patient or an age group. What we do know however, is that it needs to be monitored carefully. For some women, it means the placenta is too big and covers the cervix, for others it might mean that there isn't enough placenta at all."

"Jesus Christ."

"Don't be discouraged Desiree. Most cases lead to very healthy babies. However, they are almost always premature in birth, born of cesarean means."

"Almost always?"

"Yes, there is risk involved and side effects as well."

"What am I facing?"

"Besides the migraines, some mothers experience fainting spells, and in very extreme cases, blindness."

"*Blindness?*"

"Yes, Desiree, but again those are remote cases where prenatal care is usually absent."

"I see. Is that worse case scenario?"

"No. Worst case scenario would be losing either the mother or the baby."

"I can't believe pre-eclampsia is so dangerous."

"To many it isn't, but it's to be monitored extremely closely. It would be in your own best interest as well as your babies' interest to keep as close to bed rest as possible. I do not want you to go on your walks and faint in the street with no medical attention. I would want you home for the most part and always a phone call away from reaching me or the hospital."

"The babies aren't even six months yet and they will be even smaller as twins. When would you suggest we deliver since it's obvious that I can't make it to my December 18 due date?"

"If we made it to mid-October, I would be very pleased Desiree. The babies would be 7 months by then and most twins are born at 34-36 weeks anyway, so even without the pre-eclampsia, I doubt you would have reached your due date. We will be monitoring you and the babies carefully and I want you to start coming in weekly to see me. Weekly appointments usually don't start with a normal pregnancy until the eighth month, but–"

"But this isn't a normal pregnancy?" Desiree wrung her hands desperately.

"No, at this point we would consider you a high risk pregnancy." Dr. Jashe reached across the examining table and patted Desiree's shoulder.

"This is a lot to take in. When would my quasi-bed rest start?"

"I think it would be responsible to start immediately."

Desiree looked at Dr. Jashe and shook her head in dismay, "I'll rest on Saturday and Sunday. But on Monday, I'm going to my Aunt Leslie's house for Labor Day. I guess that's my last outing before the babies come?"

"Definitely Desiree, it should be your last one."

"I knew you were going to say that."

Desiree sat back and exhaled sharply. Dr. Jashe's words were constantly on her mind. She turned towards her sofa's pillow and laid her head down. She was mentally exhausted. She had cried plenty that morning and had to stop herself for fear that she'd bring on another migraine. She didn't think she could take any more challenges. Losing Dane was painful, telling her family about her surprise pregnancy was humiliating, hearing about Sable's hysterectomy was horrible, dropping out of school was embarrassing, but this....*this* was overwhelming. She had cried a lot that morning and felt better for it. She was tired of trying to appear strong. She was scared dammit. She was scared of so many things lately, but now she was scared for the babies' health. She would gladly do bed rest to ensure that they were healthy. She longed to meet them and hold them and she wasn't going to let this condition harm them in any way. After Monday's gathering at her Aunt's house, she would stay in her apartment virtually non-stop. She didn't even want to tell her family about the pre-eclampsia. Everyone was so worried about Sable's hysterectomy on Tuesday, that she just couldn't tell them at that point. Maybe in a week or two, she thought to herself, after Sable recovered a bit.

Desiree had to chuckle to herself. With both she and Sable on bed rest, they were truly going to go stir-crazy together. Well, at least they'd catch up on old movies over potato chips and dip. She thought it would be fitting that she'd either ask Aunt Leslie or Uncle Daniel to drive her to Sable's beach house everyday so that the two convalescents could peer out onto the ocean and have some beauty to look at as they complained the day away over their aches and pains. Her Aunt and Uncle were always offering to help, so why not coerce them into a little taxiing for their favorite niece?

∾∾ ∾∾ ∾∾

"I think it's funny that we're having pizza on a Saturday night. What are we, seventeen?"

"You look seventeen, so what's the difference?"

"That's sweet Phillip, thank you. But I'm twenty eight and I know you're trying to butter me up for something."

"I am not. I just want you to know how ravishing I think you are."

"Aww Babe, thank you. You are too kind. Now, what do you want?"

Phillip laughed heartedly. "I don't want anything, except to make this weekend last as long as possible. Tomorrow will be relaxing and Monday will be great at your folks' place for the holiday."

"Yes, I'm looking forward to the rest of the weekend too. I've come to terms with not returning to *Amor Mio* any time soon. That was harder than I could really admit. And even though Miles and I didn't find the assistant manager we were talking about, I feel confident that Miles, my parents and the rest of the staff can handle things. I'll help as much as I can through email and hopefully, no big problems will arise."

"I hope not, Sable. You deserve a great rest. Between fostering the eggs for the last two months and Tuesday's procedure, you deserve a little relaxation in the recovery. Before that, you were working so hard to start the restaurant, that ironically, this is probably the first break you've had in years."

"Actually, you are completely correct. Six weeks of daytime TV hasn't happened since my UCSB summer breaks."

"Your wish is my command for tomorrow. The day is all yours. What would you like to do?"

"Hmmm, I want to wake up and have steak and eggs a few blocks down on the boardwalk café. Then we could come back here and snuggle back in bed. During the day, how about we take a bike ride? We can rent a tandem bike and ride off into the sunset."

"I couldn't have planned anything better than all that. I love the bike riding idea."

"I'm getting tired. Why don't you take me to bed lover?"

"Let's go! A man doesn't have to be asked twice!"

☙☙ ☙☙ ☙☙

They woke up the next morning and Sable rolled up on top of Phillip and started kissing his ears and neck. She could feel him develop goose bumps all over his body and she loved that affect on him. He tried to put his arms around her, but Sable playfully pinned his arms to his side.

"I'm gonna do everything to you. Let me. Just lay there."

"Wow, I don't think I've ever been so turned on. Hurt me!"

"Don't make this silly! I'm trying to have my way with you!"

"I promise, you can do anything you want to me. I'm your pussycat."

"No humor, cutie. I'm trying to be seductive!"

She hugged him and started to suck on one of his fingers, and she heard Phillip draw in his breath. She decided to stand up on the bed and Phillip looked confused for a moment. Then she playfully tried to shimmy out of her pajamas while she lowered one sleeve off her shoulder and then the other. Phillip was grinning from ear to ear and enjoying her show immensely. Then she turned around and smiled at him over her shoulder as she started unbuttoning. She drew her hair up and piled it high and turned around slowly while letting her pajama top slip to the bed.

She walked up a little closer and playfully stepped on both his legs as he peered up at her. "Are you almost ready for me?"

"Oh yes! Oh yes!"

She laughed and wiggled off her pajama bottom and threw it right into his face. She started laughing and straddled him. "I love you, Phillip. I want you to want me like this always."

"You're sexy as hell, Sable. I will always want you. I couldn't love you more."

"Show me." And he did.

"That was—I can't even describe it. You're going to be the death of me." Phillip said half breathless.

"No I'm not. You're young and healthy and you need it."

"You bet I need it," he said as he reached for her.

"Absolutely not….. don't look at me like that." Sable jumped out of bed and laughed good naturedly.

"So what you're really saying is that you crave steak and eggs and not me."

"That's exactly what that means! Let's go! Joey and I will meet you on the sand!"

An hour and a half later, Sable was slightly moaning at the café's table,

"Why did I eat so much? I hardly ever eat like this."

"I think you're overeating because you'll be on soup and crackers for most of next week."

"Absolutely, and you don't even want to know how many of my dad's special ribs I'm going to polish off tomorrow!"

"They're that delicious?"

"Yes, they are to die for. My dad could probably win a cook-off with them. You'll see."

"I trust they are Sable. Let's walk over to the bike store; I don't want them to run out of the tandem bikes. Joey's going to love running beside us."

ๆ ๆ ๆ

"Green or pink? You decide."

"Can your masculinity take riding a pink bike in a public setting?"

"With such a hot babe behind me, I would be the envy of every guy on the beach today. I assume you want pink?"

"It's so cute and that oversized wicker basket is precious. Let's do it."

"Let's."

Phillip and Sable rode all through Manhattan Beach and stopped periodically to play with Joey and to take pictures. They kissed constantly, never tiring of each other. The tandem bike was a fun and easy exercise after such a filling breakfast. The day was glorious at eighty degrees and the easy breeze cooled them as they rode. Although UCSB was famous for its bike riding and some couples had indeed ridden tandem, Sable had never done it. Today was the first time she'd ever been on a tandem and the closeness of it was both special and intimate. She looked over at the waves and wondered how different and lonely her life would be if

Phillip wasn't in it. The restaurant was rewarding, but Phillip's presence was a blessing. She had tried to be so strong and let him go once, but knew deep down that she would have regretted it forever. What a miracle it was that Dr. St. Francis had convinced her that harvesting her own eggs would indirectly give her and Phillip a second chance. She knew many families weren't successful in surrogacy, but she knew having Phillip in her life would be enough. And he had finally convinced her that having *her* in his life would be enough for him. One day, they could hopefully have children, either by the surrogacy or through adoption, and they could live the dream of starting a family. Looking at the waves gave her peace, but looking at Phillip gave her love.

"Hey, back there! I could feel your intense gaze staring at my butt!"

"I'm not staring at your butt my friend, I was staring at the waves!"

"I don't believe you! But that's ok. Wanna head back and get ready for that nap?"

"You read my mind, but let's take a soak first."

"Sounds great. It's already 3:00 and I want to cherish this day forever."

"It is indeed very memorable."

"And it's only going to get better. Mr. Bubbles never fails."

ᙙᙚ ᙙᙚ ᙙᙚ

"I can't think of anything sexier than a man who looks like you in my tub washing my hair. Please pinch me."

"You're flattering, but I'm the lucky one. I can't believe life gave you back to me. I've never been happier than the past five months, Sable. I love you."

"I love you too, Phillip. We're both pretty lucky. Let me turn around and kiss you."

"Nope, conditioning is too much fun."

"Hmmmm, it sure feels good. Hurry babe, that nap is calling our names."

After a two hour nap and after they dressed into warm comfortable clothing, Phillip came from behind Sable and gently blindfolded her with a tie he had brought in his overnight bag.

"Hey, what are you doing, Phillip?"

"I'm having my way with you. I'm taking you for a ride and I don't want you to peek at all! I've been thinking of this all day and I think you're going to love where we're going."

"You promise you're not going to tie a sign on me and leave me on the corner of a busy boulevard so people can honk at me?"

"Haha, no sorority hazing from me, Baby! I'm taking you to a place where you'll feel loved."

"More than I do right now?"

"Yes. Now let's get moving."

All through the car ride, Phillip kept glancing at his Sable. She looked so silly smiling blankly with no idea where she was headed with that tie over her eyes. She couldn't see it of course, but it was the same tie he had purchased to wear at her reunion. It was nautical which was fitting given that she lived at the beach. Sable looked silly, but so damn irresistible. Her auburn hair curled around her shoulders and half way down her back.

Phillip reached out and touched a curl. She had no idea that he was creating all this hype just for onion rings.

"Open your eyes, love, we're here."

"Aww, honey, our first date."

"Yes. Let's go inside." Phillip kissed her temple.

They clasped hands and smiled at each other as they walked in. Inside, as luck would have it, the booth where they sat for the first time so many years ago, was empty. They both walked toward it remembering.

"I think you're really pretty, Sable."

"Thank you," she blushed.

"There's a dance at school in two weeks. Do you think you'd like to go with me?"

"I would love to go. I'd have to ask my parents of course, but I think that would be fun."

"My friends will probably join us too if you don't mind."

"I don't mind at all."

"Remember how great our first dance was?" Sable asked a few minutes after they were seated.

"I do. You were awfully cute in that denim mini skirt."

"You remember what I wore?"

"Of course! Red sweater too! If you only knew how many times I looked at our dance photo over the years."

"You have so earned major points."

"Wonderful, I'll collect on that some time later tonight."

Sable smiled at that while the waitress set down a heaping platter of onion rings and potato skins.

Sable looked up to look at Phillip and the next moment felt like time moved in slow motion for her. She saw Phillip return her smile and reach into his coat pocket and withdraw a small jewelry box. Her eyes grew wide in surprise as Phillip's smile lit up his face. Their eyes locked knowingly and he slightly nodded his head. Her eyes glossed over and her hands flew up and covered her mouth.

"Sable, I knew the moment you were in my arms at the reunion that I wanted to marry you. I want you to be my wife and share your life with me. I want to make you happy and love you more each day. I want us to walk down the aisle and build a life together. You were the only love of my past and you will be the only love for my future. I brought you here today to remember the innocence and the magic. You are my magic, Sable. Will you be my love for all time and marry me?"

"Oh yes, yes, yes! Phillip, I will marry you and love you forever. You're my first love and I can't imagine my life without you. I would love to be your wife."

They reached out to each other over the table and hugged and kissed awkwardly over the onion rings until they laughed.

"We're not teenagers anymore."

"So why are we trying to eat like we are?"

"It kind of felt fitting for the occasion."

"It absolutely does, my love."

"Don't you want to look at your ring now?"

They both sat back and looked at each other lovingly for a moment before Sable opened up her box.

"Oh my God, Phillip. It is breathtaking! It is so incredibly beautiful."

"Here, I want to slip it on your finger Sable. There. I'm yours forever now."

"And I'm yours, Phillip."

☙☙ ☙☙ ☙☙

Sable walked across the room to reach for the phone.

"Oh Hi, Diane. Yes, it's on Tuesday."

"Sable, are you nervous?"

"Well, I was. But to be honest, I haven't even thought about it today."

"You haven't? How in the world were you able to put it out of your mind?"

"Diane, I had the best day ever. Phillip and I went to breakfast and then rented a double bike and had a great ride. And then we got engaged!"

"Ahhhhh! I'm so excited for you! Congratulations! Tell me all about it!"

"I'm so excited too! I haven't even told my family. I'm going to tell them tomorrow at my parents' barbecue. And the ring is the biggest diamond ever!" Sable laughed. "Phillip took me to the same diner we went to as kids when we first met. Amazingly, we even sat at the same table! It was all so nostalgic and then he surprised me. His words were incredibly touching Di, and I'm just so happy! I can't stop looking at my ring and thinking that one day, I'll be his wife."

"Oh, Sable I am thrilled. He is perfect for you. You've loved him you're whole life. What a gift to receive him again."

Sable looked over at Phillip and he knew they were talking about him and he winked at her. "Yes, Diane, he's a complete gift. My gift from God."

Twenty-Five

As Sable was inside talking to Diane, Phillip decided to take a walk on the beach by himself. He walked to the water and let his feet sink in. He closed his eyes and breathed in and let the happiness wash over him. Although he was pretty confident that Sable would say yes, he had had a small fear that Sable would reject him and bring up the potential fatherhood issue again. He had thought that they'd overcome her fears about her ability to have children, but Phillip had not been able to shake off the insecurity that made him anxious about her accepting his proposal.

Now that she had accepted and was inside gabbing like a schoolgirl to Diane, he let the tension ease out of him. "This is our time," he thought to himself. He loved her so much, he felt that this moment was beyond surreal. He would one day kiss the bride and he would age with her and he'd bring her breakfast in bed on Mother's Days and her birthdays. He would kiss her every night before they'd go to bed. And tomorrow, he would tell her parents how proud he was that he'd soon join them as a son-in-law. He shivered at the possibility. He knew he was a lucky man.

ᥫᥬ ᥫᥬ ᥫᥬ

The next morning, Phillip rolled over and looked at his beloved. He started laughing because she was staring at her ring in the morning light.

"Happy, are we?"

"Phillip, I've never been happier. I'm still not used to the idea that one day I'll be your wife. But to look down and see this sparkler every day, I just can't seem to wrap my head around it. Babe, you bought me the biggest ring I've ever seen!"

"You are very worth it. I love you enough to have that sparkler shine on your finger for all time."

"I love pear diamonds. I just love them, how did you know?"

"I ran into Toni at the mall months ago and she gave me some guidance."

"Months ago?"

"Yes, Sable. I wanted to marry you immediately."

"But then you already had the ring when we separated?" Sable looked down at her hands and then reached for his.

"Yes. It killed me to know that I hadn't yet proposed, but I prayed that you'd come back to me one day. I often looked at it at home and imagined you wearing it."

She leaned over and kissed him soundly. "I'm so sorry for that. I love you and we will never be apart again, I promise." Then she sat on his tummy and asked, "Phillip, how big is this? It's as big as a raisin!"

"It's 2.6 my love. I wanted you to have at least a 2 carat ring because this is our second time in love. That was symbolic to me. And as for the band, those are thirty six mini diamonds and it's called a Pave engagement setting and it's all in white gold."

"You are so perfect, my love! Did Toni help you with the pear shape *and* the white?"

"Yes, she did. Toni's wonderful."

"Hmmm, she knew I loved pear like my grandmother and white like my mother."

"I was lucky to have seen her at the jewelry store that day."

"Oh Phillip, my mother is going to flip when she sees how gorgeous this is. And my dad is going to flip that his little girl is going to be a bride."

"Let's hurry up and get over there. Let the crazy Franco family rejoice!"

Desiree woke up and the first thing she thought of was that her parents would be here in slightly less than a month. She found so much comfort in that. Her parents would somewhat take over her life and truly, she was going to welcome that. They were going to organize looking for a new apartment and the whole move. They were also going to unpack for her and set up the babies' room. She was even going to be spoiled with daily chores, such as laundry, being done for her. Her mother was going to make her delicious meals and her father would love to be a handyman and make sure everything ran smoothly. If she'd feel tired or had any more migraines, her mom would make her lie down and stroke her hair and temples. Her parents loved her so much; they had always doted on her. And although, she hadn't honored them with a respectable wedding, they would support her in this next chapter of her life unconditionally. Their love would really make a difference. Desiree's life had become so complicated and their presence would simplify everything.

The last two days had been a little difficult. It was hard to just lie around the house and force herself to be still. She had filled her days with reading her pregnancy books and highlighting the important information. She had chuckled that she was highlighting, but being a dedicated student meant highlighting, a habit that was hard to break. She had forced herself to lay down on her bed or sofa and only get up to go to the bathroom or to have a quick meal. Her roommates had been great in entertaining her with stories of their days or with keeping her company while watching TV with her.

Today she would be picked up by her Uncle Daniel and she'd have a glorious day with the family. She had just told him that she felt huge behind her steering wheel and he was happy to come and help. She wasn't ready to tell them about the pre-eclampsia and she was going to try to relax on her aunt and uncle's chaise lounges. They did not need to know about the bed rest yet. Today was about family and about making Sable feel at ease on the day before her procedure. Today was about love, family and normalcy, not medical problems.

When her Uncle Daniel picked her up, she was eating some grapes on the couch and got up and kissed his cheek. He helped her by picking up her sweater and purse and he locked her front door for her. He guided her down the steps and into his car. She felt herself wobbling a bit but willed herself to walk straight.

"It will be nice when my body belongs to me again."

"I remember Leslie used to say the same thing. She was only carrying one baby, but she wobbled just as much if that makes you feel better."

"It's just that as women we take pride on how we carry ourselves. We practice walking in heels since we're three when we play dress-up with our mother's shoes. Then, you're pregnant and wham! You look like you've swallowed an egg and your feet are like miniature boats."

"I don't know what it's like to be pregnant Desiree, but you and all other women are beautiful when you're carrying. I want to tell you that you're extraordinary. You should have that son of a bitch Dane telling you this, but since he's not here and your dad's a month away from arriving, you need to hear that you're doing the right thing and that you'll be a great mommy. We're all here for you and although this wasn't in your plan, we're proud of the person you are and how courageous you are to face the obstacles."

Desiree was surprised that she had tear tracks down her face and she didn't even notice until one fell and splashed on her hand, "Thanks, Uncle Daniel. Your words mean a lot to me and until just now, I hadn't realized how much I needed to hear them. Gracias."

He smiled at her and tousled her head as he had when she was a little girl. By then they reached the front of his house and she saw that Phillip and Sable were also parking. It took Desiree a moment to climb out of the car and by then, Sable and Phillip were standing there ready to hug her on the sidewalk. Desiree immediately saw Sable's new ring and the cousins locked eyes and started yelling hysterically and hugging and whirling around. They were worse than ten year olds and Phillip was laughing proudly. Daniel had walked around the car and was looking at the screaming girls in the most bizarre way.

"What's going on, Phillip?"

"Sir, I've asked your daughter to marry me. I hope you can give us your blessing." Phillip looked at Daniel expectantly.

Daniel smiled brightly, "You have my blessing, son. Welcome to the family." The men shook hands and Daniel's voice choked up slightly. "Thank you for loving my daughter. I can tell she's very much in love."

"Thank you. I love her beyond anything."

"Then let's please go tell her mother and stop this horrible screeching."

The girls were still twirling around ridiculously and the men hugged as well.

🦋 🦋 🦋

Sable walked into her mother's house with her hands behind her. Leslie looked up from the lettuce she was shredding and smiled at her.

"Hi Mom, how are you?"

"Fine, dear. You look so cute in that dress." She paused and looked closely at her daughter. "Did you change your hair?"

"No Mom. But there is something different about me. Want to see?"

"Of course honey. What is it?"

"I got engaged last night!!!! I'm getting married! Look at my rock!"

Leslie brought her hands up and clasped them together near her heart. "Sable, your ring is incredible! It's stunning! It has to be the most magnificent ring I've ever seen! I'm so happy for you two, baby!"

"Mom, I'm so happy!" And when they hugged they didn't share in the screeching Sable had with her cousin moments ago. Instead, she cried very happy tears in the arms of her mother.

ଡଡ ଡଡ ଡଡ

They all sat down to eat and Desiree was the first to ask, "So have you two set a date for the wedding?"

Phillip and Sable looked at each other and smiled, "No, we haven't prima. We're just so excited to be engaged. We haven't talked about the details yet."

Leslie said, "Sable, planning a wedding is all about details. Surely, you two must have some ideas."

"All I ask," Phillip said, "is that we don't have a long engagement.

Sable and Phillip quickly kissed each other and looked around the table. They were so happy at that moment. "What do you think, Phillip?"

"I don't know. There's so much to think about. Where we'll live, for example."

"Well, we both own our homes and we both own our own businesses. But your house is a four bedroom and mine is only a small beach cottage. Maybe we could live at your house during the week and my house over the weekend. When we have a family we'll need more space anyway."

"I love that idea, Sable. But would you mind the commute terribly?"

"Well, I don't have to be at the restaurant that early so I'd beat the morning traffic or most of it anyway. And now that Miles and I are looking for an Assistant Manager, I'd work less hours a day anyway. I promised myself, I'd give my health a lot more attention from now on. I won't be overworking myself like before."

Leslie said, "I'm so happy to hear that dear. I'd like you to work less, definitely."

"Hon, I wouldn't mind selling my house and moving to a city more central of El Toro and Los Angeles where both the studio and the restaurant are."

"I'm glad you're willing to do that, but I don't think we need to for a long way off. Your house is big and comfortable and it would be fine for me to commute there four times a week. On Friday through Sunday nights we'll stay at my house and that will make it easier for my drive to work on both Saturday morning and Monday mornings."

Daniel said, "I like the way you two compromise, but I want to know when I'll be walking my little girl down the aisle."

"And I want to know when I can plan the bachelorette party," Desiree proclaimed.

"What I'd like to know is when we can go wedding dress shopping," Leslie said.

They all laughed and Sable felt loved. She didn't fear what tomorrow would bring. She felt incredibly happy. She peered down at her ring and Desiree teased Phillip.

"Phillip, that's quite a rock you bought my cousin! It's so big! And the band with all those smaller diamonds is exquisite, you have quite the style!"

"Thanks Desiree. I fell in love with it and knew it was perfect. Just like your cousin here."

"Sweet talker you are, Phillip. I like that in a man!" Desiree laughed. "My cousin is lucky to have you as you are her. But you two need to stop side stepping the wedding date question."

"We're not side stepping the question! It's just that we barely got engaged last night! Phillip, help me out here."

"Well, June's a great month. If we wanted to have an outside reception, June would be ideal."

"That's nine months away, is that enough time to plan a wedding?"

"Of course it is. I planned my wedding in five months, Sable."

"You did, Mom? I didn't know that."

"Trust me, nine months is plenty of time to plan a very special wedding. Phillip, when will you tell your parents?"

"I'm going to call my parents as soon as we leave here. My mother will never forgive me if she's not in the loop immediately."

"I remember meeting your parents just briefly when you two were younger. I would love to see your parents and get to know them."

"Mom, even I haven't seen them in years. Phillip, do you think they'll approve?"

"Sable, I've talked of you constantly since your reunion. They know how much I love you, trust me. They'll be thrilled."

"Well, that's a relief."

"Sinclair's already agreed to be my Best Man."

"Sinclair already knows we're engaged?"

"Kind of. I told him I was going to ask you a while ago."

"Aww babe. That's so sweet."

"So what do you think of June?"

"June sounds wonderful, love."

"Who is ready for another round of ribs?"

"I am!" Everybody chorused.

A few hours later, Sable and Desiree were laying down on the chaises drinking Shirley Temples when Sable said, "Desiree, I want you to be my Maid of Honor. I love you like a sister and I want you there by my side."

"I'm honored cous. I would love to. And by June I should be skinny again."

"Of course you will be. You will be as cute as a button as you always have been."

"Cute? I prefer to think that we would be some hot babes that day."

"That's hilarious, but I don't think I want to be a 'babe' that day. How about 'gorgeous'?"

"Of course you'll be gorgeous! I can't believe you're getting married to your high school sweetheart. Talk about a young girl's dream come true."

"Yes, it's pretty spectacular. I can't stop smiling and I can't stop looking at my ring."

"Sable, I remember you crying for him when I was a little girl. What an incredible thing to have him back and love you as intensely as you love him."

"Des, I'm blessed. I think about tomorrow's procedure and although it's horrible, I still feel lucky you know? I know it's crazy because my whole female anatomy is being butchered tomorrow, but at the same time, I know I'm lucky because of my family and because of Phillip. I feel loved and his proposal last night made me feel so special."

"You are Sable. You've always been wonderful and you deserve this. This is your time. Your time to feel overwhelming happiness."

"It's your time too, Desiree. Those twins will be the luckiest little babies ever."

"I can't wait to meet them. I love them so much already."

"This is our time, little cous, this is *our* time."

Twenty-Six

$\mathcal{S}$ able arrived at the hospital at 6am with her parents and Phillip. She was both mentally and emotionally prepared. This summer had been painful, but she had gotten through it. She had the support of her family and friends and she was engaged to the love of her life. She was thankful for her blessings and although she felt that her body had failed her, she had decided to not feel like a victim. She would have happiness, she was certain of it.

Dr. St. Francis had pre-registered her so she didn't have to wait for the paperwork process. She hugged both her parents together with all the love she could muster and said, "Thank you for all your support and thanks for being the best parents a girl could have."

"We love you, honey," they said, "good luck in there."

Next, she hugged Phillip with an intensity that tore at his heart.

"I love you, Sable. You're my family now too."

"I love you too, baby. Thank you."

She walked into the corridor and felt warmed by their encouragement.

ೕ೧ ೕ೧ ೕ೧

Desiree was just getting out of the shower when she heard the phone ring. She was trying to hurry because she wanted to be at the hospital before noon to see her cousin. She wrapped a giant towel around herself and sat down on her bed.

"Hello?"

"Hello, Desiree, this is Dane."

"Dane? You call now? I haven't heard from you in almost four months. What do you want?"

"I want to know how you are. How you're feeling. How the baby is."

"So much has happened since we last spoke. I had wanted your attention and concern at the beginning, but frankly, I don't want to talk to you now."

"Come on, Desiree. You know how hard this is for me."

"How hard for you? How the hell do you think it's been for me? I had to drop out of college! Can you even imagine? My career is on hold. And you didn't care at all about your responsibilities. You left me in a heart-beat. You said you were falling in love with me and then bailed on me almost immediately afterwards."

"I'm sorry, Desiree. Of course, it's harder for you. But we're in our twenties and this wasn't in the plan.

I'm sorry I didn't have all the answers. I was in shock and not ready to be a father."

"Well, I'm not ready to be a mother. But here I am. I'm doing it. My body has medical issues I have to deal with and you're nowhere to be found. You're a jerk."

"I am Desiree. I know. I'm sure this will haunt me when I'm older, but I just can't right now."

"Listen, I heard all this garbage months ago. Why do I need to hear it again? What do you want?"

"I want to know how you are. I want to know about the baby."

Desiree leaned back against her headboard and closed her eyes. There was so much going on and so much he had already missed. Should she be forthright with him or should she be dismissive? She thought she'd give him minimal information and let him go.

"Listen Dane, I really don't want to play catch-up with you, but I'll give you the gist: I'm not having one baby, I'm having two. A boy and a girl. Their names are Farrah and Beau and I've already decided I'm not writing your name on their birth certificates. Their last name will be Castile, like me. However, if they should ever ask, I will give them your information and they could try to find you. My due date is in mid-December but there is a very strong possibility that I will deliver in mid-October."

"Wow, twins, I can't believe it…"

"All the more reason to run from your responsibilities, right?"

"I know you're angry at me, Desiree. I deserve it. I wish I could've been a better man for you. But I can't disappoint my parents nor can I jeopardize my future."

"It's pathetic how disappointing your parents is more important than disappointing your children. Good bye, Dane." Hanging up on him felt good. Real good. For about five minutes. Then sadness flooded her soul and tears consumed her. What a day. Her cousin was having her ability to reproduce taken away from her, while Dane so easily rejected his own babies. The irony never ceased to overwhelm her.

๑๑ ๑๑ ๑๑

At the hospital, Dr. St. Francis came out to talk to Sable's family.

"Everything went as well as I would have liked. Sable had no complications and I would now consider her system clean and very healthy. We were able to take out all the fibroids and polyps before they compromised any other area. I would fully expect her to have an excellent recovery."

"Thank you, Dr. St. Francis for being so thorough. When will you be releasing Sable?"

"She will be here for 48 hours. So we'll be sending her home Thursday, late morning."

"When can we see her?" Daniel asked.

"She's in the recovery room now and should be in her own room in the next two hours."

"Thank you Doctor, we appreciate it," Phillip answered.

Leslie and Daniel were going to join Desiree who had just arrived and have lunch together. Phillip told them he had a meeting and would return in about three hours. He walked into the gift shop downstairs and ordered two huge bouquets of roses to be sent up to her room. On the first card, he wrote, "I love you always" and on the second card he wrote, "Wishing you a speedy recovery, Mrs. McNeil." He smiled at himself thinking of the special years to come and drove to his meeting.

Surprisingly, his meeting only lasted twenty minutes and he looked at his watch. He knew Sable was still in the recovery room, so he decided to drive to his office and return some calls and some emails before he headed back to the hospital.

As soon as he got to his office he remembered that he still hadn't spoken to his parents about their engagement. He had meant to do so last night but when they arrived at Sable's house they were both so full from all the ribs they had eaten, that they'd fallen asleep on the couch watching the Late Show.

He didn't want to delay any further and picked up the phone to dial his mom.

"Hi, Mom. It's Phillip. How are you?"

"Love! I haven't talked to you in a week and a half, how are you?"

"I'm doing very well. I have so much to tell you and Dad. Is he around?"

"No, he's at the hospital all day."

"Oh, I was going to have him grab the other line and listen in."

"Well, I promise I'll tell him everything. Why don't you tell your Mother the news?"

Phillip laughed and said, "Mom, I'm engaged! I proposed to Sable Sunday night!"

"Phillip, that's fabulous! I'm thrilled for you!"

"We are so happy, Mom. It's been a long time coming."

"But son, you two only rekindled five months ago. Is that enough time to know?"

"Mom, I knew the first day I saw her that I wanted to be with her forever. I went ring shopping a few months ago and showed considerable restraint, I think, in waiting as long as I did."

Rose McNeil couldn't feel happier for her son. "I'm very happy for you dear, congratulations. Your father will be just as happy to hear this great news."

"Well, I feel there's more that you should know about our relationship."

"Okay…"

"Sable underwent a partial hysterectomy this morning." His voice was soft as he said it.

"Oh Phillip, that's horrible, she's so young."

"Yes, it is mom. She had benign tumors in her uterus and uterine polyps as well. They had to be proactive since these sometimes lead to endometrial cancer in the future."

"I'm heartbroken for her. And for you too. How do you feel about this?"

"I wouldn't have wanted any kids with another woman anyhow Mom, so that part didn't matter. Luckily, they allowed her two months worth of egg harvesting to see if a surrogate can be used in the future. Usually two months worth of retrieval isn't enough, but it was all the time her specialist was willing to give her. Sable was thrilled with the chance of using her own eggs at some point in the future and that gave her a lot of inner peace. As for me, we can adopt and I'd be just as happy. I love her and I know I want to be with her for the rest of my life."

"I raised a fine young man. I'm proud of you Phillip. I really am." Phillip could actually visualize his mom smiling.

"Thanks Mom. I have to go and head back to the hospital soon."

"Wait, before you go, give me the name of the hospital, I want to send her get-well-soon flowers and I'd also like to call her tomorrow when she's not so groggy and welcome her to the family."

"Thanks, Mom. I love you for that."

☺☺ ☺☺ ☺☺

Sable was tempted to doze off again when another floral delivery came in. She had already received two amazing bouquets from Phillip, one from her parents and one from the *Amor Mio* staff. This next bouquet was so fragrant with the most alluring scent that she knew they were star-gazers before she opened her eyes. The card shocked her and warmed her heart more than she thought imaginable.

"Dear Sable," the card read, "I want to wish you a very speedy recovery. I wish for you a wonderful recuperation and I look forward to the day when you will indeed be the mother of my grandchildren. For you see, my dear, children are born in the heart, not necessarily in the womb. With Love, Rose McNeil"

Sable was smiling, but she couldn't help the tears that welled up in her eyes. What a touching moment this was, she felt. Incredibly sweet. Phillip walked in at that moment and went right to her and hugged her softly and kissed her.

"Love bug, who made you cry? I'll beat them up for you."

That made Sable laugh and cry harder. "I think my hormones are already out of whack. The person you'll be beating up would be your mother."

"Oh. Let me re-think that."

"Here, read this."

"Wow, that's profound. I'm a lucky man to have both of you in my life."

Sable nodded and wiped at her eyes and leaned into his embrace.

☙☙ ☙☙ ☙☙

"Phillip, I know I should be incredibly sad, but right now I feel okay. Even hopeful. I had thought I'd be an incredible crazy woman today, but I'm feeling positive."

"That's great, Sable. But to your credit, you've had a little over two months to prepare yourself."

"Sure, but that was the theoretical and today it became reality. And still, I feel positive and hopeful about the future. I don't know how loca I'll be tomorrow, but I'm enjoying feeling tranquil today."

"That's good hon. Maybe your grandmother Olivia is here with you today. People often find strength in believing things like that."

"You're right. The funny thing is that I feel like she's always with me, today's no different."

"What would she say about our engagement?"

"She would be thrilled. She really did like you when she knew you. She would have worn a floral dress to our wedding if she would have been there."

"That's sweet that you knew her style so well."

"Absolutely. I idolized her growing up." Sable smiled remembering her grandmother. "You know, Phillip, the idea of June is really growing on me. I would really love an outside reception."

"Then that's what we'll have. What do you envision?"

"I can see our reception in a garden with topiaries all around. The centerpieces would be really full and plush with red roses. I'd like a head table not of our wedding party but of us and our parents and Sinclair. I'd like a big dance floor and I'd like a way to display some of our photos from when we dated as kids. It would be fun for our guests to see how we looked the first time around."

"That would be great, Sable. Do you also want to get married outdoors?"

"I don't know, what do you think?"

"If we're going to have an outside reception, I would love for us to get married outside as well. That way our guests don't have to travel from one location to another."

"I like that idea. That would actually lengthen our overall wedding time. Good thinking McNeil. Do you want to wear a suit or a tux?"

"A tux definitely. I need to look my best for you."

"I love that answer sweetie."

"How many guests did you have in mind?"

"Probably 75 on my side; how about you?"

"I was thinking around 75 myself. I've always liked medium sized weddings the best."

"Yea, I agree......Guess who called me today?"

"Hmmm, I have a feeling the old Mrs. McNeil called the new Mrs. McNeil."

"Yes! She must've told you!"

"Yes, she asked for the number here. She told me she wanted to welcome you into the family."

"She did. We spoke for a few minutes and I was able to thank her for the bouquet of star-gazers. She was very sweet, Phillip, I feel really touched."

"My mom's great. I promise she won't fit into the mother-in-law stereotypes."

"I'm sure she won't. She's absolutely amazing. I was really happy that she made an effort to call and talk to me. She loves you very much I can tell."

"Of course Sable, everyone does!"

"Especially me! But I have a favor to ask of you. Phillip, would you be able to run to my house and get something for me? They wouldn't let me wear it during surgery and I really miss it."

"Are you talking about your rock?"

"Well, yes, I'd love to wear it," Sable said sheepishly.

"Great minds must think alike in the Franco family. Your mom called me earlier and suggested that you might want to wear it. So, I swung by your place before I came over here and," he reached into his coat pocket and smiled proudly, "here it is. Let me place it on your finger."

"My mom is something else! And as for you, I love you so much, Mr. Fiancé. I'm a lucky girl."

Twenty-Seven

$\mathcal{A}$fter two weeks of recovering, Sable felt strong again. The cramps were gone and her scar was healing nicely. She realized that most of her healing was internal, but she couldn't imagine staying home another four weeks. She had easily slipped into the routine of lying in bed until ten and then taking a leisurely bath. At around eleven, she had brunch on her balcony and read magazines or did a crossword puzzle. At noon, she usually went into her home office for four hours and did light work for *Amor Mio*, whether it was emailing Miles, calling contacts, placing orders or doing record keeping. Although her parents were helping around the restaurant, there was always so much to do. She was grateful that no real emergencies had arisen since her convalescence. Around 4pm she usually wandered into the kitchen and made a meal for herself and Phillip who usually arrived an hour later. Some evenings, her parents would come over with either take out or some of Leslie's cooking, and they would all dine together. After 5pm she'd lay on the couch for the rest of the evening bullied into doing so either by her parents or Phillip.

Desiree usually spent Tuesdays and Thursdays with her and on those days, she skipped computer work for the restaurant. They'd go for slow, leisurely walks on the beach and have lunch at one of the cafes. They'd walk back home and lay down for the rest of the afternoon and complain about their tone-less bodies and how all that rest was driving them crazy. They both fantasized about getting back to work or school and getting some exercise.

They also spent a lot of time talking about Farrah and Beau. There was so much to do for their arrival. But with Desiree's parents flying in in two weeks, it was easy to postpone all those baby tasks until they got there.

Sable had already done the bulk of the work that was necessary for Desiree's shower that was in two weeks' time. She had Miles talk to one of his pastry chef friends and Sable had ordered the most splendid cake decorated in a pink and blue harlequin design. It had three levels and the top layer was decorated in red and white hearts. It was delightful. She had already ordered the balloons, the flowers, the food, the chair covers and the favors. Desiree had asked that they not play games, so she didn't have to worry about prizes. Desiree just wanted to sit back and enjoy the party with family and friends. Besides, every time she'd ever gone to a baby shower, the gift opening took upwards of 90 minutes and she didn't want to add silly games to the afternoon.

Sable asked Desiree, "Do you know what you're going to wear to the party?"

"Nope, I've outgrown all the maternity clothes I own and I'm not buying any more casual wear. But I will indulge myself in a party dress next week. That would only be a week before the party and hopefully I won't grow much beyond that. I shudder to think how badly my skin is going to sag after the babies come. I'm beyond maximum capacity here!"

"You sure are gigantic, Desiree. I had no idea those twins could stretch you so far. And to think that realistically, you still have ten weeks to go."

"Well, in theory I do, but we all know I won't make it to December. Dr. Jashe assumes I'll have the babies by Halloween."

"They'll be so cute, I can't wait to meet them. Listen, I'm going to start driving again next week. Do you want to spend the day at the mall?"

"I can't spend the day at the mall Sable. Just walking here for an hour, tires me out for the next two days. How about if I look online and see which stores have the dresses I like the most and then we'll just visit those stores?"

"That sounds perfect. Let's do that. Excuse me, I'm going to go to the bathroom."

"Go ahead, I'm going to take a peek in your fridge."

A few moments later, Sable walked into her kitchen and Desiree was laying on the floor. After she tried to shake her awake, she reached for the phone.

"Yes, 911. My cousin has just fainted and she's 28 weeks pregnant with twins. Yes, that's the correct address. Please hurry!"

ଚଚ   ଚଚ   ଚଚ

She grabbed Desiree's wallet and found Dr. Jashe's office phone number. She quickly called and told them that they were heading to the hospital. Then Sable called her parents and Phillip and told them that she was riding in the ambulance with her cousin.

Sitting there, with Desiree lying so still on the gurney, frightened her so much. Desiree looked so young, she was only twenty. She held her younger cousin's hand and prayed. She prayed for her and her babies. Dear God, please let my cousin be alright. Please save her twin angels and help them that they all come out through this safely. Please, please.

The sirens blaring around her seemed so surreal. Suddenly, Desiree started to convulse violently and Sable yelled, "She's having a seizure! Please help!" They flew through the traffic and were at the hospital in five minutes. Sable was pushed along to talk to one of the nurses, while Desiree was rushed into the ER. She had given the EMTs as much information as she could back at her home and now she was filling out the admittance papers. She was so scared. Her cousin was only twenty, how could she faint? How could she be having a seizure? She prayed it was only a dizzy spell, but knew the episode was too severe for just that.

She had been waiting for about half an hour when her parents finally arrived. They all hugged and Sable could feel herself strengthen a bit with her parents' presence. Leslie said she wasn't going to call her sister Sara, Desiree's mom, until the doctor came out and talked to them. About ten minutes later, Phillip arrived and they all continued to wait anxiously for any news.

Finally, Dr. Jashe came and found them. She remembered Sable and Leslie from earlier appointments when they'd accompanied Desiree.

"How is she, Dr. Jashe? We've been so worried."

"Thankfully, she's just woken up. But her blood pressure is very high and she says she's seeing in double vision. There's protein in her urine which is another sign of pre-eclampsia–"

"My cousin has pre-eclampsia?"

"Yes, I'd assumed she'd told you. That's why I had ordered bed rest."

"She didn't tell us she was on bed rest. We simply assumed that her body was slowing down and that she was taking it easy. We didn't know it was on doctor's orders. Did you suspend her driving also?"

"Yes, fainting is always possible and we tell the mothers to stop driving immediately."

"She told us she wasn't comfortable behind the wheel any longer…..are the migraines a symptom of pre-eclampsia as well?"

"Absolutely. Desiree needs to be very careful from here on end. She's less than three months from her due date, but she will never reach that date given her condition and given that she's carrying twins."

"What else can happen to my cousin?"

"Pre-eclampsia can be very dangerous. Severe seizures can lead to comas. In some cases the babies grow a lot smaller than expected. There's no cure for pre-eclampsia or eclampsia, but we need to monitor both mother and babies carefully. From now on, the babies will have to be on a baby monitor."

"When will Desiree be allowed to go home?"

"We're going to leave her overnight because we need to order blood tests to check her platelet count and we need to assess her kidney and liver function. Other than that if she were to seize again, we'd leave her in the hospital until the babies are delivered."

"Thank you, Dr. Jashe," Daniel said.

Almost an hour later, they all walked into Desiree's room and it looked like she was just waking up.

"Desiree, why didn't you tell us that you have pre-eclampsia? We're in shock," her aunt said.

"Oh Aunt Leslie, I'm so sorry. I found out just a few days before Sable's hysterectomy. I couldn't mention it then, we were so worried for Sable. Besides, at that moment, I needed a little time to think about it for myself. After that, Sable and Phillip got engaged and I was thrilled for them. I don't think I could've been happier if I would've gotten engaged myself. I was so very happy for her and I just didn't want to mention something so depressing."

"But Desiree, my hysterectomy and my engagement were almost three weeks ago now. Surely, you could have mentioned something before this happened," Sable said.

"You're right. But besides the migraines, I felt that I was healthy. I was keeping off my feet and I was watching what I was eating. I was going to bed early and taking all my vitamins. I even stopped driving. I just didn't want to worry you all."

"Well you know that I'm calling your mother tonight. There's no way that my sister would forgive me if something happened to you and they didn't know."

"Yes, I knew you'd call her once you knew. My parents are set to come in two weeks, but I'm sure they'll fly out sooner once they hear that I'm in the hospital—even though I'll be coming out tomorrow."

"It doesn't matter, Desiree. They should be here even if you are receiving the best medical care."

"I know. All I care about is that the babies are healthy. That's all I care about."

∾ ∾ ∾

Miles called the next morning and Sable was grateful to talk about business. She was tired of thinking of health concerns. She welcomed the world of food and business in this conversation.

"Sable, I think I found the perfect applicant for Assistant Manager."

"Really? That's wonderful. Tell me everything."

"His name is Demetri Blanc and he's a recent graduate of Cal State LA and he graduated with honors. He majored in Business and he was an Asst manager of a local restaurant the last two years he was in school. He's young at twenty-three, but I see that as a plus. That means he'd be willing to prove himself and he wouldn't have a wife and kids who'd protest long hours. Given that he's eager, if you needed him to come in last minute to cover for you, I think he'd be very willing and I know you now need that flexibility."

"Thanks Miles, yes I do need that type of last minute coverage, I'm afraid. I like that he's young and hungry. It also means that I could teach him how to do things exactly the way I've done it at *Amor Mio* and he wouldn't be too partial to "his" way. Why don't you call him, Miles, and ask him to come in next Tuesday around 1 or 2? I'm planning on being there all day."

"You are? But that's only the 4 week mark after your surgery. Is that ok?"

"I feel healthy Miles and I'm starting to go stir crazy. Coming in next Tuesday is responsible and if I don't cramp up or have any problems, I'll come in on Saturday as well. Maybe the following week, I can also work two days. I miss the restaurant. I need to start working again, but I've promised myself to take it slow. Mothers go back to work after six weeks and heaven knows they have a much more traumatic hospital experience than I did."

"Well, as long as you think you're fine. Sure thing. I'll call Demitri and I'll email you the particulars including his resume and work history."

"Perfect, Miles, thanks."

☯ ☯ ☯

"Sable, your Aunt Sara and your Uncle Marcel are arriving on Sunday. It's only a week earlier than they planned and they just can't stay away any longer. They're worried for Desiree and they want to help her in every way."

"Of course they do Mom. She's their baby and Desiree needs their tender loving care."

"I suggested to my sister that they stay here in the guest bedroom and Desiree can spend the night here whenever she'd like in your room. The more time she spends here, the better. What do you think?"

"I think it's a great idea Mom. She needs all of us watching her like a hawk. Those babies need as much baking time as possible in that little oven."

"Well said sweetheart. Let me call our little oven next. You know how stubborn she can be."

Sable laughed at that. "You're right mom. Good luck with her!"

$\mathcal{S}$ hane walked into Phillip's office and slapped him on the back. "Congratulations! I can't believe I had to hear it from Terry!"

"I'm sorry Shane. I meant to tell you, but you were gone on your vacation, and we got so busy around here–"

"Let me guess, the beauty at the Reunion? Auburn hair, hazel eyes?"

"That's the one indeed."

"I remember us going out to lunch once and you mentioning that exact type."

"I wasn't mentioning a *type* my man, I was mentioning *her*. I never forgot her and I always had hope that I'd run into her again one day. And when the reunion company put her ten year reunion in my hands, well,

I prayed that destiny was going to take over and it did. We're getting married in June."

"That's terrific. Just six months ago you were married to *Enchanted*. Congratulations, Phillip. Have your brother call me when it's time to plan the Bachelor party."

"That's a promise."

☙☙ ☙☙ ☙☙

"Aunt Sara! Uncle Marcel! You two look great! I've missed you!"

"Sable, you look wonderful my dear! You don't even look like you've just had surgery!"

"Well, it's been three and a half weeks now and I have to admit the recovery's been great. I have a doctor's appointment on Monday and I'm hoping to go back to work on Tuesday at least for two times a week until the six week mark is met."

Leslie said, "That seems reasonable Sable. You really have healed wonderfully. I'm glad you took your time at home seriously and really let your body rest."

"I did, Mom. So tell me, how was the flight from Spain?"

"It was very long as you know. But we're excited to be home again. All we want is for Desiree to be healthy and the babies too."

"She will be. Now that she's wearing the baby monitor and is being so careful, I hope that it's enough to pull her through."

"Yes, we all pray for exactly that."

"Where is she? I thought she'd be here."

"She's actually taking a nap. She was starting to get another headache and decided to lie down. I was happy to see that she knocked out. She's very cozy in your old bed."

"Well, no wonder, it *is* the coziest bed."

"Sable, let's let your aunt and uncle unpack and you and I can start on dinner."

"Sounds perfect Mom, lead the way."

☻☻ ☻☻ ☻☻

On Tuesday, Sable walked into *Amor Mio's* with so much happiness inside of her. Yesterday's doctor's appointment with Dr. Morgan had been perfect. Her incision had healed perfectly and her ultrasound showed that there were no signs of re-growth of either the fibroids or polyps. She had left the doctor's office ecstatic. Her future seemed so bright now, her engagement to Phillip, her aunt and uncle's arrival, her little cousins Farrah and Beau would be here soon and today she was interviewing Demitri Blanc who might prove valuable to the restaurant. Yes, she thought, the future held so much promise!

She didn't walk too far into the restaurant before she was greeted with countless hugs from the waiting and kitchen staff. She was so happy to see everyone and she felt right at home instantly. She stood next to Miles as he was preparing today's special of whole beef tri trip and twice baked potatoes. They discussed Demitri. He was to arrive in an hour and Sable had already phoned his previous employer who had provided a wonderful recommendation.

Sable looked around the kitchen and smiled to herself. She loved this restaurant. The past few months had taken a toll on her both physically and emotionally, but she had come through it and was happy and grateful to have done so. She touched Miles' arm and strolled into her office.

In her office, she stroked her desk and eased into her chair. The paper work seemed in order due to her parents' diligence and her own email inquiries were up to date. She was happy that she felt current with the office end of the restaurant. She re-read Demitri's resume and waited for his arrival.

A few minutes later, Emily came in and announced that Demitri Blanc had arrived. Sable thanked Emily and went out to greet him. They shook hands and Demitri was the first to speak, "Thank you for giving me this opportunity to interview with you, Ms. Franco."

"And I thank you for coming, it's nice to meet you."

"Your restaurant is charming. The ambience is very inviting."

"Thank you. Yes, I would definitely agree with you, Demitri. Let me show you the kitchen and introduce you to Miles who you've already spoken to on the phone and then we'll talk in my office."

The interview went very well and both Sable and Miles liked him very much. Although he was young, he seemed very knowledgeable of the intricacies of restaurant management. He had a professional presence about him and he seemed very personable and kind which was very important to her. She knew he would be willing to work very hard since this was his first career job and stay long hours on the nights that she would need him to do so. Although Miles had set up two other interviews for later that day, it was his resume and recommendation that were leading. Sable decided to sleep on it and promised to call Demitri within a few days.

☯ ☯ ☯

On Thursday, Sable and Leslie, along with Toni's help were organizing the last minute details of Desiree's shower. Sable called the bakery, the florist and Miles to confirm the deliveries. They purchased all the vases for the flowers and all the favors. They rented all the linens, tableware and stemware. They bought all the wine, the ciders, sodas and waters. They picked up the chair covers and organized all the music they would play. They made a poster as a guest sign-in and finally, they rented the helium tank for the hundred balloons to tie around the yard. Sable also confirmed that Phillip would be there to photograph the party and he chuckled and told her, "Of course, babe, I'll be there."

The three women were absolutely exhausted by the day's end. They decided to go to a restaurant and indulge themselves in a great meal and several glasses of wine. After a lot of debate, they decided on four appetizers.

"I can't believe all this planning. If this baby shower is this much work, what am I really facing in planning my wedding?" Sable said.

Leslie responded, "Don't look at it that way honey. Today's run-around isn't far off from what a bride does for her own wedding. The only other details you would include are the dress, the DJ and the limousine. Everything else is basically what we've done here today. You'll be fine honey, don't stress. Besides, the wedding venue helps out so much with the details."

"Please Sable, at least you have a handsome man! I'm still looking!" Toni playfully complained.

"You're right, Toni. I am grateful for everything, especially Phillip. But all this planning definitely seems a bit overwhelming."

"What I would do to have such a problem!" Toni chastised and Sable hugged her as they laughed.

"Here you go ladies, enjoy," the waitress announced.

The women spent the next few hours laughing and eating and having a fabulous time. Sable felt like she was finally relaxed.

ꕥ ꕥ ꕥ

Desiree decided to splurge on Saturday morning and get her hair done. She felt happy with the impromptu decision and was so excited to see everyone at today's shower. She had bought the palest, pink, flowing, chiffon dress. It had small capped sleeves and clung to her tummy in the most adorable way. The saleslady had said that she looked ethereal and in fact, she had. She wanted to finish her look today by indulging in a beautiful, but loose and casual, up-do. She would feel loved by her family and guests today and she wanted to embody the loveliness that surrounded her.

Her mom drove her to the salon and they talked a lot about all the guests they would see, some whom they had not seen in years. This week, she and her mother had already caught up on all the issues that Desiree was dealing with. Of course, she and her parents already had talked a lot during the course of this problematic year, but it was so much more meaningful to talk to her parents face to face about all her concerns and worries for the future. Just having her parents back home eased her anxiety significantly. At twenty years old, Desiree welcomed their gentle safekeeping. It was nice for Desiree to completely assent to all their decisions and for her to feel, for the moment, taken care of and utterly protected.

The hairdresser curled all of Desiree's dark waist length hair at the ends and at the crown for volume. Then she picked it up and started to pin it up in criss-cross pieces. The effect was very sweet and delicate, almost angelic. She was so happy, she knew her hair and her dress would complement each other nicely.

On the way back home, mother and daughter held hands and knew that they were sharing a wonderful moment. Sara often thought of how funny life was. She herself had tried to conceive for well over a decade and her daughter was able to conceive the first time she had been careless. Either way, Sara was a believer in fate and knew that the babies would be a blessing, regardless of the circumstances of their arrival.

☙☙ ☙☙ ☙☙

When Desiree walked into the party, she drew in her breath. The backyard was absolutely awe-inspiring. There was about seating for fifty and all the chairs had been adorned with stylish chair covers that had the cutest ribbons tied in large bows on the back. The glassware on the table sparkled in the daylight. The buffet table looked incredible in its arrangement and also in its spread. The cake table was a show stopper, wrapped in adorable blue and pink tulle, displaying the cake as a magnificent art piece. There must have been hundreds of balloons tied all over the yard and the huge floral centerpieces were grandiose.

She walked across the yard where Leslie, Sable and her mother were working on hanging a poster board and hadn't noticed her arrival.

"This has to be the most enchanting party décor I've ever seen. I love you all!"

The women whirled around and all took turns hugging her and squealing in delight. "Desiree, you look gorgeous!"

"Sweetheart, you look like an angelic Aphrodite in that whimsical dress! Your father is going to love it!"

"Dad's going to be allowed to be here?"

"Yes, we thought that since Phillip is going to be here photographing the party, that we'd let your father and Uncle Daniel attend as well."

"That sounds great to me. I look around and I can't believe the transformation. It is awesome back here! Oh- I just noticed the giant polka-dot 'F' and 'B' to hang on their walls! How sweet to-" her voice choked up-"use it here as an accent!"

"Hey, hey, no tearing up! Your mascara is going to run and your guests are going to arrive any minute!"

"Ok, ok. But I have to say, I really love you all. I am blessed."

Sable said, "Mom, I have corsages for both Aunt Sara and Desiree. Here. Why don't you pin your sister and I'll pin my little sister's." All four women basked in that sweet moment.

Within the hour all of Desiree's guests had arrived and she was so happy to see everyone. Phillip had also arrived and was taking great group shots as well as candids.

Sable was so happy with the turnout, the food and the décor. It was just the party that Desiree deserved. Sara was the beaming grandmother-to-be and both Desiree and Sara wore their corsages with pride.

When it was time to open gifts, Desiree was overwhelmed with gratitude. She received absolutely everything she could need for the first year of the babies' lives. Desiree opened countless presents of the most darling clothes, shoes, blankets, bibs, hats, even hair accessories and bows for Farrah. She was also given the baby bathtub, baby monitors, two car seats, a double stroller, towels, toys, baby videos, books, even art work. Other special gifts included baby jewelry, a miniature chandelier and baby mobiles. Farrah got her fill of dollies and teddy bears, while Beau got plenty of trains, planes and sports toys. Desiree's roommates got her an enormous basket filled with probably 400 diapers and countless bottles of shampoo, baby wash, creams, lotions, ointments and even a first aid kit. Her parents gave her two bassinettes as well as a generous gift certificate to buy the two cribs when necessary. Sable's parents gave the babies a high chair, a playpen, and a video camera to record all the precious moments. Sable bought Desiree a very comfortable glider with ottoman as well as an old fashioned rocking chair. Phillip gave Desiree a digital camera and six photo albums to fill.

After Desiree had opened up all the gifts and the guests had eaten the delicious cake, she walked around and personally hugged and thanked all her guests for coming and for spoiling her so. After she had walked around, she stood next to the cake table and asked for everyone to grab a glass.

"I just want to say how eternally grateful I am for all the amazing love I have received here today. It wasn't easy to tell my family and friends about my condition earlier this year, and I have received nothing but unconditional support. I am blessed to know each and every one of you. My babies are now spoiled beyond comparison and will be cocooned with all your precious well wishes. I want to thank my parents for flying thousands of miles to be here with me and for always helping me and treating me like a princess. I'm everything because of both of you. I also want to thank my Aunt Leslie and Uncle Daniel for hosting this party in my honor at their home and for loving me so. Finally, I want to thank my dear cousin, Sable. She is truly my sister and this day would have never been this special without her touch. I love her so deeply and I will always fall back on her for everything I need in this world, this I know. She and her fiancé Phillip will be my babies' Godparents and this will mean more spoiling for Beau and Farrah! And to my beloved Grandmother Olivia, I miss you, but I know you're watching over me today! I'm so lucky to have all of you to help guide me in this new adventure of my life. So lift up your glasses, Salud!"

👁👁 👁👁 👁👁

The next morning, Sable woke up in Phillip's arms and jokingly said, "Hon, I can't breathe!"

"Oh, sorry Sable! I guess I was squeezing you too hard!"

"Yes, you were!" Sable sat up and leaned up against the pillows and headboard. "I am so happy with yesterday's party. Everything was just perfect! Desiree looked divine. I can't wait to see the photographs you took."

"They'll be great. I was happy every time I clicked. The weather was great, the lighting was in our favor and everyone wore smiles all day long. The pics will be very beautiful."

"All those gifts! I just can't believe that she received so much! They're just going to leave everything in my parents' garage for a couple of weeks until my Aunt and Uncle get Desiree moved into her new place. No reason to move it all twice."

"She's one lucky girl."

"Yes, she is." Phillip picked up her pajama top and kissed Sable's new scar.

"It doesn't repulse you?"

"Are you kidding? It's not that big at all. And you can have them all over, I'd still desire you like this." He started kissing her all over her tummy and was starting to work his way up.

"Phillip, mmmm, you know I can't. Dr. Morgan said specifically six weeks and it's only been four."

"Sable, Dr. Morgan said four, I'm sure she did," he was kissing her neck and ears and his hands were exploring everywhere.

"Phillip stop, she said six I'm sure of it. You have to stop that….right now…..cut it out!"

"Ok babe, I'll stop…" Phillip whispered.

"Well, maybe she did say four….."

☙☙ ☙☙ ☙☙

Desiree wasn't feeling well. She had spent the night at her Aunt and Uncle's house since her parents were guests there; and because she had been having so much fun, even hours after her baby shower, that she just hadn't wanted to go home.

She had gotten up and eaten a light breakfast with the family, but she felt queasy and dizzy. She decided to lie down in case she had another fainting spell. She didn't want to scare her parents, but she had a feeling, she would be calling Dr. Jashe today.

It wasn't even two hours later that she told her mother, "Mom, I really don't feel well. I'm feeling a little disoriented and now my stomach seems to be cramping. I don't want to wait until it gets worse. I need you to call Dr. Jashe for me. She'll tell us if I should come in and see her."

"Okay, love, let me call her and see what she says."

Desiree doubled over in pain just as her mother came back into the room. "Dr. Jashe says we need to drive to the hospital immediately. Cramping is a bad sign of a complication. Let me help you, oh my God, let's hurry."

ლ ლ ლ

Three hours later, Dr. Jashe and Desiree were talking in her room alone. Dr. Jashe was re-reading something on her chart and was frowning.

"How bad is it, doctor?"

"Your pre-eclampsia, which most people think of as 'toxemia,' has matured into eclampsia. Your blood pressure is very high and there is a large amount of protein in your urine. You haven't had any more seizures which is a great sign. However, the fact that you're still getting migraines and that now, you also have nausea and abdominal cramping, is very concerning to me. Another problem I see here, although less alarming is that you're also deficient in several vitamins."

"Are the babies in danger?"

"No, at this point the twins are thriving. My main concern is for you. We will need to hospitalize you until the babies' birth."

"I can't believe this pregnancy is so difficult," Desiree sighed and rubbed her eyes. "But I understand and want to do everything to ensure that my babies are born healthy."

"Of course. Desiree, now I'm going to talk to you about something that might seem alarming to you. When other mothers are admitted to the hospital to give birth, we ask them if they have a living will if anything catastrophic should happen during their delivery. Most mothers don't give it much thought assuming that because either they're married or young and healthy, that the paperwork becomes a formality. But since eclampsia can be dangerous to both mother and babies, I wanted to discuss your living will."

"I don't have anything in place Dr. Jashe. I've never thought of that issue."

"Well, now that you are to become a mother, you'll soon find that you need to think of your children's well being at every given moment. I'll give you time to think about it and I'll bring in some hospital forms later for you to sign."

"I really don't need time to think about it extensively. I would choose my first cousin, Sable Franco, to raise my son and daughter if anything were to happen to me."

"Not your parents or their father?"

"Their father does not want to be in the picture. And although my parents are the most loving people, they are both in their mid-sixties and they live in Spain. They wouldn't have the energy to handle two babies. No, I don't need to think about it. For sure, I would select my cousin Sable."

"I understand Desiree. Go ahead and take a nap and I'll tell your family in the waiting area about the complications and to return in a few hours."

☾☽ ☾☽ ☾☽

Outside, in the waiting area, Sable was raging mad. Her eyes were full of anger and her jaw was clenched.

"How in the world do *both* of us have medical problems in our reproductive systems at the same time? It's so unfair, I can't stand it!"

Leslie answered, "I know it's hard Sable and it is unfair, but in a way, it makes sense."

"What do you mean by that? Nothing makes sense."

"I know you're angry, we all are. But what I mean is, you two are first cousins. Genetically, you're pretty close. Both of your mothers are sisters who had problems ourselves. I was only able to conceive you Sable, I was never able to get pregnant again, although I was always hopeful. And your Aunt Sara tried for sixteen years to conceive Desiree. Your mutual Grandmother Olivia had several miscarriages in her own lifetime. I know it's hard right now for all of us. All we can do is pray."

"I'll pray later. Right now, I feel like remaining angry. I'll see you all later," and she stormed out the door.

hen Sable returned to work, she welcomed the responsibility and the fast paced momentum of the day. She could lose herself in her work and not have much time to think about medical problems-either hers or her cousin's. This whole summer had been consumed with worry and constant doctor visits and now she welcomed that *Amor Mio's* needs were pushed to the forefront.

Of course Desiree was still in the hospital, but it made Sable feel less anxious about her cousin, knowing that she was being monitored around the clock. It had only been four days since her hospitalization and she was bored there, but nonetheless, getting the rest she needed.

Sable turned her attention back to her cost analysis report and heard Demitri and Miles speaking in the hallway. She had decided to hire Demitri and had already been impressed with his work ethic. He was proving to be quite an asset and it had only been a couple of days that he had been brought on. Sable was training him on the way *Amor Mio* ran its business, but he had quite a bit of background knowledge from his experience at restaurants during his college years. She found that she didn't have to monitor him too closely as he was incredibly self-sufficient.

Demitri was only working six hours a day for the first month. She had wanted to gradually bring him on as Assistant Manager, while she also got back into the swing of things at the restaurant herself after her leave of absence. She enjoyed working eight hour days and then going home feeling satisfied with what she had accomplished. Before the hysterectomy, she had easily worked twelve to fourteen hour days, but she couldn't handle that physically any longer.

She knew that it was time for a balanced life in order to be her healthiest self: time for the restaurant, time for Phillip and time to rest. Sable knew that when the babies came, she'd be able to take a few days off to help Desiree and could leave the restaurant in very good, capable hands with Demitri and Miles.

Since she was thinking of her, she picked up the phone and called her cousin, "Hey, how are you doing?"

"I'm watching my second soap opera today and am going crazy I assure you!"

"I remember staying home too, it was for the birds."

"I know I need to be here. And I'm trying to stay positive. How's the restaurant?"

"It's really great. My new Assistant Manager is working out great. I'll be giving him full shifts and trusting him to take over in no time. I just wanted the restaurant a little to myself as I transitioned back. I didn't want to be talking about procedures all day. Him being here 6 hours is plenty right now."

"That was a really smart move. Plus, I'll need your help when Beau and Farrah come."

"Absolutely. I've already thought about that and will definitely be able to stay with you a few days while you're getting used to the little dolls. Are you scared about the nursing?"

"No, I'm actually really excited about the nursing. But when I see pictures of moms doing simultaneous nursing of twins, I get kind of overwhelmed. I think I'll want to just nurse one baby at a time."

"I completely agree! It will give your boobs some down time too."

"No doubt! Haha."

"What have you guys decided about your new place?"

"The new apartment search is being pushed back a few weeks. My folks are always here now…"

"Yea, that sounds fine. No need to rush and have them get you something you don't like at all. Listen, I'll swing by the hospital tonight on the way home from work. I'll probably be there around six. Anything you want me to bring you?"

"Yes! I'm craving vanilla ice cream. And bring me a couple of slices of garlic bread from the restaurant."

"Yikes, what a combination!"

"Hi Baby, how are you?"

"Phillip! I'm great, how are you?"

"I'm missing you. I haven't seen you in two days. That's too long."

"Phillip, you didn't see me for thirteen years, two days is nothin'!"

"That will *never* happen again Sable, and you know it."

"Yes, I do. Never again. So what are you up to tonight? If you want to come over, I should be home from the hospital around 9."

"Great, I'll meet you at your house. I don't have to go to work until noon tomorrow. Want to sleep in and then have breakfast in bed?"

"That sounds decadent. It's a date."

ೲ ೲ ೲ

When Sable reached the hospital, Desiree was just waking up from a nap. She sat up groggily and smiled up at her older cousin.

"Quite a life of leisure you have here, I see."

"Are you kidding? Both our moms were here from 11-4 and they tired me out! With all the advice and pointers they give, I told my mom to run downstairs to the gift shop and buy me a notebook so that I could jot it all down. They finally got the hint! I know they mean well, but they mentally exhaust me!"

"Oh, don't be such a baby. They love you and are trying to help."

"Just wait until you have one, they'll do it worse to you because you'll be older and might use a surrogate or adopt. They'll have a field day lecturing you on all those side issues."

Sable laughed. "I'm afraid you're absolutely right. They'll have a multitude of topics to harass me with. Most of which they have absolutely no knowledge on."

"Ah, the power of being old. You can say whatever the heck you want and pull it off as so-called wisdom."

The cousins laughed heartedly and Sable handed her cousin a big book with a huge red ribbon tied on it. She said, "Here, a present from Phillip."

"Oh my goodness, what is it? Ohhh, it's the photo album of the shower!" She amazingly turned the pages, "It's amazing! Look at these! I'm speechless."

"They really are amazing photos." Sable and Desiree enjoyed looking through the album together. Everyone had been so happy and Desiree had had truly a wonderful day. The pictures of the food, the décor, the guests, the gift opening, even the toast, made Desiree feel so much joy.

Sable reached into her purse again and withdrew her water bottle and a small package and said, "I brought you the ice cream you asked for and splurged on some sprinkles. Here. Let me go grab some napkins."

After setting aside the album and devouring the first couple of spoonfuls, Desiree said, "This is delicious, thanks! Where's the garlic bread?"

"It's in my purse in a foil bag to keep it warm for later. Wait–don't tell me you want it now," she made a face at her younger cousin.

"Guilty. Hand over the goods, Sable."

"Oh Desiree, you're pretty disgusting!"

"I can blame it on the cravings. No use for name calling!"

Once again the girls laughed and relaxed with each other.

"I'm glad my mom and Leslie were here for so long earlier because that means they won't come in for a pop visit later on. I really wanted you all to myself for awhile because I have to ask you for something."

"Sure, what do you need?"

Desiree exhaled greatly and tried to gather up some courage, "Dr. Jashe explained to me that all mothers who give birth nowadays are asked if they have a living will in place. Most mothers are married so if there were to be a problem with a delivery where the mother passes, the children obviously are the father's. However, in my case, I'm both single and not in communication with Dane.

"What I'm asking you, Sable, is that I'd like to put your name on the legal documents that you become the guardian of the twins if something should happen to me."

"Well, of course Desiree. I'll do anything for you and the babies. But you're scaring me. Are you sure this is just a technicality?"

"Actually, no." Desiree looked at Sable intently. "I have a dismal feeling deep in my heart that my condition is worse than they tell me or worsening day by day. My migraines are still constant and the abdominal cramping hasn't subsided. Now that I have full-blown eclampsia, instead of pre-eclampsia, I feel very nervous about all this. Eclampsia is one of the leading killers of first time mothers. I'm overwhelmed with emotion, but am trying to act levelheaded and not freak out."

"That's a very smart move, prima. If you become an emotional mess, it would only complicate your well-being further." They reached out and held hands and looked deep in each others' eyes for a moment without words.

"I'm scared, Sable."

"Me too," Sable whispered.

"I need you to sign some other papers as well, because I don't want Dane to have a change of heart down the road and try to contest you for custody."

"I'll do whatever you want, baby cousin. But won't your mom feel hurt if you were to give the babies to me?"

"Sable, my parents are in their mid-60s. Although they are fantastic and in great health, how long could they endure the intense schedule of two babies? The middle of the night feedings, the running around, colds, teething, temper tantrums? They would be wonderful for a short time, but Beau and Farrah would ultimately tire them out and age them considerably. Plus, even if they were to survive the early years, they'd be in their 80s during the high school years....no, I don't want them to raise the babies. I want you."

"Anything, anything for the family."

"I feel selfish about imposing the babies on you if something were to happen because of your new marriage to Phillip. You wouldn't get a chance to be real newlyweds if–"

"Hush! Nothing is going to happen to you, Desiree. I know doctors have to discuss worst case scenarios, but you're a 20 year old healthy woman. You'll be fine, dammit. The discussion you had, Desiree, was a just a hospital duty. You won't need me and Phillip to raise your babies, although we would do it with all the love in the world; I would love them as if they were born out of my body because you're my sister. But this is all a mute point, so relax. Don't be so literal about those hospital forms. Your eclampsia is touchy, I know, but you're here and you'll be monitored until the delivery. You'll go home with them and you'll be crazy and sore and sleep deprived—life will be perfect, you'll see."

"Yes, I guess you're right. I shouldn't be such an alarmist when my head is splitting or when I feel dizzy or when my cramps feel *so* bad it feels like a large man is kicking me. Of course this is all normal, what was I thinking?"

Sable and Desiree hugged fiercely then and Desiree cried in Sable's arms and Sable consoled her younger cousin. They continued talking for a few hours and held hands during the whole time. They imagined Farrah in her first dance recital and giggled at the idea of Beau being a bowling champion since Dane's father was on a Seniors bowling team. They imagined the kids fighting over stuffed animals or TV channels. They thought of trips to the park, the beach, to Disneyland. They imagined them riding bikes and the first day of Kinder. Finally, Desiree was getting sleepy and Sable kissed her forehead, adjusted her blanket and walked out the door.

Outside, a few feet from Desiree's room, she leaned against the hospital corridor wall, and the tears finally came. She covered her face in her hands and sobbed. She was afraid for her cousin and wanted her to be healthy and happy. She wanted to erase the great fears she had seen in her eyes and she prayed to their Grandmother Olivia to save beautiful Desiree.

" $\mathcal{M}$ om! Mom! I can't understand you! Please stop crying, I don't understand!" she looked over at the clock and noticed that it was 2:40 in the morning.

"Sable, it's your cousin. The hospital just called. She was having what they called adult respiratory syndrome. She was having trouble breathing and–"

"Mom, you're scaring me. Stop crying! What else, Mom?"

Leslie caught her breath and tried to speak but she barely uttered a whisper, "And then the seizures happened. They think she had a brain aneurism. She's slipped into a coma, baby. We're on our way. I'll see you there," and Leslie quickly hung up.

Phillip interrupted Sable's erratic thoughts, "What's happened?"

"My cousin just slipped into a coma. Oh dear God. We have to go *now*."

At the hospital, she found her parents, her aunt and uncle all huddled around the doctor. She heard her father ask, "Why did my niece slip into a coma? She's been monitored very closely here all week."

Sable noticed that her aunt and uncle gripped each other's hands and waited for Dr. Jashe to answer.

"We really don't know why. Eclampsia is not a clear cut condition, it looks different to different women. It usually happens to first time mothers, more so with ones who carry multiples. We see patients with various genetic factors, problems with the central nervous system, vitamin deficiencies, kidney disease, diabetes or hypertension. Many also have problems with the placenta, although that wasn't the case with Desiree. I believe what has happened here tonight is that Desiree had a cerebral hemorrhage."

"Oh my God!" Sara exclaimed, "When will my daughter wake up?"

"We just don't know, Mrs. Castile. We will have to wait and see. But we can't wait too long or her babies will be in danger."

"But they're too young," Sara insisted, "they are only thirty weeks along."

"Twins are usually born early anyway. I had hoped they would reach 32-34 weeks of gestational age, but we need to keep them safe if your daughter's condition were to worsen. We don't want the babies to have intrauterine growth retardation or go into fetal distress if they're not receiving the proper nourishment necessary for development. I'm so sorry to have to tell you this."

Sable asked, "What is the worst case scenario Doctor?"

She looked around at all of them and answered as gently as she could, "Worst case would be that she loses her vision or that she not pull through at all."

Sara and Leslie started screaming and crying and the men gripped each other's arms. Sable covered her mouth to stifle a cry that never came. She started to walk backwards away from her family and the doctor whose words she hated until she collided into the wall and slipped down to the floor.

☙☙ ☙☙ ☙☙

For three days, they waited for Desiree to wake up. They spoke to her, kissed her, held her hands, played music for her, but nothing roused her. They didn't want to despair, they kept praying and praying that she and the babies would be safe from danger. Sara and Marcel were desperate for their daughter to wake up. It was hard to even look at them without crying, they were so weakened by the possibility of losing their daughter or grandchildren.

They kept strong by talking to the many visitors who came to see Desiree. Her roommates, her friends, her old co-workers. Everyone loved Desiree and it was hard to imagine what the possible dire consequences might be. Sara and Marcel spoke to all the visitors with hope and supplication of the possibility of recovery. They prayed constantly and filled her room with love.

Sable walked up to her uncle and put her arms around him. Marcel looked so fragile when he spoke.

"I was just thinking of when Desiree was a little girl. She had straight, long black hair and the longest eye-lashes you'd ever seen. When she was three or four, people started comparing her to Snow White, because she was just so cute and pure. Then, when she was six, she developed into quite a mouthy little character and we'd wonder, 'where does she pick up this lingo?' and although we should have scolded her, we'd laugh at her ridiculous and outrageous comments. Because, you see, when you become a parent at such a late age, everything they do is so memorable and wonderful, even when they're naughty. I love my daughter so much, I can't believe I'm about to possibly lose her, when it's my life that should soon be over, not hers."

"I don't know what to say. I love her so much. She's like my sister. Those babies need her, we need her."

"Yes, we all need her. My world won't work without her. She's my sunshine."

Sable couldn't hold back the tears and tapped her uncle on the shoulder and left the room so that he could have some time alone with Desiree.

The next day, a surprise visitor came that shocked all of them.

Dane walked into the hospital room. He looked a mess. His eyes were bloodshot and he kept wringing his hands and running them through his hair. His pres-ence surprised them and although Desiree's parents had never met Dane, they knew exactly who he was immediately.

It was Sara who spoke first, "Why are you here? No one wants you here."

"I'm sorry, Mrs. Castile. I really am. I can't believe this is happening to Desiree. She's so beautiful and good. I'm just so sorry."

"Young man, you are pathetic. My daughter would call me in Spain to tell me how you two were falling in love and how the future seemed so promising. Do you think this is a future for my daughter? Do you? She's dying because she's carrying *your* children! Because of *your* irresponsibility! Then, she got ill because her poor body couldn't deal with it all, the stress, the babies, the loneliness—all because of you, you bastard!" Sara jumped up from her chair and ran across the room and slapped Dane hard, then she slapped him a second time just as hard, before her husband and Phillip held her back.

Dane was crying openly now. "I'm so sorry, Mr. and Mrs. Castile. A thousand times I'm sorry. I should have proposed to Desiree the moment I found out we were expecting. But I was scared and selfish, I only thought of myself. I hurt her so profoundly. If only I could have supported her emotionally, maybe she would have been ok."

"Don't you understand? Her bottled up feelings, her fears, her stress, probably all attributed to the migraines, to the hypertension—and now we're here battling with the possibility of losing her. The unthinkable possibility. But you get to walk out the door like nothing ever happened because you dropped her the moment it was too hard. You're a disgusting coward!" Sara seethed.

"Yes, I am. I'm just so sorry. I will regret my behavior for as long as I live. May I ask that I have a few moments with Desiree to apologize to her?"

Before Sara could object or yell at him again, Marcel whispered to her, "Let the poor boy cleanse his soul and his conscience."

The whole family walked out of Desiree's room and left Dane alone to atone for his negligence and beg for forgiveness. Sable looked at him and thought he looked so fragile.

Phillip took Sable's hand and said, "Let's go for a walk."

They walked hand in hand outside the hospital and walked for a bit until they found a bench in front of a pretty fountain.

"This is so surreal, Phillip. I was just talking to her four days ago and now I might never talk to her again. I'm so scared."

"I know babe. This is so incredibly unbelievable."

"I miss her. I feel that she's already gone in a way. I'm afraid the babies will start to be in danger if she doesn't wake up soon. I didn't tell you this the other day, but Desiree signed me over as guardian of the babies on her living will."

"Good, that Dane character can't take care of himself, let alone two babies."

"You mean, you're ok with that?"

"Of course. Desiree is your family and when you and I get married, we'll be family too. If Desiree needs us to raise her angels, we will. We'll love them as our own and it will be fine, I promise you."

"I was worried that it would be overwhelming for you given that we're not married yet and we wouldn't have anytime for ourselves."

"Sable, I don't care about that. It's very possible that Desiree needs us *right* now. It would be selfish of me to want anything else at this moment. I've lived alone for many years now. I'm ready to start my life with you and all that you bring with it. I've always wanted kids, you know that. Those babies are a blessing."

"I'm so scared," her voice was barely a whisper.

"I know. We'll do the best we can."

Sable nodded a few times, fell into his embrace and sobbed in Phillip's arms. She prayed her cousin would open her eyes. Waiting for her to do so was tormenting all of them.

⟐⟐ ⟐⟐ ⟐⟐

Two days later, while Marcel was holding Desiree's hands, he noticed that her face was twitching and he felt hopeful that maybe she was waking up.

He rushed out to call the nurse who paged Dr. Jashe. Within minutes Dr. Jashe was there and witnessed the facial twitching herself.

"Mr. Castile, I'm afraid the facial twitching is not a good sign. What I'm seeing on this monitor here is that she's having a mild seizure. That tells me that instead of her brain healing, it is indeed becoming more jeopardized. I'm sorry."

"How many more days are we going to wait before we know truly what my daughter's fate will be?"

"Today, your grandchildren turn 31 weeks and every day is a milestone for them in their shared space. Later today, Desiree will have a cranial exam to assess her brain activity and a team of doctors and I are going to have a meeting to discuss her progress. We can talk more at length at that time."

"Gracias, Dr. Jashe."

At 6pm, Dr. Jashe came in with her colleague Dr. Ramsey. Desiree's parents, Sable, and her parents were in the room. The family collectively already had a feeling for what the news would be. Desiree had slipped into the coma six days ago and there'd been no sign of improvement. Now they felt anxious for the babies as well. This whole experience was absolutely unbearable.

Dr. Jashe said, "Family, we have tried our best. Desiree's assessments unfortunately tell us that Desiree's brain activity is virtually inactive. Her cerebral hemorrhage was a lesion that we couldn't stop from developing. I'm so very sorry. For all intents and purposes, she's gone."

The family held hands, but nobody was able to speak. The women started crying and the men also wiped at their eyes. How very vacant this moment felt, with the realization that Desiree was not going to wake up. After a few more silent moments, Dr. Ramsey moved forward closer to Sara and Marcel.

Dr. Ramsey said, "As horrible as this news is, we need to focus on the babies now. Desiree would want her babies saved and we feel it is imperative to act swiftly. We suggest a cesarean section would be our next, but immediate, course of action."

The room was quiet again for about two minutes and the doctors gave them the time to process the bad news they had imparted.

"My wife and I are completely destroyed. But you don't see your daughter in a coma for a week and not know that, what you're telling us, is a grim possibility. We have the rest of our lives to mourn our daughter, but it is our responsibility now to look to our grandchildren and make sure they arrive into this world safely. With a very heavy heart, we will consent to your recommendation."

Sara stopped crying for a moment and asked, "When exactly do you intend to operate on my daughter?"

"I can have an OR ready in less than an hour Mrs. Castile."

"No, I don't want that. You see I'm a very spiritual woman and tomorrow would have been my mother's birthday. I thought, in my naiveté, that we would experience a miracle tomorrow. My mother helped raise my daughter and they were so very close. It would mean a lot to me and my daughter if my grandchildren were born tomorrow."

Dr. Ramsey said, "But, then that also means that your daughter's life medically ends on your mother's birthday as well."

"For me, I will see it as all my personal angels sharing the same special day. I know it might seem silly to you as you are a person of science, but for me, I would like Farrah and Beau Castile to enter the world on the 14th of October. Just as my mother did. And too, as my baby leaves it." Sara covered her mouth to keep from screaming the torment that she felt within.

Dr. Jashe said, "I respect your wishes ma'am. I will schedule the OR for midnight tonight and the babies will probably be born ten to fifteen minutes later."

"Is that when my daughter will pass?" Marcel whimpered painfully.

"Sadly, yes, Mr. Castile. We are very sorry."

When the doctors stepped out, everyone started hugging Desiree and kissing her and sobbing hysterically. It was as if they were being brave in front of Dr. Jashe and Dr. Ramsey, but now the sadness was overwhelming. Desiree was only twenty, it was so unbelievably unfair.

Sara climbed into bed with Desiree and laid next to her. She kept kissing her temple and holding her hand. She said, "I'm so sorry I couldn't help you my love. I wish it were me. It should be me. I love you more than anything on this earth, sweetheart. I wasn't the person I was meant to be until I became your mother. I love you Desiree, I love you so much."

Sable couldn't stop crying after she heard her aunt's words. But she felt she had to step forward and share her thoughts with Desiree as well.

"I love you little cousin. I remember the day you were born, I was eight. I was so proud. I thought you belonged to me. I remember telling Olivia that you belonged to me and she said she'd fight me to get you first and we laughed at how silly we were being. But the point is, you were irresistible. We are all proud of you. You have looked angelic pregnant, and you've given those babies life while forsaking your own. And that's exactly what a real mother would do. I promise to love those babies eternally. Phillip and I will love them as our own. We'll inspire them to follow their talents and their dreams. I promise to speak of you all the time. They will love you and feel your presence. I love you prima, with all my heart! I love you, I love you little cous. Say hello to Abuela in Heaven for me."

Sable sank in her chair and cried for all of them, cried for Desiree, cried for her poor aunt and uncle who were completely destroyed and finally, for the twins who would miss out on their mother's presence. She was exhausted with grief. The disbelief overwhelmed her and she closed her eyes and wept some more.

ᐏᐏ ᐏᐏ ᐏᐏ

At 12:17 am Farrah Castile was born. She was 4lbs 2 oz and measured 16 inches. Two minutes later, Beau Castile joined his sister weighing 4lbs 1oz and was 15 ½ inches long. The family was so relieved that they were born virtually healthy. They were told that the babies would stay at the Neonatal Intensive Care Unit for several weeks. They would stay there until they could breathe on their own and be assured of complete organ development.

Everyone stood outside the window of the nursery and were shown the babies. It would be a few hours before the family would be able to go into the NICU and touch the babies. And although, the moment was shadowed with Desire's absence, it was also the sweetest moment any of them had ever experienced. Leslie held her sister's hand and they cried happy tears this time. Desiree would be so happy and they internalized her joy. The twins would be cherished by everyone and they would be reminded of their mother's love and beauty. Sara and Marcel embraced for a very long time and promised each other that Farrah and Beau would be the best loved babies ever.

Sable moved forward and looked at the little faces of her new baby cousins, while both pride and panic washed over her. She had always wanted to be a mother, but had never imagined having babies in this way. She was already worried about the babies' sizes and development. She chuckled to herself and thought that mothers always worry and that she had taken on that trait immediately.

"I love you little Farrah and Beau. I'm not your real mommy, but I already love you so much and I will love you for as long as I live. Phillip and I will be honored to raise you and your mommy will watch over all of us. We'll be fine– your mommy is going to make sure of it."

The next morning, Sable walked out to the beach and sat down on the sand. She was devastated to lose her cousin. It seemed completely unbelievable that Desiree was not here to meet her babies. It was so surreal to think that her babies were now about ten hours old and had not been held by their mother.

Sable threw some nearby sticks into the ocean and felt anger rise up inside of her. Desiree would have been a great mother! Sure, she was nervous and young and overwhelmed, but she had the basics: love, patience and a strong sense of family.

Sable noticed a young family a few feet away and shook her head. Dane could have married her cousin or at least supported her emotionally and perhaps this situation would have played out differently. But even

Desiree believed in destiny and if she were here sitting next to Sable she'd say, "I was their vessel to come into this world. Their presence is meaningful. I've played my part."

Sable half-smiled at the words she had created for her own cousin and stood up abruptly. She had so many things to do today, but her heart was so heavy.

She walked into her living room and called Demitri. She quickly explained what had happened and asked him if he could handle the restaurant, along with Miles' help, for a couple of days. Luckily, Demitri was very accommodating and was willing to put in the extra hours to compensate for Sable's absence. He offered Sable his condolences and assured her that *Amor Mio* would be well taken care of.

She drove over to her parents' house where her parents and aunt and uncle were all sitting around the dining room table drinking coffee. Everyone looked horrible, red eyes from tears and lack of sleep, not to mention the look of overwhelming and unbearable sadness.

Sable went around the table and kissed everyone's cheek and sat down with them.

"Tia Sara, have you decided on funeral arrangements?"

"We have. We're not going to have one. Everyone she loved was at her shower less than two weeks ago. She looked like an angel that day, blessed by the upcoming birth of her children and the love that surrounded her." Sara stopped to look at her husband and wiped away a tear from his eye.

"We don't want any more sadness. Our hearts are broken and funerals exasperate that emotion even further.

We, all here, spoke from our hearts to her the moment she passed. *That* is the memorial that matters."

Sara stopped again to choke back a sob and took a sip from her coffee.

"Your uncle and I have decided to donate as many organs as possible to other people who might benefit from them. That way, our Desiree, will live on this Earth for many more years. It's a gift for others, but we will find peace that Desiree's eyes or heart or kidneys will provide others with the longevity that she was robbed of. We spoke to Dr. Ramsey and set it all in motion. Later, there'll be a cremation and we'll spread her ashes."

After a few silent moments, Sable said, "I'm proud of you guys. It's very selfless and admirable. Desiree would have loved the idea of organ donation."

"Yes, she would have," her father agreed.

"Well, I'm ready to go to the NICU to hold some babies. Who's coming with me?"

They all smiled softly and all stood up to go to the hospital. Once there, they spoke with the head nurse who gave them positive news. Although they would be spending 4-6 weeks in the NICU, the babies were fairly healthy and strong. They needed time to develop, of course, but the nurse assured them that for 31 weeks and for their birth weight, they were thriving.

They all spent about four hours in the NICU that day taking turns touching the babies through the arm slots in the incubators and talking to them. Sable thought her heart would break when she saw her Uncle Marcel start reading to the twins a book about animals. The simplicity of the gesture screamed to her, that Desiree wouldn't be here to read to her own children. She had to rush out the door and run to the bathroom and lock herself into the stall. The amount of tears surprised Sable. She couldn't believe that she would have any left to shed, given that she'd been crying for about two days solid.

Finally, around 4pm they all left, kissing the plastic boxes that protected the babies and headed home. Sable drove to her own house and was making herself a sandwich when Phillip called. She caught him up with everything and he asked if he could come over.

"Phillip, I'd love to see you, but I think I'm going to crash right after I eat this sandwich. I'm so emotionally drained and sleep deprived. I know it's only dinner time, but I'm crawling into bed in probably ten minutes and it wouldn't surprise me if I slept 16 hours."

"I'm happy you're going to rest early tonight, I really am. How about if I let you sleep and I pick you up in the morning around eleven and we'll have breakfast and spend the rest of the day at the hospital with the twins?"

"That sounds like a wonderful idea, hon. I love you Phillip. I really do."

"And I love you too. See you in the morning."

As Sable was walking towards her bedroom, the phone rang and it was Diane.

"Sab, I can't believe about poor little Desiree. We were just with her at the shower. I'm heartbroken."

"Oh Diane, she was my little sister. I had always assumed that we'd grow old together. Now, I'll be without her and I can't wrap my head around it."

"I know, it's unbelievable. When will the services be?"

"My aunt and uncle decided to not have any. They say they just can't go through with that ordeal. They feel that everyone who loved her was at the shower and that the words that were to be spoken about her about love and memories were spoken when she passed by the few of us who were in the room. They just can't, they're so devastated."

"I understand that. Whenever a person passes away and your heart and brain start to take it in and process it, a funeral always rips you to pieces again. And no one should see their daughter in a casket."

"I agree. A funeral seems to throw families into deeper sadness and my family just can't bear it. They're trying to focus on the babies and not on their grief at the moment."

"How are the little bundles of joy and when can we visit them?"

"They are completely precious. Pretty big for pree-mies, I think. They're both four pounds and just beau-tiful. They still need time for further development, but the doctors assure us that they'll be fine and are, thankfully, passing all their little assessments and reach-ing their mini milestones. Farrah and Beau will be at the hospital for at least a month, maybe more. Sorry Di, they won't be allowing visitors into the NICU, other than their immediate family."

"That's wonderful that they'll be staying in the NICU just for growth and not for medical concerns. That's a miracle right there. Desiree's hand over them, I'm sure. I understand about not visiting them right away, because of their little immunities. Sable, will your aunt and uncle take them back to Spain with them?"

"No, Di. I'm sorry I hadn't told you any sooner, but our world has been upside down and I haven't had a chance to tell you. Desiree gave me custody of the ba-bies in her living will. She spoke to me about it a few days before she died. It breaks my heart that she might have had a premonition about her own death, she must have been so afraid." Sable's voice broke and she stayed quiet for a few moments. "I'll love them to the best of my ability and those babies will love Desiree, I assure you."

"Sable, I'm so happy for you. You will be a wonderful mother! Desiree gave you an amazing gift."

"Yes, she did. I don't know if, later on, the eggs I harvested and the surrogacy plan would even be successful, but now I'll be a mom. I just hate that her fate was robbed so that I could have babies in my life. It's hard for me to reconcile all of this in my heart. I feel a lot of guilt."

"Don't feel guilty, Sable. You are a wonderful person and there's no one on this Earth who will take care of those babies like you will and Desiree knew that. Her parents are older folks, so that probably was another factor in her decision. Don't waste time feeling guilty, my friend. Embrace this as the most amazing gift your little prima could've ever given you."

"I will, Diane. I'm just so shattered right now, I hope I can do it."

"Even natural mothers feel anxiety and self-doubt, so don't be so hard on yourself. You've had a roller coaster of events happen to you this year. These babies will ground you and Phillip into a solid family. How does he feel about it?"

"He's just such a dear. He's so excited to be their dad. He says they'll be cherished by us beyond belief. I love him for being so accepting of all the changes….In the meantime, there's so much to think about. Where will we live? How much will I work at the restaurant?

Will the legal proceedings of actually adopting the twins be difficult? And the one that terrifies me right now is, will my aunt and uncle ultimately hate me for taking the babies?"

"It will all work out in time, I promise. Your aunt and uncle will never hate you, Sable. When are you going to talk to them?"

"I'm going to talk to them about all of this tomorrow. Right now, I'm heading off to bed. I've slept so little in the last few days, I can barely keep my eyes open anymore."

"Ok, Sable, have a great rest. Go easy on yourself. And when you see the family tomorrow, please give them Clark's and my condolences."

"I'll try to rest. And your wishes will be delivered, Di. Talk to you soon."

👁 👁 👁

The next morning, instead of Phillip coming at eleven, he came at 8:30 and let himself in. He tiptoed into Sable's room and saw that she was still under the covers. He kicked off his shoes, climbed in behind her and encircled her waist and nuzzled her neck.

"Quick, call the police, there's an intruder in my house, Phillip."

"This intruder couldn't wait 'til eleven, I'm sorry. And how did you know it was me?"

"Maybe the cologne I bought you a few months back?"

"Ah. Forgot that detail."

Sable turned around and put her arms around Phillip. She breathed in his scent and smiled. She felt safe and was happy that he was back in her life during this troubling time.

"Thanks for being here for me, hon."

"I always will be. Always."

Sable sat up cross-legged and rubbed her eyes. She faced Phillip and he propped another pillow behind him guessing that she had something on her mind.

"We need to talk about some things."

"Sure, doll, anything."

"We need to make plans about where the babies will live. My house is only a two bedroom and the office would have to be cleared out if I were to bring them here. But what I was thinking, is that when the babies come home, we'd all move into your house."

"I'd love that. We'll get married next year anyway, and it seems like the natural step for all of us. My four bedroom house has been lonely long enough. Time for toys and books and diapers to be strewn all over!"

Sable laughed at that. "Well, I'm too much of a neat freak to let stuff be thrown all around. But I'm sure, family life will make me a bit more flexible, so I'll learn to be okay with some baby clutter. Will you be okay with all this Phillip? You're suddenly getting three of us, and our wedding was supposed to be months away."

"If it's okay with you, I'd like to keep our wedding plans exactly as they are. That would give us months to just be parents to the babies who will need so much attention. Besides, I doubt you would want to celebrate a wedding, when the whole family is in mourning."

"Well, we could have a small civil ceremony and have a reception later. What do you think about that?"

"No babe, I wouldn't want that. A small civil ceremony right now would still be overshadowed with family sadness. When I marry you, I want it to be the happiest moment in our lives, Sable. I want you to wear the big white dress and even the babies will wear fancy outfits. That's what I'd like."

"You're right, Phillip, I want that too."

"Listen, I have plenty of space. They can each have a bedroom and we'll have a blast decorating. I would love for you to move in with me now, way before the wedding. It would be best for the babies to feel their home settled right away. There's no need for them to feel any more emotional setbacks."

"You're right, hon. I'm actually excited about all this. Let me take a shower and we'll head off to breakfast, then the hospital."

"Can I join you in there?"

Sable laughed, "No! But why don't you be a sweetheart and make the bed?"

"Wow, rejection *and* chores! I feel married already!" Phillip laughed.

⚭ ⚭ ⚭

Later, at the hospital, they all took turns being in the NICU two at a time. The babies were so cute and responded to their touch. The family longed to hold the babies in their arms, but they weren't allowed to yet. They all missed Desiree terribly, but these little miracles softened their pain.

"Aunt Sara, I need to talk to you. Will you come downstairs and have coffee with me?"

"Sure. The men want to come in and have a turn with the babies anyway."

"Nothing cuter than a man with a baby, I've recently learned."

"That's for sure. After sixteen years of marriage with your uncle, I never loved him more than when we had Desiree. To see a man change a diaper or spoon feed them their cereal or worry when the baby has a fever, there's a manly gentleness to it, that is too precious."

"I can definitely imagine that." They had reached the hospital cafeteria by then. "Here, sit down, while I run and get our coffees."

Sable soon returned with some muffins and the coffees.

"How are you feeling, Aunt Sara? I know it's a dumb question, but..."

"No honey, it isn't. I'm destroyed and empty. But somehow, those two little angels upstairs, make me smile. They're part of my daughter and they help your uncle and I more than we can describe."

"I wanted to talk to you about the babies. I was afraid to mention this before, but I wanted to ask that you not hate me over the living will. I'm so scared that you will."

"Sable! How can you be so foolish? I can never hate you, you are my niece. And until I had Desiree, you were my little girl as well."

"Yes, but Desiree left me the babies. And I'm so afraid that you and Marcel will be angry over it—if not now, then perhaps, eventually."

"Sable, don't you know that Desiree and I spoke of this decision? I supported her decision fully and agreed with all the same reasons she had in choosing you."

"You did? Desiree didn't tell me the two of you had spoken of it. In fact, I felt that she was just being nervous about the living will and that it was a hospital administrative formality."

"No Sable. Desiree spoke to me before she even mentioned it to you. I knew my daughter very well and I saw it in her eyes that she was afraid she was going to leave this Earth. It made me panic, but I felt I needed to hear what she had to say. She chose you because your uncle and I are both 66 and we won't have the energy to raise two little bundles of crazy chaos. I understand that and agree with that. Also, she wanted you to have the babies because you're young and dedicated in all that you do. Because you and Phillip would provide a nurturing and respectful home, full of love. Because you are the closest person to her and she trusted you completely. And also because," Sara stopped and grabbed both Sable's hands and looked her lovingly in her eyes, "because if the surrogacy fails, Desiree wanted you to be a mom and have a real family."

Sable felt the wind knock out of her and her stomach flip-flopped inside of her. Her shoulders started shaking and it wasn't until the tears had fallen, that she even realized she was sobbing. She lowered her head on her aunt's hands and cried for the cousin she missed so desperately and for the gift of the babies. She also cried because her aunt was so unbelievably selfless and wonderful. It seemed all too precious and bittersweet.

*S*able called Demitri into her office and told him that she would be, unfortunately, working even less in the next few months. She explained that she would be working about three to four hours a day, either in the morning, before customers came in, or late at night when *Amor Mio* closed. She decided to give him a bonus and was relieved when he was enthused about the further added responsibility. Lucky for Sable, he was young, lived alone, and was eager to prove himself.

Over the next two weeks, the family fell into a routine. In the early mornings, Daniel and Leslie would spend two hours at the hospital with the babies, then would work at *Amor Mio* until two or three in the afternoon and then go home. Their assistance at the restaurant was a big help to Miles and Demitri, and made the transition of Sable's waning schedule become a bit more manageable.

After Leslie and Daniel left the hospital, Marcel and Sara came and usually spent four to five hours with the babies. By this time, the nurses had allowed the babies to be held, so they loved sitting in the side by side rocking chairs and cuddling them. They were even allowed to bottle feed them and change them on occasion. They loved the quality time they were spending with their grandchildren and knew that Desiree would be happy with their bonding.

After they left the hospital, they would load up their rental car with more baby supplies from the Franco's garage that Desiree had received from the baby shower and take the drive down to El Toro to Phillip's house.

At Phillip's house, Sable and Phillip would already be there working on some sort of task in readying the house for the babies' arrival. In these past two weeks, they had painted one of the baby rooms mint green and had assembled the two cribs and placed them next to each other under a big window. They had also assembled two dressers and baby book cases. The glider and ottoman were in place and they were working on hanging curtains and putting up shelving on the walls, as well as placing the mobiles over the cribs.

The other room, they decided, would act as a changing room and play room. They had painted that room yellow and had assembled the changing table with an adjacent wall unit that held nine wicker baskets with cute, yellow and white gingham lining to house all their diapers, wipes, lotions, creams and other little supplies. On a shelf in the wall unit was a beautiful photograph of

Desiree laughing at the baby shower holding her tummy lovingly.

The rocking chair was also in that room, as well as a 6x8 colorful rug of alphabet letters. There, they still had to hang curtains and Phillip and Marcel were currently in the process of hanging a miniature crystal chandelier over the changing table.

There was still so much to do. They wanted to put all the finishing touches in the two rooms, hang and fold all their little clothing and assemble at least one of the playpens. They needed to put all the crib bedding on and put together the swing and one of the bouncie chairs. They needed to hang the artwork and the giant "F" and "B" letters that Desiree had loved at her shower. They needed to install the baby camera monitor and a ceiling fan. They additionally wanted to decorate the kids' hallway bathroom, but they would leave that task for last being that they wouldn't be potty training for almost two years. They also left the high chairs in their boxes in the garage since the babies wouldn't be sitting up to eat until they were at least four months old.

Sable also worked everyday in moving her own things into Phillip's bedroom and bathroom. She had decided to leave most of her furnishings at her place, since she had decided not to sell the Manhattan Beach house. But just bringing all her clothes, shoes, toiletries and a few special items such as picture frames and mementos, had been a lot of work and time consuming. She was trying to take care not to crowd Phillip in his bedroom, since the rest of the house was being stuffed with baby gear. However, Phillip didn't seem to mind and loved his new job as Baby Handyman. His employees at *Enchantment* had taken over some of his assignments and duties so that he could work on the house.

So everyday, baby items were taken to Phillip's house by either Marcel and Sara or Daniel and Leslie and unloaded and set up in its proper place. The acts of getting the house ready for the babies and in visiting Farrah and Beau everyday, kept them all busy. They all went to bed exhausted and this helped with the grief. When one falls asleep immediately, there's less time for tears and reminiscing, and there was a bit of relief to that.

Slowly, but surely, the Franco's garage got emptied out, and Phillip's house filled up with all of the necessary items the babies would need. The last items that had to be built were the two bassinets and all three men, Phillip, Daniel, and Marcel set them up as the last project. They were placed in Phillip's and Sable's bedroom so that they could attend to the babies immediately in the middle of the night. Babies usually slept in bassinets until four or five months, when they outgrew them. But with the twins being so small, they might stay in the bassinets until seven or eight months.

Sable was so tired lately. Whether she worked at *Amor Mio* in the morning or in the late evening, she still put in a day's worth of work at the house. But, she knew this was called "nesting" and she was excited to bring the babies home soon. She visited the babies daily, even if sometimes, she could only spare an hour, and kissed them to pieces. Dr. Jashe encouraged affection towards the babies assuring them all, that babies needed human contact constantly. Between Sable, Phillip, and the "four grandparents," Farrah and Beau received more attention than any other of the babies at the NICU.

Sable's parents had recently suggested to her that they would be willing to work six hours a day at the restaurant from 10-4, so that the afternoon shift could be covered by Demitri allowing her to stay home for the first month with the babies. Sable loved the idea and ran it by Demitri who consented as well. They were expecting the babies home in about two weeks, and all was almost ready.

ඏ ඏ ඏ

The babies finally came home on the Monday before Thanksgiving and the Francos, Castilles, and Phillip and Sable were beyond excited. The men had installed the two car seats in Sable's Jeep the week before and they all caravanned from the hospital to El Toro. Once there, everyone was so excited to hold them, kiss them, be photographed with them, place them in the bouncie seat or the swing and baby bottle feed them. With six adults running around, the babies were very well taken care of.

Sable went to the kitchen to prepare some pasta, garlic bread, and a salad while all the others cooed over Farrah and Beau. Just recently, the babies' features had really become prominent. Because they were so tiny and their skin so translucent when they were born, it was hard to see their real features. But now that they were six weeks old and weighed six and a half pounds each, their little faces showed their true beauty. Farrah had dark black hair and black eyes and very fair skin. Her lips were very bright pink and she had long eye lashes. Beau, although he looked similar in features, had very different coloring. His skin was very tan and his hair was very light brown. His eyes were also very light brown with some flecks of yellow. Beau was longer and leaner than his sister and had big hands. Farrah was dainty like her mother. Farrah was also the louder of the two and seemed to be more stubborn as well.

Sable was just finishing pouring the wine when she heard a baby wail. She heard her Aunt Sara say, "Feisty, feisty, just like your mother! She was demanding just like you, little Farrah!"

Her Uncle Marcel answered, "No complaining, she's perfect. I can't believe God gave us another little Snow White, she's almost identical to her mother."

"That she is, in looks and in temperament, so far."

"Poor Beau," and they all laughed at that.

ᏧᏩ ᏧᏩ ᏧᏩ

Sable didn't return to work until the beginning of January. Her Aunt and Uncle had returned to Spain just three days before. They promised to return in the summer for the wedding and would stay for six weeks.

When Sable returned to work, she took the babies with her in the morning and dropped them off at her parents' home by 9:30 and worked from 10-4. Her parents would no longer be helping at the restaurant, but would stay at home babysitting the twins. To save on traffic time in the afternoon, Sable's parents dropped off the babies at the restaurant at exactly 4 so that Sable's commute was only 45 minutes. On Fridays, Sable worked the evening shift from 3-11 and on that day, she dropped the babies around two while her parents later drove the babies to the beach house around seven and Phillip would meet them there. They always spent the night at the beach house on Friday nights because Sable had to work her 10-4 shift on Saturday. Usually, Phillip drove down to El Toro after the babies were fed lunch and later met Sable at home. Sable didn't work on Sundays and had recently made the decision to close the restaurant on Mondays. Demitri had truly become a blessing and Sable had given both he and Miles a $2,500 Christmas bonus to show her gratitude.

The babies were such a joy. They had all worked together to make a routine for the babies and they were flexible. They were hardly fussy and were happiest when they were being held or when they were lying next to their sibling. Although Farrah was the stronger of the two in terms of personality, they were both constantly smiling and cooing.

Sable and Phillip were overjoyed to become a family and loved taking them out for walks in their double stroller with Joey in tow. The dog loved the babies as well, and for the first time in months, Sable felt at peace. There were no more medical concerns to worry about or doctors and specialists to see. They were just a couple in love with sweet, healthy twins. Their pediatrician said they were in the tenth percentile for both weight and height and considering they were born so early, the pediatrician felt that developmentally they were at par with other newborns. They were happy, healthy babies and Sable and Phillip felt very fortunate.

There wasn't a day that passed that Sable didn't think of her cousin. She spoke of Desiree often to the babies and although, she knew that the babies didn't understand her words, Sable felt happy when she told the babies stories about their mom. She knew it was a tradition that she would foster their whole lives.

After Sara and Marcel had returned to Spain, Phillip's parents had flown down for the weekend right after the New Year. Because his father was the head cardiac surgeon at his hospital, he wasn't often able to get away, but the McNeil "grandparents" were just dying to meet the babies.

Sable was very pleased at how loving they were towards the twins. She didn't really know what to expect, but they were darling. They spent the whole weekend carrying and doting on Farrah and Beau. Phillip's mother, Rose, had even insisted that they move the bassinets into the guest room for both nights so *they* could give the babies their middle of the night feedings so that Phillip and Sable could get a much needed full night's rest, and plus have the luxury of sleeping in.

"Oh, you don't know what this means to us!"

"Oh yes I do! My two boys didn't sleep through the night until they were both almost one! I very much remember what it felt like to go around all day like a zombie. Now you two get some rest. Grandma and Grandpa will be just fine with these little angels."

Sable and Phillip had gone to bed that night happy that Blake and Rose were so quick to love the babies. But they didn't think about it for too long, as they were both fast asleep in sheer moments.

🦋 🦋 🦋

By mid-March, Phillip wanted to start looking at wedding venues. It was pretty late to begin planning for a June wedding in March, but considering that they had just become new parents, there'd been little time to look. Also, since Phillip had so many connections with the world of weddings, he knew that he could contact some of his friends if he needed a hand.

One Saturday morning, Sable's parents drove down to take care of the twins so that they could look around. Both Phillip and Sable wanted a location where they could get married and have an outside reception immediately afterwards. They didn't want their guests to waste part of the day driving. They visited two hotels that were very nice, but unavailable for June. They also visited a country club that had an impressive garden. Then they visited an old mansion in South Orange County that had been restored and had a huge lawn. Both Phillip and Sable fell in love with the place immediately. They decided they would set up the altar at the front of the house and have the amazing mansion as the backdrop. The back of the house, would be where they'd set up the reception with probably fifteen round tables and they would rent a dance floor.

Sable and Phillip wrote the wedding coordinator a deposit check and decided on Sunday, June 2nd. They would marry at noon and would have the venue until 7pm. They decided on an earlier end time so that they could drive off to their hotel and still enjoy part of their evening all to themselves, before they caught an early flight the next day to Cancun.

The remaining details quickly fell into place over the next few weeks. Sable worked with the wedding coordinator and asked for advice and recommendations about what other brides had done at this location in the past. She quickly ordered the flowers, red and pink roses, and selected the caterers. She didn't want to have *Amor Mio* cater it, because she wanted her *Amor Mio* family including Miles and Demitri and the rest of the staff to celebrate with her. She ordered the wedding invitations and chose an officiant. Sable ordered the most luscious 5 layer cake with angels carved into the sides. To go along with her Angel theme, she also ordered an ice sculpture of two angels. She selected a DJ and scheduled two bartenders. She ordered the party favors: a picture of her and Phillip at a dance fifteen years ago imprinted on a large candle with the words, "Love is Eternal."

Sable also enlarged one of the pictures they took in Santa Barbara into a large portrait and displayed it at the entrance of the reception. The photo was of Sable kissing Phillip's cheek by surprise and catching his open-mouthed laughter.

Sable had already discussed her hair options with her hairdresser and she would be meeting Sable early the morning of the wedding. Sable had decided on a traditional up-do. She also scheduled the hairdresser to bring two make up artists to work on the bride, the two bridesmaids, Toni and Diane, and all the mothers, Leslie, Sara, and Rose. Shane from *Enchanted* would be shooting the wedding along with an assistant.

Sable's final detail was the wedding dress. She had decided to leave that detail for last because she hadn't wanted it to consume all her time. Now that all the other details were set, she could enjoy her fittings, and concentrate on finding the ideal gown. She and her mother went shopping and Sable loved walking through the boutiques and selecting the prettiest pieces to try on. Sable's parents were paying for the wedding dress and the honeymoon. They had wanted to pay for the whole wedding, but Sable and Phillip had insisted that they had lived on their own for many years, and as two adults, they wanted to pay for their own special day.

After trying on a dozen dresses over a two day shopping venture, Sable was able to streamline what she loved the best and what suited her body type. She loved the dark ivory colors because it set off her auburn hair and her hazel eyes. She loved strapless dresses with full satin skirts, but did not want a train or bustle. She really liked the bodice to have some crystals to sparkle, but not too much, and she especially loved the veils that were extra long in length and would reach down almost to the hem of the back of her dress.

On the third day of shopping, Sable gasped when she saw the one she had to have. "Mom, look! This is perfect!"

"Try it on, honey. I love it!"

When Sable came out of the dressing room, both Leslie and Sable locked eyes. "It's the one, Mom. I love it. I can't imagine any other dress."

"Then it's perfect, because I love it too."

"But Mom, it's too expensive, I can't let you buy it for me."

"Sable, you're my only child and you're insisting on paying for the wedding that I had always dreamed of hosting. Please let me buy you the dress of your dreams. How much is it?"

"It's $3,900 Mom, I just can't let you buy it."

"Okay dear, we'll argue over it later. Why don't you go back into the fitting room and I'll beckon the sales girl to bring us some veils and tiaras."

As Sable went back into the dressing area, Leslie quickly walked over to the manager and handed the manager her credit card and said, "You need to charge this immediately. I'm buying my daughter that dress and I don't want her to make a fuss."

The manager chuckled and said, "As you wish. The mother of the bride is always the boss."

☙☙ ☙☙ ☙☙

In mid-May, Phillip's parents flew in from Texas again. Phillip's father, Blake, had been able to take some time off of his busy schedule at the hospital. Sable knew that they had been trying to come again since their weekend trip in January, but he was the head surgeon there and other doctors kept referring complicated cases to him.

He and Rose were beyond smitten with the babies. By now the babies were seven months old and they could crawl a bit, sit up, clap and even hold up their arms when they wanted to be carried. They had grown so much that no one would have guessed they were preemies at birth. Farrah weighed twelve pounds and Beau weighed a pound more. They were precious and much loved by everyone.

Phillip's parents had insisted that he and Sable leave for the night and go out and have some fun. They wanted the babies all to themselves and they wanted Phillip and Sable to have one restful weekend to themselves before the chaos of the wedding in two weeks' time.

Sable decided to work her usual 10-4 shift on Saturday and after that, Phillip met her at the beach house and they napped for three hours. Then, they went to dinner and a movie, and slept in until almost eleven the next morning. Sable called every few hours to check up on the babies, but she knew they were being taken excellent care of. On Sunday, they laid out on the beach for a few hours and got some sun. By five, they were driving back home and felt very rested. They couldn't bear to stay away from the babies a moment longer and burst through the door to hug and kiss them. Farrah reached for Phillip's arms and Beau reached for Sable's. The four of them hugged and kissed many times, while Blake and Rose stood by laughing. On impulse, Phillip threw on the radio and Barry White's "My First, My Last, My Everything" came on and the four adults and the babies all danced and twirled each other around in laughter and the moment was indeed a tender one.

$\mathcal{S}$ able woke up on her wedding day smiling. As soon as she got out of bed, she kneeled on the side of the bed and clasped her hands to pray.

"Thank you God for giving me back Phillip over a year ago. He and I belong to each other and fulfill each other's path. He's my story and my life could have only been this meaningful with him. Today, I become his wife and I couldn't be prouder.

"Abuela Olivia, you helped raise me and helped me to become the person I am. You filled me with confidence and love. You made me feel special every day of my life. You taught me to have high expectations and to never settle. You, along with my parents, gave me the most loving childhood. Please watch over me today, for I know you will be here.

"Desiree, little prima, how I miss you. I miss your smile and your laughter, but I have you in my heart. That sounds so cliché, but I do. Your babies are total cutie-pies, smart, healthy and happy. Thank you for allowing me to become their mom and for letting me love them as my own. I know you will be here today with us too. My wedding theme is Angels, not only because you gave me two of them, but because I know I will feel yours and Abuela's presence with me today. You're still my maid of honor and I know you'll be standing beside me. I love you so much and if you can just help me with one little favor. Farrah is wearing a little red gown and Beau is wearing a little white tuxedo. If you can watch over that they don't get too dirty out there, that would be fabulous."

Sable wiped at her happy tears and smiled. She got up to shower and knew that it would be an amazing day.

☙ ☙ ☙

Daniel stepped into the mansion and held his breath as he saw his daughter.

"Honey, I've never seen anything more precious than you right now."

"Thanks Dad. I feel like this is the best moment of all time. I can't believe I'm about to marry my High School Sweetheart. And to think, I almost didn't go to that reunion!"

"That wouldn't have mattered; he would've found you eventually."

"Yes, I think you're right." Sable hugged her father very tightly.

"Thank you for believing in me Dad. There's nothing like a Dad's love."

"And there's nothing like a sweet daughter's love. I love you baby."

"I love you too."

"I hear the processional, we have to go."

"Okay, I just have to slip on my gloves and put on my pear-shaped earrings from Abuela. She would be happy that I'm wearing them today."

"Yes, she would."

Moments later, all the guests rose to their feet as Sable and Daniel started to walk down the aisle. Halfway down the length of the aisle, awaited her Uncle Marcel. Sable wanted him to experience walking a bride down the aisle and he had been very touched. She locked arms with both men and smiled broadly. Sable looked at her mother and aunt and for a moment, she thought she saw Desiree and Olivia in their faces. She blinked and looked again and her aunt and her mother were smiling proudly at her. Sable smiled knowingly.

At the end of the aisle Sable kissed both her father and her uncle and her father shook Phillip's hand and whispered in his ear. "Honor and love my daughter. Take care of her always."

Phillip replied, "I will sir."

Phillip and Sable looked at each other and held hands. It was Sable who felt strong now and it was Phillip who wiped at his eyes. Sinclair reached out and patted his older brother's shoulder. She smiled at Phillip then and winked and he grinned broadly.

When Sable slipped Phillip's ring on his finger, she never felt happier. She had engraved in his ring,

"Forever, My Destiny." And when they said their vows and said, "I do," Farrah let out a loud squeal and started clapping and everyone laughed. Phillip and Sable kissed and their guests applauded happily. It was magical.

When the reception started, Phillip and Sable made their grand entrance and they were announced as "Mr. and Mrs. McNeil." They took their position on the dance floor and the Beatles song, "And I Love Her" came on and the guests erupted in applause and cheers. They swung each other around and kissed many times. When they danced cheek to cheek, Sable took in the moment and knew she was so much in love. A boy she had met at fifteen had become her husband and her whole life. She closed her eyes and said, "I love you Phillip. I'll never stop. In fact, I never did stop loving you."

"I've always loved you, Sable. Only you. We will always feel this, I know it."

"Yes!" Sable squealed as Phillip gave her a surprise dip with a passionate kiss and the crowd cheered again.

"I think you've made my dad a happy man by bringing his beloved Beatles to our wedding."

"Anything for your parents Sable, they're great."

The song was winding down but Phillip and Sable walked over to pick up the twins and the four of them spun around in laughter.

❧ ❧ ❧

After dinner, Sable walked over to her father and asked, "Are you ready cutie?"

"I am dear daughter!" The music filled the space and Frank Sinatra's "The Way You Look Tonight" came on. It had been a big secret, but Sable and Daniel had been practicing a ballroom dance for the past two weeks. Everyone started clapping and Sable and Daniel beautifully danced around the dance floor. They twisted and twirled and were very light on their feet. Their routine took them to all corners of the dance floor in the most delightful way that could only be shared by a father and a daughter.

Leslie asked Phillip, "When in the world did these two come up with this routine? They look like two professionals out there!"

"I don't know, but I can't keep my eyes off of them!"

For the last twenty seconds of the song, everyone could tell that they dropped the routine and just hugged and hugged each other. It was darling and unforgettable.

The next song was Phillip's turn to dance the Mother/Son Dance and Phillip was so excited to show off his mother.

The soft, sweet sound of Frank Sinatra's was replaced by the edgy and fun song of Queen's "Crazy Little Thing Called Love." Phillip started a rock and roll fast pace with his mom and she kept up perfectly. They had precise footwork and even sang along to the words to everybody's surprise. The audience was having the best time and Sinclair told his father, "I don't think I've ever seen Mom let loose like that, she looks like a teenager!"

"Your mom and brother look like showstoppers! I'm proud of them—Oh no, what's he doing!"

To everyone's surprise, Phillip scooped his mother under her arms and flung her between his legs and shot her back up high in the air and set her back down in time for a final spin just as the song was ending! Everyone was clapping and cheering, it was quite a moment. Rose and Phillip were absolutely beaming and also laughing pretty hard.

When Phillip finally walked back and joined Sable after he had high-fived his father, brother and quite a few of the male guests, Sable said, "When in the world did you and your mother practice *that*?"

"You think you're the only one with secret rehearsals around here? You just married into a very talented family!"

"No doubt, you were spectacular!" Sable beamed.

"So were you babe!"

"Come on, everyone's dancing now, let's join them."

"Let the celebration continue!"

Three Years Later

arrah and Beau were healthy and the best little toddlers a family could ever ask for. They said the funniest things and brought their parents and their six grandparents, Marcel and Sara, Daniel and Leslie, and Blake and Rose, the utmost joy.

Sable continued working part time at *Amor Mio* and Demitri practically ran things full time now. He was resourceful and gifted in the restaurant business and *Amor Mio* was more successful than ever. Sable worked about twenty hours a week and that was plenty since she wanted to spend the majority of her time with the twins. However, lately, she had been thinking of hiring on an Assistant Manager for Demitri and becoming a full time mom.

Later that day, her Aunt and Uncle were flying in from Spain as they did twice a year and everyone was going to gather at the Franco home for a grand party.

Early last year, Phillip and Sable had tried to conceive with the surrogate twice, but both efforts had failed. They were sad for a time, but knew that they had one more try left. Miraculously, they tried seven months later, and the pregnancy had taken and had been an easy one for the surrogate. Although Phillip and Sable were nervous all the time, the pregnancy had been a success.

The journey they had taken with the surrogate, Nina Johansen, was a remarkable one. Phillip and Sable decided to go through an agency. They wanted to feel confident that the person they chose was physically and psychologically sound. They needed to feel secure that she was emotionally balanced and that her medical history and background were thoroughly investigated. Upon looking through the agency's extensive database, they found and selected Nina after just one meeting with her. She was healthy and intelligent and was using the fee she would collect to finish graduate school.

Gestational surrogacy was used with Sable's eggs and Phillip's sperm to produce a child that was one hundred percent genetically *theirs*. The process was done through In Vitro Fertilization and on their third attempt, Nina had carried their baby to full term with no complications. Sable had benefited from the emotional support that the agency had offered in their workshops and their professional staff had been an astounding resource. She spoke to them often about her concerns and they were always reassuring. Nina and Sable had also talked about once a week to keep in contact. Sable had welcomed their conversations because she could ask Nina about her well being or diet or her doctor visits and had grown to really trust her. She felt that Nina was being healthy and as nurturing as she could be with their child. Nina had been very friendly to Phillip and Sable from the start and the baby was a mutual product of their shared commitment to add to the McNeil family.

Two days ago, Olivia Desiree McNeil was born weighing seven pounds, 2 ounces and was 21 inches long. She was precious. She had hazel eyes like Sable and seemed to have red fuzz as hair. She was small and perfect. Sable and Phillip had been in the delivery room with Nina and from the moment Baby Olivia was born, she was already loved beyond reason. Big brother Beau and Big sister Farrah had waited outside with Leslie and Daniel and had cheered when their dad came out to hug them and announce the baby's birth. A few hours later, they had been allowed to see the baby and they had kissed her so sweetly. They were all so excited that the baby was coming home today.

"When will baby come?" asked Farrah.

"We're going to the hospital in just a few minutes, love."

"And the baby will stay here forever?" Beau asked.

"Yes, honey bunny, your little sister will be with us forever."

"And her name is after Grandma Livia and mommy in heaven?"

"Yes, after Grandma Olivia and your mommy in heaven. She'll be very special just like you both are."

"Are we going to have more babies?"

"No Beau, Olivia Desiree completes our family."

Farrah then asked, "But can we get new puppies?"

Sable laughed, "Yes, I think we can ask Santa for a puppy this year. Joey will love that."

Phillip entered the house and said, "Is everyone ready? I just installed the infant car seat."

"Perfect, I'm finished packing all the diaper bags and things we'll need to go to my mom's later."

"Yay! We're gonna see Abuela Sara and Abuela Leslie and Abuelo Marcel and Abuelo Daniel!"

Phillip laughed, "Good job with all those names son! Now who wants to get in the car and pick up the baby?"

"Me! Me!!"

Once in the car, Phillip reached across and kissed Sable. "I love you, hon."

"And I love you."

"Look back there and tell me what you see,"

"I see two toddler seats and an infant seat, two diaper bags full of stuff, three stuffed animals, plus the portable bouncie!"

"You know what I see, babe? I see a carload of kids. What I've always wanted."

The End

Made in the USA
Lexington, KY
23 July 2010